WALKING BY NIGHT

Kate Ellis

This first world edition published 2015
in Great Britain and the USA by
Crème de la Crime, an imprint of
SEVERN HOUSE PUBLISHERS LTD of
19 Cedar Road, Sutton, Surrey, England, SM2 5DA.
Trade paperback edition first published
in Great Britain and the USA 2015 by
SEVERN HOUSE PUBLISHERS LTD.

British Library Cataloguing in Publication Data

Ellis, Kate, 1953- author.
Walking by night. – (Joe Plantagenet series)
1. Plantagenet, Joe (Fictitious character)–Fiction.
2. Murder–Investigation–Fiction. 3. Police–England–
North Yorkshire–Fiction. 4. Detective and mystery
stories.
I. Title II. Series
823.9'2-dc23

ISBN-13: 978-1-78029-073-7 (cased)
ISBN-13: 978-1-78029-556-5 (trade paper)
ISBN-13: 978-1-78010-643-3 (e-book)

Except where actual historical events and characters are being described for the storyline of this novel, all situations in this publication are fictitious and any resemblance to living persons is purely coincidental.

All Severn House titles are printed on acid-free paper.

Severn House Publishers support the Forest Stewardship Council™ [FSC™], the leading international forest certification organisation. All our titles that are printed on FSC c[illegible] FSC logo.

MIX
Paper from responsible sources
FSC® C013056
FSC www.fsc.org

Typeset by Palimpsest Book Production Ltd,
Falkirk, Stirlingshire, Scotland.
Printed and bound in Great Britain by
TJ International, Padstow, Cornwall.

WALKING BY NIGHT

The Joe Plantagenet Mysteries from Kate Ellis

SEEKING THE DEAD
PLAYING WITH BONES
KISSING THE DEMONS *
WATCHING THE GHOSTS *
WALKING BY NIGHT *

* *available from Severn House*

ONE

Debby Telerhaye's footsteps echoed in the fog like hammer blows as her tottering heels hit the stone pavement. She shuddered, hugged the thin jacket she'd bought in the sales the previous Saturday around her body and walked on, hurrying like a mouse who fears a cat is watching from the shadows.

The city was shrouded in fog, milky white and yellow where it blended with the sickly glow of the street lights. She could only see six feet ahead, and every so often she heard voices that sounded as if they were coming from some distant world. Debby hated fog. Fog conceals all kinds of wickedness.

She'd had a good time at the Abbott's Head that evening: the music had been loud and the company raucous, up for anything. It had probably been a mistake to consume so many vodka shots, but she'd been caught up by the moment and the desire to follow her friends' example. They'd urged her on. *Come on, let's have another. Let's get hammered.*

They'd been in a far worse state than she was, but they'd taken a minicab home. As she'd watched them clamber in, giggling, she'd wished she was with them. But they lived in the opposite direction so there was no chance of her sharing the ride, and she had no money left for a cab of her own because she'd put her last tenner into the kitty for the final round of drinks. She had to walk. There was no choice.

She'd just reached the corner of Marketgate when she stumbled on her vertiginous heels. She carried on walking, but by the time she reached the main road her ankle had started to throb so she stopped. As she came to a halt she heard a soft footstep echoing the sharp click of her stilettos. She turned her head, but when she saw nothing behind the blanket of mist she told herself that it had probably been her imagination and limped on.

He'd been watching her all night, sitting in the corner of the bar at the Abbott's Head while she laughed with her friends. He'd heard their chatter growing louder with each drink they'd downed – and they had downed a lot over the course of the evening.

He'd been trying to make his pint last because he wanted to keep a clear head, and when she'd stood up to leave he'd drained the glass and followed her, careful to keep his distance. He'd seen her friends get into the minicab while she set off home alone. Vulnerable.

Some things were meant to be.

Debby crossed the road to the Museum Gardens, trying to ignore the pain in her ankle, and she felt her heart thumping as she braced herself to flee if she saw some silent vehicle bearing down on her. But the street was empty of traffic. Nobody in their right mind would drive on a night like this. She turned right and walked parallel with the railings, putting out a cold hand to touch them and finding the solid feel of the metal reassuring. The fog was denser now, and fear of getting lost in its enveloping embrace crept into her mind like mist seeping through an open window.

Her heels were slowing her down and her ankle was getting worse. She stopped to take off her shoes, feeling a sudden urge to run for home and flee this unearthly landscape where the familiar had turned frighteningly unfamiliar. But she wondered whether home was any safer, now that her mother had moved Sinclair in. He made her flesh creep. But her mother didn't see it: she'd let him into her life because she feared being alone. There's none so blind as the desperate.

As she bent to slip off her shiny beige stilettos, she heard the sound again. Footsteps that stopped a few seconds after hers, like a delayed echo. She was scared now, so scared that she ignored the pain when her unprotected feet met a patch of gravel. Someone had stopped when she had stopped. Someone was out there in that dense wall of mist. Following her; watching each move she made and assessing her vulnerability.

She saw Eborby's main library looming up on her left, and she knew it wasn't far to the undercroft, the only part of the medieval monastery of St Peter still standing after centuries of destruction and neglect. In its sheltering covered passageway lovers met and tourists wandered, but at this time the night people took over – the drug dealers and the up-to-no-good hangers about.

But if she could slip inside and wait till her pursuer had passed, she might throw him off. To her vodka-fuddled brain it seemed like the perfect solution to her problem.

She limped into the undercroft's dank passageway on tiptoe, her shoes dangling from her left hand and the cold numbing her feet, and to her surprise and relief the place was empty. As she flattened herself against the wall, her fingers came into contact with something soft and damp. Moss which felt like dead men's flesh. She breathed in deeply, and when the chill, moist air hit her lungs she started to splutter, the noise sounding like gunshots in the silence. She covered her mouth with her free hand and waited, half expecting to see a figure looming at the end of the passageway but nothing happened. Perhaps the footsteps had been in her imagination. Or a trick of the fog.

Both ends of the tunnel-like undercroft were blocked by a wall of grey-white mist. But, even in the darkness, she could make out the shape of a huge stone Roman sarcophagus which stood against the stone wall, its mass looking vaguely industrial against the barrier of fog. As her eyes grew accustomed to the gloom, she opened the little denim bag she'd slung across her body to foil any passing muggers and, inside it, her fingers came into contact with the comforting shape of her mobile phone. But who would she call? Not her mother; telling her mother would be like telling Sinclair and that was a prospect she couldn't face. Not the friends who'd abandoned her so blithely. Calling the police would be an overreaction, and she'd probably be charged with wasting their time. She felt tears welling in her eyes and a warm trickle of moisture running down her cheek. She'd read about people who'd died of exposure. But was being attacked, maybe raped and strangled, any better?

If she waited another five minutes, she reckoned it would be safe to leave her shelter. Hopefully, he'd think he'd lost her and give up, turn his evil attentions to some other unsuspecting girl on her way home after a night out. She crept further into the tunnel, fingering the phone that could be her lifeline if events took a turn for the worse.

Her ankle was aching now, and she was as sure as she could be that it was swollen. As she bent to rub it, her eyes were drawn to something lying on the ground near the other end of the passage, outlined against the ghostly light seeping in through the far entrance. At first it looked like a bundle of old clothes that someone had discarded, and she stared at it for a while before curiosity made her take a few halting steps towards it, glancing behind her to make sure her follower hadn't appeared, looming against the fog. As her courage grew she took another step, then another, gasping as her bare foot came into contact with a tiny stone.

There was no sound in the blanketed silence apart from her own breathing. She was alone with the thing on the ground, and when she heard a soft sigh, she didn't know whether she'd made the sound or whether it came from someone or something else. The thing on the ground, perhaps.

As she drew closer, she thought the shape looked human, but it was too dark to be sure. Someone asleep, maybe. A vagrant, sleeping rough. As her eyes adjusted she thought she could make out long dark hair falling like a mask where the face should be. And clothes; something long and dark which showed no flesh.

She suspected it was a woman, but she couldn't bring herself to touch her; to feel cold cloth wrapped around dead flesh. Because her senses told her that this woman had become a corpse – a still, cold cadaver – and the sigh had come from somewhere else. Perhaps whoever had ended the woman's life.

She looked round, fighting the panic that had started to overwhelm her, and out of the corner of her eye she caught sight of a shape, half-formed in the swirling mist. It looked like a figure in long black robes. A thing with no face, there for a split second before the fog reformed itself into a white wall, and then it was gone, leaving only fear behind. She let out an involuntary scream and clamped her hand over her mouth. If it was a killer, the last thing she wanted was to draw attention to herself. When nothing happened she told herself she must have imagined the figure. But those following footsteps and the body lying there on the ground were all too real.

Terror made her forget her pain as she tore through the undercroft entrance and out into the fog. She opened her mouth to shout for help but thought better of it. Instead, she fumbled for her phone with clumsy, panicked fingers, and when she dropped it she squatted down and felt around for it in the shadows.

There was no sign of the phone. But she needed to get away, so she abandoned her search and ran out, hardly aware that one of her shoes had slipped from her hand. It wasn't far to the centre of the city, and the pubs would be throwing out now. There was safety in crowds, and she could summon help. As she crossed the road by the art gallery she narrowly avoided a bus that was driving too fast for the lack of visibility, but panic blinded her to danger as Boothgate Bar reared up in front of her out of the fog. She knew there was a pub at the other side of the city gate. If she could get there everything would be fine.

She staggered under the great stone gate, ignoring a small group of jeering men relieving themselves in the shelter of the archway, and spotted the welcoming golden glow from the Mitre's leaded windows to her left.

She stumbled in through the open door, and when she screamed, the bar fell silent.

He knew she hadn't seen him. How could she? But something had spooked her.

She'd tried to hide from him in the undercroft, thinking he'd be fooled. With all that drink, she hadn't been thinking straight, and her fuddled brain had underestimated him. She'd almost made it too easy for him – until she'd torn out of there and made for the city centre.

But there'd be another time. He could find her whenever he wanted.

TWO

Over the years Joe Plantagenet had become used to drinking alone, to sitting in the corner watching his fellow drinkers and imagining their lives. The passivity of enjoying a quiet pint of Black Sheep made a welcome change from police work. In his local he didn't have to solve anybody's problems.

He looked at his watch. It was time to go. If he had any more he'd wake up with a hangover and be plagued with a headache all day which was the last thing he needed. Besides, he'd promised his boss, DCI Emily Thwaite, that he'd be at the police station early because she had a meeting with the superintendent and she needed him to deal with the morning briefing. He drained his glass and stood up.

He took his glass back to the bar, earning himself a nod of thanks from the landlord. Then he zipped his leather jacket and walked out into the night. The fog outside hit his lungs as soon as he stepped out of the pub doorway, and he began to cough. Eborby was prone to fog, always had been since the Roman invaders decided it was the perfect location for their military headquarters in the north of England. He wondered what those soldiers from Italy and the warmer parts of the Empire had made of the Yorkshire weather. Probably not a lot.

The wall of white cloud was so thick this time that a stranger to the city would have had difficulty finding their way around. But this was terra cognita to Joe. He could find his way back home to his flat in the shadow of the city walls blindfold. It had been built in the 1990s, but he'd always felt that the proximity of history more than made up for the soulless architecture.

Fog plays strange tricks with sound, and the shouts and screams seemed to be feet away. Without a second thought he moved towards the sounds. Even off duty his policeman's instincts drew him to trouble. After a few moments he realized that the noise was coming from a pub a few doors down the street: from the Mitre, a cosy place he'd almost chosen for his evening drink, but when he'd poked his head round the door he'd found that his favourite corner had been taken so he'd walked down to the Cathedral Vault instead.

The entrance to the Mitre stood out, bright and welcoming in the mist, but Joe knew from the sounds drifting out of the pub that something was amiss. His first assumption was that there'd been some kind of drunken altercation, although the Mitre's landlord, in Joe's experience, ran a tight and law-abiding operation. But it was a female voice that rose above the rest, terrified and close to hysteria.

Joe straightened his back and strode into the pub. Inside, the drinkers, a mixture of regulars he recognized and tourists in search of Eborby's quieter night life, sat staring at the main event

– a motherly barmaid and the landlord ministering to a girl who was sitting between them on a bar stool with a glass of something comforting in her shaking hand.

'What's happened? Is she OK?' Joe asked as he approached the little group.

The landlord, a small, wiry man with a hairstyle that reminded Joe of a monks' tonsure, turned towards Joe, a 'what's it to you?' expression on his round face. Joe, realizing that although he'd been in there countless times the landlord had no idea what he did for a living, pulled his warrant card from his pocket and showed it discreetly to the man.

The landlord's attitude changed in an instant. He looked round the bar and lowered his voice. 'She came rushing in here as if the devil himself was after her. She says she's found a body. My wife's already called your lot, but they've not arrived yet. That was over ten minutes ago,' he added reproachfully.

Joe squatted down and brought his face level with the girl's. She was in her late teens, he guessed. Slightly overweight, with long brown hair that had frizzed in the damp air. She had a small nose and a rosebud mouth, and she looked a wreck. Her thick make-up had smeared, leaving dark tracks of eyeliner and mascara running down her cheeks. Her clothes, inadequate for the chill of the night, had bunched up, showing a long expanse of thigh. Her tights were intact up to her ankles, but the feet were torn, revealing filthy, bleeding flesh beneath. A single beige stiletto lay discarded on the floor.

'Hi, love. My name's Joe. I'm a policeman. What's your name?'

She took a deep, shuddering breath. 'Debby. Debby Telerhaye.' She sipped her drink, and Joe saw her hand was still trembling.

'Debby, can you tell me what happened?'

It took a few moments for the answer to come. 'I went for a drink with my mates in the Abbott's Head, and while I was walking home I got the feeling I was being followed.' She paused to take another drink. 'Anyway, I was scared so I nipped into the undercroft; you know, the old building by the library.'

'I know it. Go on.'

'Well, I thought I'd shaken him off, and I was going to carry on walking home when . . .'

She stopped speaking, as though what she was about to say was too painful to contemplate. Joe knew that if he tried to rush her, she'd clam up altogether. This needed patience.

After a long silence she began to whisper. 'It was dark and with the fog . . . I thought I saw something on the ground.'

'What?'

'I thought it was a bundle of clothes at first, but then I saw it was a woman. I didn't touch her.'

'So you don't know if she was dead or just unconscious?'

'I was sure she was dead but . . .' Her eyes met his. 'Do you think she might have been alive?'

Joe didn't answer. He didn't want to make the girl feel bad about fleeing the scene rather than calling an ambulance right away. He touched her hand, a gesture of reassurance, and retraced his steps to the doorway. Standing in the entrance, he took his mobile phone from his pocket to make the call that would, hopefully, hurry things along. Although, on such a foggy night, the patrols on duty would undoubtedly have their hands full.

He got through to the control room and explained who he was and what had happened. A couple of minutes later he had a call from the patrol who'd just arrived at the undercroft. They were about to conduct a search.

Joe turned and went back into the pub. It was just a matter of waiting.

Driving in such thick fog was bloody dangerous, Sergeant Una O'Kane observed to the young PC sitting, arms folded, in the passenger seat. She'd seen countless nasty RTAs when people went too fast for the conditions. As she said the words a van loomed in front of her, seemingly out of nowhere. She hit the brake pedal and swore loudly.

When she reached their destination she pulled the car off the road. It would be tempting fate to park on the road so that some idiot could canon into them. Una had never had an optimistic view of human nature.

They climbed out of the car, and Una's young colleague put on his cap. 'Who reported it?' he asked.

'A lass on her way home from a night out. She thought she was being followed by some weirdo, so she hid in the undercroft in the hope he'd go past. Stupid thing to do, if you ask me,' she said with a snort. 'What if he'd seen her go in? She'd have been cornered in there. At least out on the street she'd have a fighting chance of someone passing by.'

'Did he corner her?'

'No, but . . . Well, I wouldn't have done it.'

''Course you wouldn't, Sarge.' He could have added that it would be a brave weirdo who'd follow Una O'Kane, but he was too scared.

'Let's see this body, then.'

'Shouldn't we call for backup? The pathologist and—'

'Let's see what we've got first. We don't want to call out the whole team only to find that it's only a drunk sleeping it off.'

Una went ahead, flashing her torch into the mouth of the undercroft. It lit up the rough stone walls and the vaulted ceiling of what had once served as a storage area for the long-destroyed abbey. As either end was open, it was little more than a passageway joining the Museum Gardens to the library area. Una swept her torch over the ground and shook her head.

If there had been a body, it wasn't there now.

THREE

Joe was tempted to call the patrol to find out what was going on, but he stopped himself. They'd ring him as soon as there was news.

Debby had been taken into the back room behind the bar by the landlord's wife, a no-nonsense bottle-blonde who, Joe sensed, was beginning to lose patience with the girl, who'd consumed at least three double measures of liquid comfort since she set foot over the threshold. Joe had told her she should wait for the patrol to come and take a statement, but after half an hour he was becoming restless. The girl needed to get home. She'd told him she lived with her mum, so at least she'd have a shoulder to cry on when she got back.

He'd already suggested that Debby should call her mum, but

she'd seemed reluctant, saying she'd be fine to get home by herself. The landlord's wife took the same size in shoes, and she'd lent her a pair of old and sensible loafers, so the walk wouldn't be a problem. Joe told her the patrol car would take her back, but this suggestion was met with a disapproving silence and a 'no thanks'. He wondered why she'd refused and concluded that she might have had an unpleasant encounter with the police in the past. But he wasn't going to interrogate her. When the body was found she'd have to answer plenty of questions whether she liked it or not.

He looked at his watch. It was almost midnight, the pub was empty and the staff wanted to go home. Joe was almost losing patience when his phone rang.

The female voice on the other end of the line announced herself as Una O'Kane. Sergeant. 'No sign of a body here,' she began. She sounded relieved. 'No blood or drag marks either. Either the girl was seeing things after a night on the sauce or she panicked when she saw some vagrant taking a nap.'

'She seemed pretty sure it was . . .'

'It could have been someone trying to scare her. Might have been some comedian's idea of a joke.'

If this was a joke it wasn't funny, Joe thought. And Debby certainly wasn't laughing. She still looked shaken, sitting staring at her hands as the landlord's wife tidied up around her.

'Have you searched the area?' Joe asked.

'Of course,' the sergeant answered, as though the question had been a particularly stupid one. 'There's nothing suspicious.'

'She said she dropped her phone there. Did you find it?'

'Yes. I'll take it back to the station, and she can pick it up tomorrow. Why don't you tell her to go home and sober up?'

Joe ended the call, and when he entered the back room, Debby looked up expectantly.

'That was the patrol. They've found your phone, but there's no body in the undercroft. Are you sure that's where you saw it?'

'Yes. I told you. I'm not lying. I saw it.' There was no uncertainty in her voice.

'OK.' He raised his hand in appeasement. 'Let's get you home. It's on my way so I'll walk with you. I can explain what happened to your mum if she's worried.'

'There's no need,' she said, with an anxiety which suggested to Joe that she found the prospect of a policeman talking to her mother more alarming than the ordeal of discovering a corpse. But he was probably wrong. The girl was exhausted. People say odd things when they're in that state.

'You will let me walk with you? I don't like just leaving you.'

She hesitated, but one look at the landlord's wife's impatient face decided her. 'OK.' She slipped on the old shoes. They fitted, but she shuffled out as though walking caused her pain.

Joe wondered whether to support her arm, but he feared the gesture might be misinterpreted. In fact, he knew it was probably foolish to be alone with a vulnerable woman like that. But he'd done a lot of foolish things in his time, so what was one more?

They walked slowly, and when their arms brushed by accident, Joe flinched at the contact.

'What do you think you saw?' he asked when they reached the main road.

'A body. I think she had long hair, and she was wearing something long and dark . . . a skirt or a coat. I couldn't see very well in that light.'

'Perhaps she wasn't dead. Perhaps she was drunk and she collapsed and then she came round and wandered off.'

'No. She was dead.'

'How could you tell?'

'I just could,' she said, a note of impatience in her voice.

'But if you didn't touch her . . .'

'She was definitely dead.'

They'd reached Debby's address. It wasn't far from Joe's flat, just over the main road that ran alongside the city walls and up a little street of Victorian terraced houses. She stopped at the front door and took her key from her bag. 'I left my shoe in the pub. I dropped the other when I . . .'

'I can get it for you, if you like,' he said, thinking that one shoe wouldn't be much good.

'No, it's OK. I'll have to take these back to the landlady tomorrow, and . . .'

'Well, the offer's there. And make sure you go to the station tomorrow to get your phone back.'

Their eyes met, and she gave him a nervous half-smile. He

watched as she fumbled to get the key in the lock. The house was in darkness. Nobody had waited up.

'You sure you don't want me to . . .?'

'No.' She lowered the key and turned to face him. 'This sounds really stupid, but I think I saw a shape in the fog at the far end of the undercroft. I might have been imagining it, but . . .'

'Can you describe it?'

Debby hesitated, then she gave a little laugh. 'You're going to think I'm crazy.'

'Try me.'

'It looked like a nun.'

FOUR

Joe had already given the morning briefing when DCI Emily Thwaite arrived in the CID office. The previous night he'd feared that they might be starting a major murder investigation that morning but, as it was, it had turned out to be a false alarm. However, as he'd been trying to get to sleep last night, some nagging voice in the back of his mind told him that once the fog had lifted and the daylight arrived, the body Debby Telerhaye was convinced she saw might yet turn up.

But there'd been no call. They were off the hook.

It was nine thirty when Emily bustled in. She had the harassed look of someone who'd just been landed with work they considered burdensome and unnecessary. She caught Joe's eye as she passed his glass-fronted office, and he stood up and followed her. She looked as if she wanted to talk . . . or at least to have someone to share her troubles with.

Emily sat down as he entered her office. Hers was larger than his with her name and rank inscribed on a brass plate on her door and blinds for privacy. Emily Thwaite's round face was what many would call pretty, framed by unruly fair curls. She was plump, forever on a diet of one description or another. In a moment of rash boldness Joe had once told her to move more and eat less. She'd pretended she hadn't heard him.

'I believe that damsel in distress you rescued led us a merry dance last night,' she said. 'Think she was having you on?'

Joe shook his head. 'No. She was genuinely scared. Whatever she saw – or imagined she saw – terrified her.' He hesitated. 'She said it was a dead woman, even described what she was wearing.'

'It must have been dark in there. How could she have seen anything?'

'She said there was enough light for her to make things out.'

'And was there?'

Joe felt unsure of himself. 'I don't know. Once the patrol had given the all clear I didn't think it necessary to go there and have a look. But there was a full moon behind all that fog – and street lamps, so I suppose . . .'

'If you ask me, she'd had too much to drink and started hallucinating.' She paused. 'I hear you walked her home.'

'I didn't like to leave her to go home alone.'

'You should have asked the patrol car to drop her off if you were that worried.'

'I suggested that, but she was quite adamant.'

'Think she's got something against the police?' The question was sharp.

'Or her mother has.'

'What was this girl's name again?'

'Debby Telerhaye.'

Emily frowned, as if she was trying to recall some elusive fact. Then a gleam of recognition appeared in her blue eyes. 'Telerhaye. You sure?'

'Yeah. Why?'

'While I was in Leeds there was a case involving a family called Telerhaye. Their little boy, Peter, went missing and he was never found. The mother called in a medium – or rather the medium volunteered his services. Turned out to be as much good as a chocolate tea pot, but the mother hung on his every word. Sad.' She thought for a few moments. 'I seem to remember there was a sister, and I'm sure her name was Deborah. I think she was a couple of years older than the missing lad.'

'When did all this happen?'

'It was around ten years ago. I was only a humble DC back then, and I was stuck in the incident room dealing with the routine stuff so I didn't have much to do with the family. But I do remember our SIO moaning about this medium lurking about like a bad smell.'

'Medium. As in seances?'

'Yes. Or was he a psychic? Anyway, the mother became very dependent on him, even started ignoring police advice.'

'Debby told me she lives with her mother . . . and her mother's partner. I got the impression that the partner was bad news.'

'I remember hearing that the Telerhayes' marriage broke up under the strain of the kid going missing. It's sad, but it happens.' She paused. 'You've got me intrigued now.'

'How do you mean?'

'I'm curious to know how Debby's turned out and how the mother's coping now. But I don't expect you'll be seeing her again.'

'Unless they find the body she thinks she saw.'

Emily looked Joe in the eye. 'I worry about you sometimes, Joe. All this drinking alone.'

Joe had been about to leave the office, but now he turned back to face her. 'Nothing wrong with a quiet pint.' He knew he sounded defensive, but that's how he felt. He sometimes wished that Emily would keep her interfering instincts for those who appreciated them. 'And it's better than sitting watching bad cop shows in an empty flat.'

Before Emily could reply, DS Sunny Porter poked his head round the door of Emily's office. He was a small, wiry man with a permanently glass-half-empty expression. The name bestowed on him by his optimistic parents was Samson, but years ago someone with a sense of humour had named him Sunny, a title he had never lived up to.

'Can I have a word, ma'am?'

'You can have as many as you like, Sunny. What's up?'

'A woman's been reported missing. She's only been gone since last night but, in view of that wild goose chase in the undercroft . . .' He glanced at Joe. 'An actress called Perdita Elmet who's in the latest production at the Playhouse. She didn't return to her digs after the performance last night, and she hasn't turned up at the theatre for a rehearsal this morning.'

'When was she last seen?' Joe asked.

'She told the girl she's sharing with that she was going for a drink with someone after last night's performance and said she'd be back before midnight. She walked into the fog just after ten thirty and hasn't been seen since. They started worrying when she didn't arrive at this morning's rehearsal. Apparently, it was an important one and she said she'd be there. She's normally pretty reliable.'

'Do we have a description?'

'Aged twenty-five. Average height. Long dark hair. Slim. Last seen wearing an ankle-length black velvet coat over a long floral skirt. There's a photo of her up in the Playhouse foyer, apparently. I said we'd pick up a copy.'

Joe caught Emily's eye.

'What's on at the Playhouse?' Emily asked.

Sunny examined his notebook. 'Something called *The Devils*. Apparently there's a lot of nuns.'

Debby's head hurt as though a thousand small blacksmiths were going about their business in her brain. And she had a raging thirst which made her down a large glass of tap water as soon as she crawled out of bed. When she opened the thin curtains of her tiny bedroom she saw the fog had dispersed overnight leaving a trace of mist lurking in the tree tops. And the sun was shining behind a blanket of pale cloud, turning the sky a dazzling grey.

The events of the previous night seemed unreal and distant now. The daylight had robbed her of last night's certainties. Had fear made her imagine that figure on the ground? She could no longer be sure.

She thought of the policeman. He'd asked her to call him Joe, and he'd been different, somehow, from the police officers she'd encountered in those terrible days when her family's world had shattered and her mother had surrendered to shadows and despair.

Maybe she should try to see Joe again. He was older than she was, probably in his thirties. And he was good-looking with his blue eyes and his black hair, worn long enough to cover his ears. He had a generous mouth and freckles on his nose, and there was something about him that made you want to confide your innermost secrets. But she told herself that he was a policeman. They hadn't been much use before, so why should things change now? Nobody could protect her from Sinclair – he was too clever for that.

She opened her bedroom door and looked up and down the landing, just to make sure Sinclair wasn't about. Once she was sure, she staggered to the bathroom, her arms full of clothes. The bathroom lock was broken, so Sinclair could walk in on her whenever he liked, but if she pushed the chair against the door she was safe. He entered her bedroom whenever he thought he could get away with it, and when she'd mentioned it to her mother, she'd made some excuse for him. Just as she always did.

It was Saturday so there was no college that morning, but she still wanted to get away from the house. She wanted to be anywhere she wouldn't have to see Sinclair. Now, fully dressed in jeans and sweatshirt, hair straightened, brushed and swept up into a pony tail, she crept downstairs, alert for any tell-tale signs of Sinclair's presence.

When she entered the kitchen she saw that it was tidy. Mum had cleared up after him. He wouldn't have done it himself; he never did. She switched the kettle on and took a tea bag from the canister before raiding the bread bin, relieved that he hadn't had the last of the loaf. Then she looked out of the window. His car was still there. The old BMW that had been resprayed egg yolk yellow at some time in its dodgy past. He was still around somewhere. Lurking. Watching, like he always did. His eyes stripping off her clothes, staring into her soul.

As she dropped two slices of white bread into the toaster she heard a noise behind her and swung round. He was standing in the doorway. Five foot eight, tattooed arms, short red-tinged hair turning prematurely grey. His face was thin like a rat's, his eyes ice blue and his lips turned up slightly at the corners in an expression of permanent amusement. He got away with so much, Debby thought, because he made anyone who challenged him seem a foolish prig who couldn't take a joke. But there was nothing funny about him. She'd seen his dark side. She wasn't taken in.

'You got in late last night,' he said, walking towards her slowly. To a casual observer the movement would have appeared harmless, relaxed. But she saw only menace in his approach.

She turned to watch the toaster. Sometimes if she ignored him he got the message and went away. But today wasn't one of those days. He was standing close to her now, so close that she could feel his breath on her neck.

She stepped to one side and turned to face him. 'Where's mum?'

'Gone to work. It's just you and me,' he said with a smirk.

'Was it you last night? Were you following me?'

When he reached out a hand and pinched her cheek, she flinched at his touch.

'Why shouldn't I follow my favourite girl?' he said in a suggestive whisper. 'And someone else was taking an interest too. I think you've got an admirer.'

Debby pushed past him and ran out of the kitchen. She'd rather go hungry.

FIVE

The powers-that-be at Eborby's Playhouse Theatre liked to court controversy from time to time, and ever since the Artistic Director had watched Ken Russell's film version of *The Devils*, with a fascination verging on the prurient, she'd longed to include the play in the repertoire. So far it seemed that the people of Eborby didn't share her enthusiasm for witchcraft, torture, exorcisms and lustful writhing nuns. But she hoped that word of mouth and favourable reviews would soon turn her production into a box office hit.

Normally, the police would respond to such an early report of a missing healthy, independent adult with bland reassurances and the matter would be dealt with by uniform. But after Debby Telerhaye's strange experience the previous night, and because of the fact that her description of the body she'd seen bore certain similarities to the missing actress, Perdita Elmet, Joe was eager to find out more. Emily thought he was overreacting, but she said she fancied a bit of fresh air after being cooped up in her office for days so she'd go to the theatre with him.

They decided to go on foot as the Playhouse wasn't far from police headquarters, and they walked side by side in silence. Since she'd questioned his nocturnal drinking habits earlier, she guarded her words carefully in case she came across as interfering.

However, that didn't mean she wasn't itching to meddle in his life – it was in her nature – but she knew it would erect a barrier between them if she made it too obvious, so she said nothing.

It was Joe who spoke first. 'I was thinking of going to see this production.'

'I thought it sounded a bit gruesome.' Emily, who had to arrange babysitters for her three children whenever she ventured out at night, only tended to choose entertainment she was guaranteed to enjoy. Certainly, scenes of death and torture weren't on her list of things to see – she had enough of that sort of thing at work.

They reached the theatre, a Victorian edifice with a modern glass frontage. The row of identical posters outside depicted a sea of twisted faces on a blood-red background with a crucifix superimposed on top. Joe glanced at the image and looked away.

'Appeals to you, does it, all this churchy stuff?'

'Not when it's done by people who know nothing about it,' he said quickly.

Emily could never forget that Joe had once trained to be a priest before he met a girl who made him rethink his plans for a life of celibacy. She didn't know why, but this part of Joe's life had always held a fascination for her, even though she'd never considered herself particularly religious, just the usual weddings, funerals and Christmas sort of Anglican.

Joe's story had stuck in her mind: how he'd married Kaitlin, the girl who'd led him from the path of holiness; how she had died soon after their wedding in a tragic accident – a fall from a cliff path in Devon. Then, some time later, Joe had joined the police, and he'd been shot and injured whilst on duty in his native Liverpool and his close colleague had been killed. The bullet wound in his shoulder still gave him trouble from time to time; a niggling reminder of mortality. In an unguarded moment she had once asked whether he feared that it had been some kind of punishment, regretting the words as soon as they'd left her lips. He'd told her it didn't work like that. But there'd been a lot of bad things in Joe Plantagenet's life. And since his girlfriend, Maddy, had moved down to London a couple of years ago, he'd lived alone, which Emily didn't think was healthy. But she tried to suppress her inner mother. Joe had to live his own life.

'I'm just remembering what Debby Telerhaye said. When she found the body that wasn't there, she thought she saw a nun in the mist.'

Emily rolled her eyes. 'She'd had too much to drink. Nuns and bodies make a change from pink elephants, but—'

'You didn't see her, Emily. She was terrified. She ran through the streets barefoot. Her feet were bleeding.'

'I acknowledge that something gave her a fright, but I draw the line at ghostly nuns.' She noticed the cast photos arranged on the foyer wall and walked over to examine them. 'Which one's our missing actress?'

As was customary in theatres, the photographs of the cast were artistically posed professional efforts, enhanced to make the most of the performers' looks. Joe's eyes were drawn immediately to Perdita Elmet's. She had even, almost feline features with lustrous dark hair that tumbled around her shoulders. The legend beneath the photograph told him that she was playing the part of Sister Jeanne of the Angels. Joe, not being familiar with the play or the film, wasn't sure how substantial the role was, but he assumed from the prominent position of the picture that Sister Jeanne must be an important character.

'An actor called Jonas Ventnor reported her missing,' said Emily. She pointed to a photograph of an earnest-looking young man with the name printed underneath. 'He said he'd meet us here. Apparently, they're having some sort of rehearsal for the understudy at the moment in case Perdita doesn't turn up in time for tonight's performance. Could be someone's lucky break.'

'Let's hope not,' said Joe, suddenly serious. He couldn't get Debby's description of the body she claimed to have found out of his head. The hair; the long dark coat. But when the patrol had gone to the undercroft, there'd been no body.

Emily pushed open the swing door with the polished brass handles that led into the auditorium. Joe could hear voices coming from the direction of the stage, but they stopped as soon as Emily let the door swing back.

A man and a woman stood in a well of bright light behind the proscenium arch. They turned and watched as Joe and Emily walked down the central aisle between the red plush seats, and once they were close to the stage the man spoke. 'Sorry. This is a private rehearsal.' The words sounded peevish, with a hint of self-importance.

Joe took his warrant card from the pocket of his leather jacket and held it up like a charm to ward off evil. 'Police. I'm looking for Jonas Ventnor.'

'That's me,' the man said meekly, a hint of nervousness in his voice. He was in his twenties, skinny, dark and intense.

'You reported one of your colleagues missing?'

'That's right. Come round the side. I'll meet you.' He turned to the woman. 'Sorry, Charlotte. Won't be long.'

He hurried off the stage, leaving the woman staring. She had long waves of golden brown hair and a face that, although not classically pretty, her nose being a little too long and her chin a little too prominent, was striking. She picked up her script and began to study it as Joe and Emily made their way to the door beside the stage.

Once through the door the theatrical opulence vanished. Backstage was strictly utilitarian and smelled of paint and something else Joe didn't recognize. Jonas Ventnor was waiting for them, his face solemn. He looked worried. But Joe recalled that he was an actor. Appearances might be deceptive.

'Thanks for coming. We were just going over Perdita's scenes.' He led the way into a shabby corridor with doors either side – dressing rooms, Joe guessed. Jonas pushed one of the doors open and Joe followed him inside. The dressing room was cluttered with make-up and cards from well-wishers, and a pile of paperback books, crime novels of the more lurid variety, stood in the corner of the long counter below an illuminated mirror. Costumes hung from hooks on the wall opposite the mirror: a priest's robes, then some kind of long gown, then more priest's robes, more tattered this time, then a torn and bloodied shift, the sort a victim of torture might be found in. These costumes, Joe imagined, charted the downfall of Jonas's character. He was suddenly intrigued and wanted to ask more. But that wasn't what they were there for.

They were invited to sit on two sagging armchairs while Jonas perched on a stool by the mirror.

'Is there any news?'

'I'm afraid not,' said Emily, assuming her most sympathetic

expression: the one she usually kept for breaking news of the unwelcome variety.

'But you're obviously taking it seriously. I was expecting some uniformed constable or . . . You've found something, haven't you?'

'Not yet,' said Joe, suddenly feeling that the visit might have been a mistake. Apart from Debby Telerhaye's bizarre statement, they had no idea what had become of Perdita Elmet. For all they knew she might have decided to bale out of the production for reasons of her own. Perhaps when they questioned her fellow actors, they'd get a better idea.

Joe let Emily ask the questions while he listened, taking notes occasionally. He watched Jonas's face. He seemed sincere enough as he recounted how Perdita had behaved perfectly normally yesterday. The director had called a short rehearsal in the morning to iron out some glitches in Act One, then they'd all gone their separate ways until the performance. Perdita had said she was going back to the flat off Boothgate she shared with Hen, who was playing the part of the young and vulnerable Philippe Trincant, the daughter of a magistrate in the French town of Loudon where most of the action took place.

Jonas had spent the afternoon using the computer in the library to send emails, and then he and Hen had met for something to eat in the theatre cafe. Perdita had turned up slightly late for the half, the thirty minutes or so before curtain-up when all actors are expected to be in the theatre preparing for the performance, looking rather flushed. Then at the end of the play she shot off, saying she was meeting someone and telling Hen not to put the latch on the flat door because she'd be in before midnight. She never came home, and she didn't turn up the next morning when the director, Louisa, was due to give some important notes. There had been no hint that anything was amiss at the previous night's performance. It was a complete mystery and totally out of character. That was why everyone was worried.

'Has Perdita fallen out with anyone?' Emily asked. 'Any arguments in the company?'

'Absolutely not.' He eyed the bloodstained garment on the hanger. 'In spite of the rather gruesome nature of the play, we all get along well.'

'Is Perdita friendly with anyone in particular?'

'Hen probably knows her best because they're sharing accommodation. And I believe she knew her understudy Charlotte from when they were in the same production in Leeds.'

'Are they friendly?'

It was hard to read Jonas's expression. 'I wouldn't say they were unfriendly.'

'Why did everyone leave it to you to report her missing?' Joe asked sharply.

Jonas's face coloured a little. 'It was just the way it worked out. Hen was worried, so I volunteered.' The words were casual, but Joe sensed a tension behind them.

'Is there anyone here Perdita doesn't get on with?'

'No. She's cool. Everyone likes her.'

Joe watched Jonas's face. He looked as though he meant what he said. But Joe was sure that, in the precarious world of the theatre, some backbiting went on behind the mask of camaraderie. It was only human nature . . . and he knew what that was like.

'Tell us about Perdita,' said Emily. 'What sort of person is she?'

Jonas considered the question for a moment. 'Quiet. Not the gregarious type. She doesn't often come to the pub with us after the performance. I get the impression she has another life outside the company, if you know what I mean.'

'Do you know whether she's involved with anyone?'

Jonas said nothing for a few seconds, as if he was considering the answer carefully. 'She's always keeps quiet about her private life . . . unlike some. But Hen might know more.'

'What about her family?'

'She's never mentioned them.'

'Where can we find Hen?' Joe asked.

'In her dressing room. I'll show you.' Jonas stood up, as if he was eager for the interview to be over.

'What's your relationship with Perdita?'

Jonas blushed. 'We're colleagues,' he replied quickly.

'She's your leading lady, isn't she? You must work closely.'

'I play Urbain Grandier, a priest who opposes Cardinal Richelieu. He's accused of bewitching the Mother Superior of the local convent, and the powers-that-be destroy him. Perdita plays the crazed Mother Superior, Sister Jeanne of the Angels. Hardly boy meets girl but, yes, we do work closely. The whole cast do.' He moved towards the door. 'I'll show you to Hen's dressing room. She shares it with Perdita.'

'What about Perdita's understudy? Charlotte, is it?' Joe asked.

'That was her you saw on stage. She's good.'

'As good as Perdita?' said Emily.

Jonas opened and closed his mouth, unsure of the appropriate answer. 'She coped really well at the rehearsal, considering.'

'How do you think she'll react if Perdita shows up and robs her of her big chance?' Emily asked with a hint of mischief.

Jonas didn't answer. He opened the door, and they followed him down the corridor to a door with a piece of card bearing the names Hen Butler and Perdita Elmet attached to it with a drawing pin. Jonah knocked and waited until a female voice told him to come in.

When he pushed the door open Joe saw a young woman sitting on a sofa upholstered in tattered blue velour, her feet tucked to one side. She looked up, straightened her back and put aside the book she was reading. She had short dark hair and a heart-shaped face. But her best feature was her eyes, which were large, brown and expressive.

Joe saw a smile of greeting on her lips, the sort of smile a woman gives when she's pleased to see a man. But the smile vanished when she realized that Jonas wasn't alone.

'Hi, Hen. Er . . . these people are from the police. They want to ask you about Perdita.'

'We're all worried about her.' Her voice was deep and resonant; an actor's voice. 'It's not like her to let people down.'

'How long have you known her?'

'Only since rehearsals for *The Devils* began six weeks ago. Isn't that right, Jonas?' She looked at her colleague for support, and Joe knew his initial impression had been correct. There was an attraction there. But from Jonas's reaction, he suspected it was one-sided.

Joe saw Emily give Jonas a look. After a few seconds he took the hint. 'If you've finished with me . . .?'

'Thanks. But we might need to speak to you later,' said Emily.

As Jonas left, Hen gave him a brave smile and watched him leave the room with more than a casual interest.

'When did you last see Perdita?' Joe asked after he'd shut the door.

'When the performance finished last night. I was going straight back to the flat we're sharing, but she said she was meeting someone for a drink and not to bolt the door. She said she'd be back before midnight and she'd see to it then. Only, she never came back.'

'What can you tell us about her?' said Emily. 'Does she have a family?'

'I think her parents live somewhere down south, but I don't think she has much to do with them. She has a sister in Australia and a brother, but that's all I know.'

'Is there a boyfriend? Girlfriend?'

It was a while before Hen answered. 'There is someone.'

'Who?'

'She never talks about him, but he came to the flat once when I was there. I think she was embarrassed that I'd seen him, if you know what I mean.'

'Well, don't keep us in suspense,' said Emily, as if Hen's reticence was trying her patience.

'He's . . . he's on the Arts Committee of the Council. Chair or something.'

'What's his name?' said Joe, preparing to write in his notebook.

'Alvin Cobarn. Councillor Cobarn.'

The name was familiar to Joe, but he couldn't put a face to it. He gave Emily a quizzical look, and she responded with a little nod.

'I know him,' she said quietly. 'He's my local councillor.'

Emily lived with her husband, Jeff, and their three children in the well-to-do suburb of Pickby. It was the sort of district where people would alert their local councillor to any minor upset to their well-ordered world.

'He's a lot older than Perdita,' said Hen. 'But good-looking. Distinguished. We weren't introduced, so I never actually spoke to him.'

'Are you sure they were having a relationship? I mean, might he just have called round about something and . . .?'

'Absolutely not.' She gave an incongruous wink. 'I could tell by the body language. They were definitely an item.'

'What did Perdita say about it?'

'Nothing. But then we've never had that sort of relationship. Perdita's not an easy person to get to know.'

'And you've no idea where she might be now?' Joe asked.

'No. But she's worked really hard on this play so I can't see her just taking off like this and letting everyone down. Something's wrong.'

'You said you don't know her well,' said Emily. 'Perhaps she's done this sort of thing before.'

Hen shook her head. 'The theatre's an incestuous world. She was working in Leeds for a while before she came here. It isn't that far away, so if she was in the habit of walking out on productions, someone would have heard by now. Besides, I think Charlotte worked with her there, and I'm sure she would have mentioned it.' She hesitated. 'That's why I'm worried. We all are.'

'It would help if we had a look at her room in your flat. Have you any objection?'

'No. Of course not.'

Before Joe could say anything more the door burst open. He recognized the girl standing in the doorway as the understudy, Charlotte. Her lips were slightly open, as if she was about to ask a question. But when she saw Joe and Emily, the words left her, and she stared at them in stunned silence.

'They're here about Perdita,' Hen said. There was something about the way she said the words that told Joe that these two young women weren't the best of friends; a note of distrust, maybe.

'Has she turned up?' The words came out in a rush.

'Not yet.' Joe stood up and introduced himself.

She looked him up and down anxiously. 'You are looking for her, aren't you?'

'We will be. Can you tell us anything about her?'

She glanced at Hen. 'Only that she's lovely. A really nice person.'

'I believe you worked with her in Leeds,' said Joe.

'We were only in one production together, and I wouldn't say

I know her well. But I like her. You should be out looking for her,' she added accusingly.

'You've never seen her with anyone? You're not aware of any relationship she might have?'

'No, sorry. Like I said, I don't know her that well.'

'She didn't say anything to you about going away or . . .?'

'No. Nothing like that. It's a mystery. If there's anything we can do to help find her . . .'

'All you can do at the moment, love, is tell us everything you know about her,' said Emily. 'We need to speak to any friends she might have had outside the theatre as well. Any ideas.' She looked at Hen. 'Apart from the gentleman you mentioned earlier.'

Charlotte gave Hen a quizzical look, then both women shook their heads.

'If we can have your address and the keys to your flat,' Emily said to Hen. 'I'll bring them straight back. Unless you'd like to be there while we . . .?'

'No. It's OK.' She stood up and opened a soft velvet shoulder bag that was sitting on the counter that ran beneath the mirror. She recited the address and handed Joe a set of keys.

'I'll get them straight back to you,' he said after he'd thanked her. Their eyes met, and she smiled. She had a smile that created dimples in her cheeks.

'I should have known something bad would happen,' said Charlotte.

'Why's that?' Joe asked. It struck him as a strange thing for her to say, and he noticed that Hen was watching her with a 'don't say anything' look on her face.

But Charlotte carried on. 'Jonas saw the grey lady. They say that when someone sees her, something awful's going to happen.' There was a slight edge of hysteria in her voice, as though she was trying hard not to panic.

Emily just about stopped herself from snorting. 'Grey lady?'

'The Playhouse was built on the site of a medieval convent – you can see the foundations in the basement,' she said quickly. 'She was a nun who was walled up alive for getting pregnant.'

'Lots of theatres are supposed to have resident ghosts, and she's ours,' Hen said dismissively.

'Sounds like a load of rubbish to me,' said Emily, her eyes meeting Hen's in agreement.

Charlotte bowed her head, as if Emily's words had wounded her somehow. She began to fidget with her sleeve. 'Perdita seemed scared when Jonas said he'd seen her.'

'I think we can discount grey ladies from our enquiries,' said Joe gently, pocketing Hen's keys. 'Try not to worry, eh? Most missing people return within forty-eight hours.'

As he left the room he knew that his words had sounded hollow. Because he didn't really believe them himself.

SIX

It was time for lunch, and Debby Telerhaye bought a hot dog from one of the stalls near the market and washed it down with a takeaway coffee from Starbucks. She'd spent the morning mooching round the shops, and after a good dose of caffeine and a break from the claustrophobic atmosphere of home, the events of the previous night had begun to fade from her memory.

Her doubts about her experience were increasing. There had been no dead body – the policeman had been quite clear about that – and the more she thought about it, the more sure she was that the woman she'd seen must have been a vagrant – or perhaps someone who, like herself, had had too much to drink and decided to sleep it off. The cocktail of fog and darkness had made everything strange, creating a weird parallel world where reality had been suspended.

She'd picked her phone up from the police station first thing, wondering if she'd see Joe, and she'd felt a little disappointed when it was handed to her by a middle-aged constable, who asked her to sign for it. However, she'd felt better once she was connected with the outside world again and had wondered, as she often did, how people had survived before the mobile was invented.

She'd seen the posters around the city. Psychic Fair. All week at the Pavilion Hall, that monstrous concrete hangar off Ditchgate. The hall had been built just outside the city walls to house conventions and exhibitions, but the planners' collective lack of architectural imagination had been breathtaking. Nobody in their right minds could have called the Pavilion Hall beautiful or appropriate to its largely medieval environment.

It was only ten minutes' walk away, and Debby knew that if she went there now, she'd be back in time to meet her mates later. Or maybe she'd go to the museum. She liked museums and old things, although she'd never have admitted this to anyone. History was her favourite subject at college too, but she wasn't as comfortable with her own past as she was with other people's.

When she reached the Pavilion Hall she paid the entrance fee to a hatchet-faced woman on the door before entering the vast building. The concrete walls gave it a chilly feel, and she stopped near the entrance, looking round at the stalls. An array of brightly coloured tables and displays lined the walls and central passageway, and she wasn't sure where to start.

His name had been on the poster, so she guessed that he was one of the main attractions, which meant that even after everything that had happened he was still trusted. Still successful. Her mother had placed her trust in him, but he'd let her down.

She walked down the central passage between the displays of tarot-card readers and new-age paraphernalia; stalls selling everything the modern follower of Wicca or paganism could desire. There were offers of palm reading and other, more esoteric ways of seeing into the future, and various psychics had set up their stalls, each claiming to be in contact with the world beyond our own. Debby was making a round of the exhibits, eyeing each with jaundiced scepticism, when an announcement came over the PA system. A special session with a world-renowned psychic medium was about to take place on the main stage at the end of the hall in ten minutes' time. When she heard the message her heart began to pound. After all these years she'd see him in the flesh again, and she was suddenly afraid.

She wondered if he'd recognize her. And if he did, what on earth she'd say to him. Perhaps this hadn't been a good idea. But she was there now, so she might as well go through with it.

She felt out of place as she made her way to the back of the hall. Everyone else was either wearing black with lots of body piercings or dressed in peacock colours accentuated by flowing scarves. In her jeans and denim jacket she felt like a spy in the ranks. But perhaps that's exactly what she was.

There was another tannoy announcement, more urgent this time. Carlo Natale would be appearing in two minutes. Would the audience please take their places. Debby's legs suddenly felt heavy. Seeing his face would bring it all back. She would be forced to relive that terrible time all over again.

She was about to turn and walk away when a woman touched her shoulder. She was a fussy little soul in her seventies with wisps of brassy hair escaping from a silk scarf wrapped around her head. 'Come along, dear,' she said, taking Debby's arm. 'You don't want to miss him, do you? I've seen him before, you know. He's wonderful.'

Debby allowed herself to be led to a vacant seat, and as the woman sat down beside her, her rheumy cornflower eyes glowed with anticipation. 'He contacted my friend's late husband, last year,' she whispered, leaning towards Debby, who could smell garlic on her breath. 'Told her things only he would know. Marvellous.'

Debby attempted a smile, but couldn't quite manage it. Some people were so gullible. And those who took advantage of them, preyed on the innocent and naive, never seemed to pay for what they did.

Music oozed from the speakers either side of the temporary stage. Music of mystery selected carefully to create the desired atmosphere. There was a ripple of applause as a man stepped out from behind the night-blue velvet curtain at the back of the stage. He was dressed conventionally in a smart suit – sharp and expensive – with a blue silk tie. He had thick dark hair, touched with white at the temples, a tanned face with a weak chin and watchful eyes. It was hard to tell his age, which could have been anything from forty to sixty-five.

Debby hardly heard what he was saying. Her eyes were focused on his face, and she was suddenly sure she'd seen him somewhere very recently, although she couldn't think where. She stared at him, trying to read his thoughts and study the tricks he was using as he, apparently miraculously, selected members of the audience and told them all about their lost loved ones. She knew it was all done with trickery because she'd seen a programme about it on TV once. Cold reading, it was called. Using clues and detailed observations and fishing for information with silken hooks baited with weasel words. Debby was convinced that if she gazed at him long enough, he'd recognize her. But he didn't. Unless he was such a skilled actor that he'd managed to conceal his surprise.

Twenty minutes later the performance was over, and Carlo Natale retreated behind the curtain once more while the audience, mostly women of a certain age, fluttered away like birds who'd just spotted a scarecrow.

It was time. Debby had lost her elderly companion in the melee, so she was able to slip unseen behind the curtain. It was time to face her demons.

It was an out of the way spot, well away from the paths used by workers and visitors taking the short cut through the park. If a thin, dank mist hadn't been swirling around the low walls like wraiths, tourists might have been tempted to explore the picturesque ruins. But as it was, the abbey was deserted.

The body lay in the ruined church, hidden from any casual passer-by between two beds of evergreen shrubs marking the place where the choir of monks had once sang the offices of the day in front of the high altar.

It had been spotted by a young apprentice gardener who'd been given the task of tidying the area in the damp mist. The gardener, a gangly lad of seventeen who was a martyr to acne, had alerted his boss, and half an hour later the calm of the isolated spot was transformed into a bustling crime scene, complete with tents and barriers of striped tape.

The dead woman had been found lying on her front, her arms outstretched and her feet placed neatly together, and something told Joe that she'd been arranged that way. She was probably in her late twenties, and she wore a long black velvet coat over an ankle-length skirt patterned with red and blue flowers. Joe noticed that she only had one shoe – a purple ballet pump. Her head was twisted to the left, and a diaphanous blue scarf had been pulled tightly round her slender neck. Her long dark hair was matted to a face that had once been beautiful, but violence had robbed her of all loveliness and life.

Once the photographers had finished their work, Emily asked someone to push the dead woman's hair back, and now Joe could see her protruding tongue and staring eyes. As he looked down on her, he offered up a small prayer for her soul, a habit he'd never abandoned over the years.

When he'd finished, he heard Emily speak. 'It's her, isn't it? Perdita Elmet?' Her voice was low, almost reverent.

'No doubt about that. The ground around isn't disturbed, and if she was strangled, surely she would have put up a fight.'

'Unless he took her by surprise. Attacked her from behind. Grabbed her scarf and pulled it tight.'

'She'd still have struggled. It's instinct.'

'Do you think she was dumped here, then?'

Joe tore his gaze away from the dead woman and turned to Emily. 'It's not far from the undercroft. Maybe Debby wasn't imagining things. What if she was killed there and the killer moved her here so she wouldn't be found for a while? Loads of people take a short cut through the undercroft during the day.'

'The killer might have been hanging about while Debby took shelter. Didn't you say she thought she saw someone?'

'If you're right, she might have had a lucky escape.'

'I'll send a forensic team over to the undercroft.'

'Perhaps we should have done that before.'

Joe hadn't intended to be critical, but he could see from the look on Emily's face that she was put out.

'We can all be wise with hindsight,' she said quickly, looking away. She stared at the body in silence for a few seconds before speaking again. 'Think he carried her here?'

'Or she was transported some other way.'

'You can't get a car down here. A wheelbarrow?'

'He might not have needed one. The undercroft's only a couple of hundred yards away, and in the fog he was unlikely to be seen. She doesn't look very heavy. Most reasonably fit men could manage to carry her that far.'

'We'll have to talk to Debby Telerhaye again,' Emily said, after she'd given the order to seal off the undercroft. 'You seem to have struck up a rapport with her, so I'll leave that to you.'

Joe thought of the girl he'd encountered the night before. There had been something about her; an air of tragedy, maybe. He'd hoped he wouldn't have to see her again. But now she could be a vital witness in a murder enquiry, so he had no choice.

His thoughts were interrupted by a female voice. 'Sorry I'm late. I was in the middle of a post-mortem.'

Joe turned round and saw Sally Sharpe, the pathologist, walking towards him. Like everyone else she'd been kitted out with a crime-scene suit at the entrance to the sealed-off area, but, unlike everyone else, she looked good in it. She had once made drunken advances to Joe at a Christmas party, and for a long time after he'd experienced a vague feeling of embarrassment in her company, even though he liked her. But a lot of time had passed since then, and now she was engaged to a fellow doctor, although, as far as he was aware, no attempt had been made to set a date for a wedding.

'Hi, Sal,' said Emily. 'This one's definitely suspicious. Sorry to add to your workload.'

Sally gave a weary half smile, but as she caught Joe's eye the smile widened. Joe didn't smile back. He'd have felt bad about being cheerful in the presence of a young life cut so brutally short.

'Looks like strangulation,' said Emily. 'Would you agree?'

Sally squatted down and began to examine the body, taking samples and placing plastic bags carefully over the hands to protect any forensic traces, any DNA belonging to the killer which might be trapped beneath the woman's fingernails as she tried to save her own life. After a while she straightened herself up.

'All the signs are that she was strangled, most likely with the scarf round her neck, and I'd say she's been dead about twelve hours. I might be able to tell you more after the post-mortem, but don't hold your breath. Accurate times of death only happen in TV cop shows.'

'Someone saw her dead around eleven fifteen last night.'

'There you are then. You've only got to find out when she was last seen alive and you've got your window.'

'You OK, Sally?' Joe asked. She seemed distant today, as though there was something on her mind, something more than being disturbed in the middle of a post-mortem.

'Fine,' she said. 'You say someone saw her dead? Wasn't it reported?'

'It was. Only, when the patrol got there the body had gone.

The girl who reported it had had a few too many, so we thought she might have seen a vagrant asleep or . . .'

'She was imagining things in all that fog?'

Joe nodded.

'Actually, I was about to mention that I think the body might have been moved, but you've beaten me to it. Where did the girl see it?'

'The abbey undercroft. It's a couple of hundred yards away.'

'Wonder why she was moved.'

'That's what we'd like to know,' said Emily.

'I think her body's been arranged carefully,' said Joe. 'If I'm not mistaken she's facing east, and she's in the classic position of a penitent prostrating themselves before an altar.'

Emily raised her eyebrows. 'You sure?'

Joe nodded.

'What kind of penitent?'

'A monk, perhaps. Or a nun.'

There was a long silence before Sally spoke again. 'Do we know who she is?'

'Her name's Perdita Elmet,' said Joe 'She's an actress – or do we call them all actors these days? She was in the production at the Playhouse. *The Devils*.'

Emily glanced at Joe. 'If Joe's right, her murder might be connected with the play. It's full of nuns,' she added by way of explanation.

Sally crouched down again and resumed her examination. Then, with the help of a couple of CSIs, the body was turned gently. Joe saw the pathologist push the hair back from the dead woman's face and frown as she eased her gloved fingers between Perdita's pale lips, pushing the tongue gently to one side.

After a few seconds she brought her hand out, and Joe could see that she was holding something between her thumb and forefinger. It was a grey metal oval, about two inches long. The metal looked like lead, and there was something stamped on it: a robed figure in the centre with lettering around the edge.

'What is it?' said Emily, bending forward to get a better look.

'Haven't a clue,' said Sally. 'Looks like some sort of seal or . . .'

'I think I know what it is,' said Joe, holding out his hand. 'Pilgrims used to buy them in the Middle Ages when they visited a holy shrine.' He paused, and Sally placed the object carefully into his palm. 'A souvenir, I suppose.'

'What's written on it?' Emily asked, her voice impatient.

Joe squinted at the thing, doing a swift translation in his head. 'It's Latin. It says: *Saint Galert, pray for us*.'

'Who's Saint Galert?'

'As far as I remember,' said Joe, 'Saint Galert of Eborby was patron saint of the city's public executioners.'

SEVEN

Carlo Natale looked older than Debby remembered. But then a lot of time had passed since he'd been part of her family's life. When she pushed her way through a gap in the velvet curtain she found him sitting in his makeshift dressing room sipping amber liquid out of a crystal glass. Whisky. Even though she'd only been a child, she remembered that whisky was his tipple. Her mother had bought bottles of the stuff to keep him sweet: spent a fortune on the best single malts.

Debby stood there for a few seconds before he looked up and saw her. She saw the shock of recognition pass across his face, there for a second then swiftly concealed. He put the glass down on the folding table next to him and gave her an unctuous smile.

'Sorry. If you want a private reading you'll have to make an appointment.'

'That's OK,' she heard herself saying.

'See my assistant. She'll fix you up.'

That smile again, knowingly sympathetic, as if he could feel her pain. But she knew he couldn't.

He picked up his glass and took another drink. 'I'm afraid I'm tired. My work takes it out of me, as I'm sure you'll appreciate.'

'You recognize me, don't you?'

There had been a split second of alarm in his eyes when he'd first seen her, but now he looked calm, only mildly curious. 'I'm sorry. Have we met before? I meet so many people that—'

He was lying, and she hated him for it. 'Peter Telerhaye. You remember him?'

This time the smooth veneer of falsehood he'd acquired over the years suddenly crumbled. 'I . . . I . . . Yes, of course I remember. Who are you?'

'I'm Debby. Peter's sister. I was only eight when it happened.'

'So you were.' He took a long drink, stood up and walked over to a bottle of Glenlivet standing on a side table. He poured some into his glass, filling it almost to the top. Then he turned to her. 'How is your mother?'

The smooth, transatlantic accent had slipped, to be replaced by the flat vowels of his native Yorkshire.

'Not good. My dad walked out, and the man she's got now is a creep. She's never got over Peter. But if you're a clairvoyant, you should know that, shouldn't you?'

He glanced nervously at the curtain. 'Keep your voice down, will you? What do you want?'

'I want you to find Peter like you promised.'

'God knows, I tried.' He was staring at his glass as if he hoped to find the missing child in its depths.

'You told my mum you'd find him alive. You said you knew where he was and that he was fine.'

He shook his head. 'Somctimes wires get crossed,' he mumbled. 'I don't often fail, but . . .'

'You're a fraud. Why don't you admit it?' She stared into his eyes, amazed at her own boldness.

He put his finger to his lips, then he came close to her. She could smell the alcohol on his breath. 'He was in that old barn,' he hissed. 'When my spirit guide saw him he was alive and well. They found one of his shoes there. Something must have happened after the police were alerted. He must have been taken somewhere else while they were on their way.'

'And you didn't *see* it?'

'I lost the connection, that's all. Does your mother know you've come here?'

'She doesn't even know you're in Eborby.'

'Best keep it that way. We don't want to upset her, do we?'

'She's kept the press cuttings. She still keeps looking at them – can't let it go. I've read them myself. I know all about what happened back then.' Debby turned to go. 'This isn't the end, you know.'

'What do you mean? What are you going to do?'

'I've not decided yet.'

She saw him close his eyes, and his face took on an expression of deep concentration, almost a trance.

'I can see something,' he said. 'It's very hazy. Comes and goes. A little boy. Fair hair. I think it's . . .'

Debby held her breath.

'I'm sorry, he's gone. But he was there. He wants to talk to you.'

Debby felt tears pricking her eyes. 'You're lying.'

Natale shook his head. 'I saw him.' He froze for a moment. 'He's in the spirit world, but . . .'

'You're saying he's dead?'

'On the other side,' he corrected with a hint of piety. 'But I can help you to find him. I know I failed, but this time it'll be different. The connection's stronger.'

She put her hand on the curtain and fingered the soft velvet. 'You won't get another chance. Not if I have anything to do with it. And you stay away from my mum.'

'She's not happy with her new boyfriend, you know. It won't last, and then she'll be depending on you to . . .' He closed his eyes again. 'Soon you'll meet someone who'll change your life. But this person will bring danger. Be careful.'

'Have you been following me?'

The eyes flashed open, and he looked at her slyly. 'Now, why should I do that?'

Debby's heart began to race. She pushed the curtain aside and shot through. This needed some thought.

Perdita Elmet's body had been taken to the hospital mortuary in a plain black van, but the CSIs were still going about their work. Sally had scheduled the post-mortem for the following morning. First thing. The delay made Joe impatient, but he knew there was a lot of work to do in the meantime.

Joe stood staring at the pilgrim badge that Sally had found in the dead woman's mouth, now swathed in a clear plastic evidence bag. And the more he examined it, the more familiar it seemed.

Emily's voice interrupted his thoughts. She seemed subdued,

as if the discovery of the young woman's corpse had upset her. 'The CSIs say there's no sign of a struggle in the undercroft, but they did find the dead woman's missing shoe just outside the entrance on the park gate side which means she was there at some point – probably when your little friend saw her. It hasn't rained recently, so the ground's rock hard between the undercroft and the abbey ruins. Even if she was transported in something like a wheelbarrow, it wouldn't have left tracks.'

'Any handy wheelbarrows around?'

Emily shook her head. 'The gardeners keep their equipment locked up, and there's no sign of a break-in. I've got someone going through the records to see if there are any similar unsolved cases on the books, here and nationally.' She scratched her head. 'I don't like this badge business. And the posing of the body.'

'It does suggest a ritual element rather than a straightforward domestic. Although the two things might not be mutually exclusive.'

'How do you mean, Joe?'

'We need to have a word with the boyfriend.'

'You mean Alvin Cobarn? Maybe her flatmate, Hen, got it all wrong.'

'I don't suppose he called round to discuss refuse collection or funding for public libraries. You seem a bit reluctant to involve him, Emily. Is there something I should know?'

Emily looked affronted as she shook her head vigorously. 'Of course not. I've just met him socially, that's all. He's chair of the board of governors at Jeff's school.'

Joe nodded. This explained the slight hesitation. Normally, Emily wouldn't have any hesitation about tackling the councillor, knocking on his door and demanding the truth about his exact relationship with the dead woman. But he held a powerful position at the school where her husband taught, and he knew who she was, so the situation might prove embarrassing. 'Tell you what, I'll take Jamilla with me.'

'No, you won't. If he's a suspect, he's going to be treated like everyone else. I've got to do the job I'm paid for.'

Joe couldn't help smiling. The old Emily Thwaite was back again. Blunt and straightforward. Yorkshire's best. 'He's not on the Police Committee, is he?'

'Thankfully not, or we would be treading on eggshells. His main interest is the arts. I met him and his wife at a drinks party to celebrate the opening of a new drama studio at Jeff's school, and I've come across him at civic society meetings and all. I suppose you could describe him as a casual acquaintance, but I wouldn't claim to know him.'

'What's his wife like?'

Emily considered the question for a few seconds. 'Ghostly is the word that springs to mind,' she said. 'I've never heard her speak. I think she might have some sort of social phobia, which must be awkward for a man in his position. She left early. He said she had a headache and put her in a taxi.' Joe could hear the disapproval in her voice.

They left the CSIs to their work and made for the car Emily had left in the car park usually reserved for staff at the nearby University Medieval History Department, which now occupied the impressive former lodgings of the abbot. A police warrant card comes with certain privileges, especially during a murder investigation.

Councillor Alvin Cobarn lived two streets away from Emily in the prosperous suburb of Pickby, not far from the race course which, in turn, had been constructed on the site where public executions took place in centuries past.

Emily pulled up outside his house and turned off the engine. 'I'll let you do the talking,' she said.

'Fine by me.'

'And watch it, 'cause he's a smooth operator,' she said. 'Wouldn't surprise me if he ended up standing for parliament.'

'Does he have a day job?'

'Lawyer. And he knows his stuff. Be careful.'

'Well, if Hen Butler's to be believed, he's also a cheating womanizer. Have they got any children?'

'I've never heard any mentioned.'

Joe unbuckled his seat belt, but Emily still sat in the driver's seat. 'Come on,' he said and watched her slowly unfasten her belt and climb out of the car like a schoolgirl making for a dreaded exam.

It was Joe who rang the polished brass doorbell of the large detached house which dated from the thirties, the period of art deco. It was an attractive house with sunburst-patterned stained glass set in the sturdy front door. The diamond panes of the windows sparkled in the weak sunlight that was trying to break through the thinning mist.

When there was no answer, Joe pushed the doorbell again. Three times, as though to emphasize the urgency of their business.

It was two full minutes before the door opened to reveal a tall woman. Joe's overall impression of her was pallor. Pale shoulder length hair; pale clothes; ivory skin dotted with dark moles.

'Mrs Cobarn?' He produced his warrant card and held it up for her examination. But her eyes strayed to Emily, and a look of relief passed across her face, as though someone had rescued her from a bore at a party.

'Mrs Timmons?'

Joe was puzzled for a second. Then he recalled that Emily used her maiden name at work. To this woman she was Mrs Timmons, schoolteacher's wife and casual acquaintance. Perhaps it was an advantage that Mrs Cobarn didn't know Emily was a Detective Chief Inspector.

'Is your husband in?'

'He's busy.'

'Sorry to bother him on a Saturday, but it is rather important,' said Emily with an innocent smile.

Joe knew this was the right approach. One mention of murder and this woman would clam up.

She stood aside to let them in, giving Emily an inquisitive look, too nervous to ask her directly what she was doing there. She said she'd fetch Alvin and left them waiting in the spacious square hallway while she vanished into a back room.

Eventually, a man appeared. He was as Hen Butler had described: tall, distinguished and good-looking for his age, which must have been around fifty. He was wearing the concerned frown of a professional politician who wished to share the worries of his constituents. But he didn't fool Joe for one moment.

'Mrs Timmons. What brings you here? My wife said it was the police.'

Emily took out her warrant card. 'I'm afraid I lead a double life, Mr Cobarn. I'm a Detective Chief Inspector with North Yorkshire Police. And this is my colleague, DI Plantagenet.'

For a moment, a look of shock passed across his face, swiftly suppressed. 'So you're here in your professional capacity? How can I help you?' he asked, almost eagerly.

'Can we speak somewhere private?' Joe asked. He knew it was possible that Mrs Cobarn was lurking somewhere, listening to their every word.

'Of course. Come into my study.'

He led them to the room at the back of the house from which he'd emerged earlier. The study was a large airy room lined with bookshelves and dominated by an impressive mahogany partners' desk. Joe noticed that although there were some law books, the majority were about the arts, especially the theatre. There was also a section on the Eborby Playhouse and its history. This man was an enthusiast, which Joe thought was refreshing in a committee man.

Cobarn sank into the large leather chair behind the desk and invited them both to sit. Emily caught Joe's eye, and he knew it was up to him to begin.

'Do you know a woman called Perdita Elmet?'

'Er . . . yes.' There was no mistaking the wariness in Cobarn's voice. 'Why?'

'One of her colleagues said you were friendly with her.'

There was a long silence, as if the man was deciding on the least incriminating answer. 'Can I rely on your discretion?'

'We can be discreet,' said Emily. 'What was your relationship with Ms Elmet?'

Cobarn rose from his seat and made for the door. He opened it and looked out into the hall. Once he'd checked that his wife wasn't in a position to overhear, he sat down again. 'We have a sexual relationship. My wife isn't a well woman, and I wouldn't want to hurt her for one moment, but . . .'

'She won't find out from us,' said Emily.

This seemed to reassure Cobarn, who leaned forward and lowered his voice. 'There was an attraction between Perdita and I from the start, and . . .' He stopped and looked from one to the other. 'Can I ask you what all this is about? Is Perdita in some sort of trouble?'

'Where did you meet?'

'At the theatre. The production of *The Devils* was going into rehearsal, and I was invited along to meet the cast for drinks. Perdita's a very attractive and interesting woman, so—'

'When was this?'

'About six weeks ago.'

'And you've been having an affair ever since?'

Cobarn looked rather affronted at Emily's bluntness. 'We've been meeting when we can. She knows I'll never leave my wife, and the arrangement suits both of us. Why do you want to know all this? Is she all right?'

Emily caught Joe's eye. It was time to tell the truth.

'I'm afraid she was found dead earlier today.'

Emily was watching the man's face, searching for any flicker, any reaction that seemed out of place. Joe watched too, but all he saw was shock.

'We're sorry to have to break it like this,' said Joe. 'But we're treating her death as suspicious.'

'How did she . . .?'

'We'll know more after the post-mortem,' said Emily, reluctant to share the details with a man who might have killed her.

'Where was she found?'

'In the abbey ruins. But her body was moved there.'

Cobarn put his head in his hands, a picture of despair. Then after a few seconds he looked up. 'I can't believe it. Are you sure it's her?'

'We've identified her from her photograph. There's no doubt, I'm afraid. When did you last see her?'

'Er . . . it must have been Wednesday. We went for a drink after the performance.'

'Where were you last night?'

'I was out at a dinner. Eborby Traders' Association at the Guildhall. I arrived there about seven, and I got a lift there and back from Councillor Rowlands. He lives nearby and he doesn't drink, so . . .'

'What time did you get home?'

'I think it was just before one in the morning. My wife had already gone to bed and she was fast asleep, but I'm sure Councillor Rowlands will vouch for me.'

'Driving must have been difficult in the fog.'

'Yes. The visibility was dreadful.' He paused. 'I suppose it was some lunatic taking advantage of the fog to attack women. You have to catch him before he strikes again.'

'We're well aware of that,' said Emily. She sounded a little peeved that Cobarn was trying to tell her her job.

'Did you leave the dinner at all?' Joe asked.

'No,' the man replied, affronted.

'We can check,' said Emily.

'Of course. Go ahead.'

'Perdita told her colleagues she was meeting someone after the play last night. Was that you?'

Joe saw a flicker of uncertainty in the man's eyes. He was uneasy about something. 'I told you, I was at a dinner.'

'Does your wife know about your relationship with Perdita Elmet?' Joe asked.

'Certainly not.' The confidence had returned. But that split second look of panic stayed in Joe's memory.

'I'll ask someone to get a list of guests from the Traders' Association,' Joe said quietly as they walked to the car. 'He could have slipped out at some point to meet the victim.'

Emily looked sceptical. 'If you think it's worth it.'

Joe got into the driver's seat. The dead woman's nervous married lover was as good a place to start as any.

EIGHT

Debby Telerhaye knew her mates would be at the cafe, but she'd catch up with them later, she told herself. Now she'd got her phone back she could text them to see where they'd be tonight – if she was in the mood. But she feared she wouldn't be much company at the moment; being there in body but not in mind would be a waste of everyone's time.

She needed to think, to wander around the city centre mingling with the tourists and shoppers. The faint mist had turned into a grey drizzle by the time she left the Pavilion Hall, and she decided to take a short cut past the rear of one of the modern chain hotels outside the city walls. But as soon as she got there her instincts told her she'd made a mistake. Whenever she'd taken that route before there'd usually been a couple of hotel employees lurking out there to enjoy a furtive cigarette, but today the place was deserted and there was an air of desolation as the breeze stirred the litter on the hard grey ground.

The passage was lined with large rubbish containers waiting to be taken away, and every so often she caught the rotting whiff of kitchen waste. She imagined tumbleweed blowing through the bleak, concrete landscape, wind whistling between the bare brick walls of Eborby's modern underbelly, and hurried on, making for the street . . . and people. The bustle of the city would help to restore some kind of normality. There's safety in crowds.

She'd faced her demon now. And she knew he'd been lying. He was a skilled actor – he had to be in his line of work – but when he'd spoken of danger, she hadn't believed a word of it. She knew he'd just intended to spook her, but his words still echoed in her head. Someone will bring danger. Be careful.

Ahead, she could see the gap in the railings that led on to Mungate. If she turned left she'd see the grey city wall jutting from its steep grassy bank a hundred yards away and, once through the tall, arched gate, she'd be stepping back six hundred years into the city's medieval heart. A place of the past; of tourists and ghosts.

When she heard a noise behind her she knew she should carry on, but something made her stop and turn her head. However, there was nobody there, just the fleeting impression of a shadow vanishing into a small doorway at the rear of the hotel. She walked on, heart pounding. She'd had this feeling of being followed so many times recently, but she was too much of a coward to retrace her steps and investigate. She started to hurry towards the gap in the fence. The main road and safety lay beyond the foot-worn path through the bushes. Once she'd reached it she'd be fine.

She was sure she could hear the beat of footsteps behind now, speeding up to match her pace and getting nearer. The gap in the railings was just ahead, but then there was a wide expanse of overgrown shrubbery to negotiate before she reached the road. He could grab her there, pull her into the tall bushes, and nobody driving along the road would be any the wiser.

She knew it was Sinclair. He was always leering, speaking in innuendoes when her mother wasn't there to hear, making veiled threats in the form of jokes. She fixed her eyes ahead. She only had a few yards to go now.

She darted through the gap and along the earth track through the bushes. The traffic roared reassuringly at the end of the path, and when she reached safety she stopped and breathed in the comforting fumes before turning left and heading for the city.

She had just begun to walk when she heard a voice.

'Are you OK?'

The voice didn't belong to Sinclair so she stopped and turned round. The speaker was a young man with dyed blond hair that protruded in spikes from his head. His nose was pierced by a gold ring, as were both his ears, and his clothes were rusty black and carefully torn. His T-shirt proclaimed the legend 'we are all artists' beneath a grey baby's head which had the sinister look of a knowing doll. She recognized him from somewhere, but she couldn't quite recall where.

'Remember me?'

She suddenly realized who he was. 'You work in the canteen at college.'

'Yeah. That's right.'

He fell in beside her. Normally, she'd have been wary, but if Sinclair was following her, he was bound to be discouraged, even though her new companion was a weedy specimen who would be no match for the creep who spent hours doing weight training and thought he was some kind of tough guy.

'The canteen job's only temporary,' the young man said. 'I'm an artist. I graduated last year, and I'm waiting for my big break. The day job keeps body and soul together.'

'Right.'

'I've got a couple of other jobs as well. Part time.'

'So when do you get time for your art?'

He hesitated. 'At night. In the early hours.'

'You don't sleep much, then?'

'Neither do vampires,' he said.

She started to laugh, but stopped herself when she realized that he sounded deadly serious.

'My name's Perry.' He put out his hand, and she took it automatically. It seemed a reassuringly old-fashioned gesture.

'Debby.'

'Something the matter?'

She wasn't usually in the habit of confiding in strangers, and she'd only met this man before in passing when he served her in the college canteen. But after her unsettling encounter with Carlo Natale and her strong feeling that Sinclair was stalking her, as he'd threatened to do so many times, she found that she was glad of the company. Besides, she felt she needed to talk to someone.

'It's my mum's partner. He's a bloody creep,' she blurted out. 'A pervert. He says he always has his eye on me. When he gets me on my own he says he watches me. He's scary.'

'My place isn't far away. Fancy a drink?'

Debby glanced behind her. There was no sign of Sinclair, but she was sure he'd been there. 'OK,' she said. 'Lead the way.'

Jonas Ventnor had made the formal identification. When an officer had gone to the theatre asking for a volunteer, he'd stepped forward. He'd been the one to report her missing, so he said he felt it was his responsibility. When he'd viewed her body his eyes had lingered on her contorted face, then he'd turned away, stunned, the blood drained from his face, leaving him ash pale. It had taken him a good hour to recover his composure.

None of Perdita's fellow actors knew much about her next of kin. As far as they were concerned she might have appeared on this earth like Venus, fully formed without the benefit of parents or family. Even Hen who'd shared her flat knew remarkably little about her life outside the theatre, except for her involvement with Councillor Cobarn, and she'd only discovered that by accident.

Emily thought all this was unusual, to say the least. And Sunny Porter commented that she must be the first woman in the history of the world who could resist sharing the details of her life and thoughts with all and sundry.

Joe saw Emily give Sunny a killing look. Then she sent him to organize the collection of any CCTV footage from the area – not that it would be much help in all that fog, she whispered to Joe as Sunny slouched out of the office.

A check had been made on Cobarn's alibi, and it appeared that he'd been at the function all evening and returned home with his fellow councillor as he'd said. But Joe knew from experience that mates often cover for each other. He gave orders that other witnesses should be questioned to back up the story, but he wasn't getting his hopes up.

Jamilla was put in charge of tracing Perdita's relatives, and the rest of the team had been allocated other tasks. But Joe was reserving one job for himself. He had taken a good look at the object found in Perdita Elmet's mouth, and he was as sure as he could be that it was a medieval pilgrim badge – the kind bought by visitors to the shrines of saints in the middle ages, purchased as a souvenir or a protection from evil. From what he could tell, this one looked like a reproduction, too perfect to be over six hundred years old. But he knew the saint it depicted. The shrine of Saint Galert – an Anglo Saxon bishop of Eborby – still stood behind the high altar in the cathedral, a shadow of its former glorious self since the Reformation caused most such holy sites to be destroyed as symbols of Catholicism. But Saint Galert's shrine had managed to survive more or less intact, minus its original adornments of gold and jewels, which had been taken by Henry VIII's commissioners to fill the royal coffers and finance wars with France.

The killer had, presumably, placed it in Perdita's mouth before arranging her body carefully, posing her in the position of a penitent. But what did he imagine she was doing penance for? What sin, real or in the killer's twisted imagination, had she committed?

There was her affair with Alvin Cobarn, of course. Was somebody on a general moral crusade against adultery, or was it something more personal? He had a feeling that the Saint Galert badge must be relevant, and he knew someone who might be able to help him with this particular problem.

He made a quick phone call to ensure that his journey wouldn't be wasted, and when he told Emily he was going out, she gave him an inquisitive look. He told her he was going to try and find out more about the badge, and she offered to go with him, her eyes lighting up at the prospect of getting away from the hectic office for an hour or so. But before Joe could reply, one of the team called her over. Joe raised a hand in farewell. It would be best if he went on his own.

It wasn't far to the cathedral. Just past the railway station and over Wendover Bridge. It was autumn, and the students were back at university. Joe stood on the bridge for a few moments watching the university rowing team practising on the river below. The sun was making its feeble attempt to shine again through the low cloud, and the fog that had brought the city to a halt the previous night had mostly vanished leaving only a few scraps of mist clinging to the water. But he knew from experience that in the Vale of Eborby it could descend again without warning, turning the world white and frightening.

He walked on past the gates to the Museum Gardens and past the undercroft, now sealed off with police tape. He could see the cathedral looming ahead, the huge edifice of golden stone dominating the huddle of buildings around it.

He walked across the paved square in front of the great west door and veered to the right, to the south door where the tourists entered, paying their money to gawp at the wonder of medieval architecture that was Eborby Cathedral, one of the finest examples in Europe.

Joe bypassed the queue and showed his warrant card to the middle-aged woman on the desk, feeling a gratifying sense of power as he breezed in which he swiftly suppressed.

He stepped into the cathedral nave. Its magnificence always made him catch his breath. No matter how many times he saw it the sheer beauty stunned him. He walked to the transept crossing and stood for the few moments, gazing at the high altar beyond the carved stone screen. Then he bowed his head. He couldn't have done otherwise. As he tried to pray, the image of Perdita Elmet's body entered his head and wouldn't leave.

She had lain, spreadeagled there before the place where the abbey's high altar would have stood. A penitent with a pilgrim badge thrust into her dead mouth. And now she cried out to him to bring her killer to justice. He shut his eyes tight, trying to rid himself of the vision. But she wouldn't leave him, so he turned to his left and walked round the side of the choir stalls towards the lady chapel behind the high altar. He had an urgent desire to see Saint Galert's shrine for himself, so he walked past the table tombs and side chapels, stepping on the ancient grave slabs set into the stone floor, until he reached the lady chapel. The first thing that struck him was the east window. A kaleidoscope of stained glass, dating from the middle ages and quite unique, it was one of the cathedral's greatest treasures. The light filtering through the glass threw sparks of colour on to the grey stone ground, and also played on the shrine, a roofed structure like a miniature house with arched niches set into the sides so that pilgrims could snuggle close to the saint's supposedly miraculous bones.

The arches were topped with stone medallions depicting the saint, right hand raised in blessing. The same image had decorated the badge found in Perdita Elmet's mouth.

Joe retraced his steps and took the wide passage that led to the cathedral's chapter house, dodging past the wandering tourists until he came to a closed door. It was an ancient door, arched and studded oak. And it bore a modern steel sign with the word 'Private' engraved in black.

He knocked, and when he heard a cheerful 'come in' he turned the wrought-iron handle and entered. As soon as the man behind the pile of paper and other debris on the desk saw him he stood up, and his wide smile of greeting suggested that he was delighted to see an old friend.

Canon George Merryweather was small, round and bald and wore a black chasuble; a neat little man, his appearance was at odds with the chaos surrounding him. Joe had heard him say from time to time that his office needed a good tidying. Somehow that miracle had never happened, although George had an uncanny ability to find things amidst the jumble of books, files, ephemera, souvenirs and other stuff he'd acquired over the years.

Many of the books, Joe knew, were about the occult and the history of the church's relationship with the opposition, the devil himself. However, as George was Diocesan Consultant on Deliverance and the Occult, this was only to be expected. To Joe, George was also a friend, the man who'd saved his sanity, his faith, and possibly his life when he'd come to live in Eborby after his colleague Kevin's shooting. A psychologist he'd seen after the tragedy had told him he was suffering from survivor's guilt. But it had been more than that. Two bitter losses in so short a time had robbed him of his long-held certainties and bruised his spirit. It had taken George's quiet wisdom to bring him a sort of healing.

'How are you, Joe?'

'Not too bad. You?'

George merely smiled. As usual he was fine. Unchanging. His life ticked along to the rhythms of cathedral life and the liturgical calendar. Only the demands of his other duties, those of Diocesan Exorcist – although he never called himself that – ever interfered with the serenity of his existence.

'Tea?'

Joe nodded, and somehow George located an electric kettle and two mugs from beneath the clutter on top of a low bookcase. There was milk, too, in a pint carton: George sniffed at it with approval and flicked the switch on the kettle.

Joe knew from experience that George couldn't be hurried, and it wasn't until the tea was in front of them that both men sat down and made themselves comfortable.

'You want to ask me something?'

'What makes you think this isn't a social visit?' said Joe.

'I heard on the local radio that a body was found in the abbey ruins and the police were treating it as suspicious. Presumably, when you're investigating a case of murder – I'm assuming it's murder – you don't have the time to pay me a visit for a cosy chat.'

Joe took a sip of tea and pulled a photograph of the badge from his pocket. 'Can you tell me anything about this?'

George took the photograph and studied it. 'It's a pilgrim badge. Used to be all the rage in the middle ages. People used to buy them as souvenirs and to boast to their neighbours that they'd visited a certain shrine. The tomb of Saint Thomas à Becket at Canterbury was very popular but, of course, you earned yourself more kudos if you made it to Santiago de Compostela . . . or Rome. In those days every religious establishment wanted their own saint to bring in the punters.' He squinted at the photo again. 'This is our own local lad – Saint Galert.'

'I know he's supposed to be the patron saint of public executioners, but what else can you tell me about him?'

'Eborby's public executioner was trying to hang a particularly vicious outlaw some time in the thirteenth century and an angry mob of the man's friends attacked him.'

'I thought Galert was an Anglo Saxon bishop.'

'So he was, but there was a statue of him at the front of the cathedral which toppled over and fell on the ringleader's head and killed him. The execution went ahead after that, and the city's executioners adopted him as their patron saint. But there's another story too, an earlier one.'

'What's that?'

'He's also the patron saint of wronged women. I'm not absolutely sure of the details, but he was said to have brought a woman back to life who drowned herself when her lover married.' He grinned. 'I don't know how true it is.'

Joe nodded. Legends and tall tales that became embellished over the centuries were all too common. He took the photograph back. 'I thought the badge looked as if it was made of lead at first, but it's not heavy enough.'

'They were often made of base metal. They churned them out by the thousand in those days. We still sell reproductions in the cathedral shop.'

Joe raised his eyebrows. This was news. 'I thought the one we found looked too perfect to be old, so it could be a modern copy. Is the cathedral the only outlet?'

'As far as I know.'

'Are there any other stories about Saint Galert?'

George rested his hands on his rotund, black-clad stomach. With his bald, shiny head and his benevolent face he looked like a chubby Buddha – or maybe a well-fed medieval friar. 'Lots. He was supposed to have had a brother who envied his piety and eventually poisoned him. Then there was the child he rescued from the jaws of a wolf by commanding the animal to release the lad. And there were various miracles attributed to his bones – healings from dire diseases and so on. But why a killer would want to leave an image of him in his victim's mouth, I've no idea.'

While Joe finished his tea, George changed the subject, probing gently, asking Joe if he'd heard from his former partner, Maddy, recently. Maddy had left Eborby to work in London, and George had seemed concerned about this loss. Perhaps more concerned than Joe himself had been. When Joe said he hadn't heard from her, George leaned over and gave him a sympathetic pat on the arm.

'I'd like to go and have a look at the shop,' Joe said as he stood up.

'Of course.' George sounded disappointed that he was leaving so soon. 'Hope we don't have fog again tonight,' he said. 'They always used to say that bad things happen in the Eborby fog.'

Joe said nothing. He left George's office and crossed the cathedral to the glass-fronted shop at the west end. It was the usual stuff: bookmarks; scented candles; CDs of the cathedral choir; pieces of modern stained glass; crosses and crucifixes of all descriptions. He found the reproduction pilgrim badges on a shelf at the far end of the shop, each one cocooned in its own little plastic bag with a piece of card explaining its significance. Their price was six pounds fifty, and they were identical to the one at the murder scene. Joe wondered whether the killer had bought it, or whether he'd come in here and indulged in a spot of shop-lifting. The price was cheap, so Joe didn't dare to hope that the purchaser had paid by credit card: unless it had been bought with other items, it would probably have been a cash transaction. Untraceable.

He approached the middle-aged woman behind the counter and showed her his warrant card. She had sleek bobbed grey hair and wore an elegantly tied silk scarf around her neck. And she looked quite unfazed at this unexpected visit from the police.

'Do you sell many of those badges – Saint Galert?'

'They're not our best-seller, but we do sell quite a few,' she said, clearly surprised at the question.

'Any records of who you sold them to?'

'Low value items are usually bought with cash.'

'Are you aware of any going missing – shoplifting?'

She pulled a face. 'Not particularly, but it does happen, even here in the cathedral. I wouldn't know for sure until the stock take at the end of the month.' She glanced up at the ceiling. 'We don't have CCTV in here because the Dean thinks it would send out the wrong message. He reckons trust is important – and I suppose he's right.' The scepticism in her eyes belied her words, and Joe guessed that she thought the Dean a little naive.

'Who else works here?'

'Oh, we're quite a little team. I'm the manager, and there's Audrey, my second in command. It's her day off today. Then we employ six part-timers. And casual staff in high season; students, mainly.'

'If I could have a list . . .'

'Of course.' She squatted down behind the counter and bobbed up again with a sheet of paper in her hand. She gave it to Joe and pointed out who was who. He thanked her, thinking that this could be a waste of time. They had no way of knowing when the thing was bought. And without CCTV . . .

The woman's voice interrupted his negative thoughts. 'Funny you should be asking about them. We sold twenty of them to a gentleman about a week ago. Gifts for visiting dignitaries, he said: souvenirs of Eborby. He liked the idea of giving them something a bit different – something to do with the city's history.'

'Do you know this man's name?'

'Of course. He's on the Arts and Leisure Committee at the Council. Councillor Cobarn.'

Joe thanked her profusely and hurried out.

NINE

'I'm warning you, there's nothing normal about where I live.'

Debby walked by her companion's side. All she knew about him was that his name was Perry and that he was a good listener. He'd listened patiently to her going on about Sinclair and how he gave her the creeps, which was something her mates never did. There was something about Perry she liked. Besides, there was no way she wanted to go home. Her mum might be worried, but she didn't care. It was all her stupid fault for moving Sinclair in, and it was about time she realized how her daughter felt about him.

So far she'd done most of the talking, but she suddenly wanted to know more about him.

'So you're an artist? What kind of art do you do? Paintings and all that?'

For a while he didn't answer, and she thought he might not have heard the question. She was about to ask it again when he spoke.

'I'm a conceptual artist. Know what that means?'

Debby shook her head.

'I have an idea. A concept. Then I make it happen.'

It all sounded a bit vague, but Debby persisted. 'What sort of ideas? What exactly do you do?'

For the first time Perry smiled. 'This and that. I left college in the summer and took the canteen job in term time. I work as a living statue too. I dress as a monk, all in white like a marble statue, and stand in the middle of Boargate where the tourists hang out. Every time someone puts money in my box I raise my hand in a blessing. It goes down surprisingly well.'

'Does it pay?'

'With the canteen job and some other casual work, it's enough to keep body and soul together. I don't starve.'

'What's it like . . . standing there with everyone gawping at you? Is it hard to keep still?'

'Kids can be a bloody nuisance . . . and dogs . . . and drunks. But most of the tourists are OK. Some of them see me as a photo opportunity.' His lips twitched upwards in a smile. 'The young Japanese girls think it's great, and some of them shriek when I move. It's funny, but I can't laugh. Sneezing can be a problem too . . . and going for a piss. But it's all worth it 'cause it helps to fund my proper work.'

'What's that?'

His expression suddenly turned serious. 'You'll see when you get to my place. You're not squeamish, are you?'

Debby shook her head, suddenly nervous. She was making for an unknown destination, somewhere that contained something that wasn't for the squeamish. But anything was better than going home.

Perry had been telling the truth when he'd said it wasn't far to where he lived. It was about a hundred yards away from the city walls in a street of small red-brick Victorian houses. Unlike much of Eborby, the area hadn't yet been gentrified, and there was an uncared for atmosphere about the place. Debby guessed that most of the houses were rented out, probably to students. The grimy windows hung with limp, outdated curtains that needed a wash were definitely a giveaway. Only a couple of houses stood out as privately owned, with freshly painted woodwork and hanging baskets swaying in the breeze.

At the far end of the street she could see a stone building, a relic from the medieval past, tucked between a small garage specializing in tyre fitting and a joiner's yard. An old oak double door was set in an arched entrance beneath a pair of gargoyles, barely recognizable after centuries of erosion.

Perry made straight for the door, took a Yale key from his pocket and inserted it into a modern lock that looked quite out of place against the ancient wood. The door opened smoothly. Debby had expected a horror film creak.

'Welcome to my humble abode.' Perry sounded a little nervous.

Debby stepped inside and looked round. It was a large space, around forty feet long and twenty feet wide. It might once have served as some sort of chapel, and only in a place with a glut of medieval buildings such as Eborby would it have remained so neglected and unloved. The arched windows were plain and boarded up in places, and the floor was well-worn stone. There was little inside: just a makeshift kitchen in a far corner and a plasterboard partition which created a small room to the side of the entrance, possibly a toilet. The main space was filled with canvasses and wooden crates, and against the left-hand wall Debby could see a mattress, made up with a duvet. Tattered red velvet drapes covering half the back wall provided the only hint of warmth and comfort in the place.

She looked down, and when she saw several grave slabs set into the floor, she suppressed a shudder. But she'd been warned that it was no place for the squeamish.

'Until a few months ago it was used to store antiques,' Perry said. 'And it was a carpet warehouse before that. I remember it from when I was a kid. I broke in when the antiques bloke moved out. Squatted and changed the lock. It's mine now. Squatters' rights,' he said proudly.

'What did it used to be?'

'I've just told you.'

'I mean before then?'

'Part of some monastery . . . or convent. Don't know which. I reckon this might have been a chapter house where they held their meetings. Like my flooring?'

'The gravestones? Are people actually buried under here?'

'They sometimes buried important monks in the chapter house, but I haven't taken a look.'

'That's really creepy. I don't know how you can stay here.'

He leaned towards her and whispered in her ear. She could feel his breath hot on her face. 'It gets better. Come and meet Fred.' He began to walk towards the back of the building, and she followed, suddenly curious.

The opposite corner to the kitchen area was gloomy and unlit, but she could make out a niche set into the wall: a space long enough for a tomb. Debby had a feeling from the way he said the words that meeting Fred might not be a routine social encounter. As she drew closer she could see that stones had been removed from the niche to reveal a wooden box inside. The wood looked ancient, its time-bleached boards eaten by worm, and when Perry lifted the lid carefully she could see the relish on his face, the gloating pleasure of a collector who'd just acquired something rare and precious to feed his obsession.

'Come on, don't be shy. He doesn't bite.'

She stepped forward and gasped as she peered down at the thing that was lying there. It had a human form, and desiccated flesh still clung to the bones. It was dust grey, as were the strands of hair attached to the skull. It seemed to be grinning at her . . . as if it knew her innermost secrets.

'That's horrible. Put the lid down.'

'I like him. He keeps me company. I call him Fred, but that won't have been his name.'

'Is it a he?'

'I reckon so. He probably lived in the fourteenth century, and he might have been a high-up monk or even an abbot. I don't know. In my head he can be whatever I want him to be. See ya, Fred,' he said as he closed the lid.

'That's really weird.'

'I am weird. It's my job.'

Debby clutched her canvass bag close to her body. 'I've got to go. I've got something to do.'

'Don't let old Fred spook you. He's harmless. The perfect housemate. He doesn't hog the bathroom or nick my stuff from the fridge. Unlike my sister. I don't know what you're worried about.'

'You've got a sister?'

'Why shouldn't I have one?'

'What about your mum and dad?'

Perry's face clouded. 'My dad walked out on us when we were little, and my mum died two years ago.'

'I'm sorry,' she said automatically. 'My dad walked out too.' She hoped this would create a rapport between them. But instead there was an awkward silence. 'What does your sister think of Fred?'

'She understands. But even if she didn't it wouldn't matter. Fred inspires my work.'

'How do you mean?'

Perry stared at the closed lid of Fred's resting place. 'I'm working on a conceptual piece about the ghosts of Eborby. They're always going on about how it's the most haunted city in the country, and I think it needs to be marked properly, not just with a few hammy ghost walks. Ghosts are restless spirits . . . the results of turmoil or violence,' he said in a whisper. 'I'm going to create new ones. Play my part in history.'

'How?'

'Wait and see.'

His eyes were shining with passion, and she suddenly felt frightened. She'd intended to tell him about Carlo Natale, but the moment had gone.

She needed to get away.

'Will I see you again?' Perry asked as she half walked, half ran towards the door.

She said OK. Maybe she'd see him around.

Joe asked himself how he could have forgotten. For years now this date in October had dominated his life. The anniversary of Kaitlin's death. But he'd woken up that morning oblivious to the significance of the day. He'd been distracted by Perdita Elmet's murder, but that was no excuse. He felt guilty, almost as though he was being unfaithful, as if he'd betrayed her memory. There'd been other women since his late wife's death, but he'd never forgotten this particular anniversary before. The day they'd quarrelled; the day she'd stormed off and never came back. She'd fallen. Her death had been an accident, although there were some, especially Kaitlin's sister, who blamed him. There were times when he blamed himself.

He tried to forget, to concentrate on the problem in hand, and as he was heading back to headquarters he wondered how Emily would take the news that Councillor Cobarn had purchased twenty of the badges. Did he now just have nineteen? Was one of them in an exhibits bag in the incident room? She'd seemed reluctant to push matters when she'd questioned him before, but now it was unavoidable.

He had almost called ahead to tell her the news, but he reckoned it would wait until his return. Then maybe they could go together to pay Cobarn another visit and put on a bit of pressure. At the moment he was the best suspect they had, and Joe wasn't going to be daunted by the man's veneer of power and respectability. Throughout history seemingly respectable men had been known to commit the most appalling acts of violence.

As he passed the library he glanced to his right. The undercroft was still sealed off as a crime scene until the CSIs were sure that they'd gleaned every available clue. He carried on past the park gates, and as he was about to cross the bridge over the river, something caught his eye.

It was a drawing low down on the wall of the medieval tower that guarded the entrance to the bridge. At first Joe took it for graffiti; a small, annoying scar of the city's medieval fabric. But a second look told him that it had been executed in chalk, which would probably wash off with the next shower. He carried on walking. Then he stopped, retraced his steps and looked again, more carefully this time.

It was a faint shape, so lightly drawn that it was barely visible on the stones. It was the size of a human being; a robed figure in spectral grey with no discernible face. Joe had the impression it was the shape of a nun in an old-fashioned habit, but he could have been wrong. The vague figure appeared to be holding something which was far clearer, as though the artist had sketched in the ghostly figure around it. Joe stared. There was no mistaking the similarity. It was a round medallion depicting a saint in his bishop's mitre, his hand raised in benediction. Joe could just make out the Latin words around the edge. *Saint Galert Pray for Us*.

Somebody had drawn the badge that had been found on Perdita Elmet's body. Perhaps the killer was trying to draw attention to himself.

TEN

Once Emily learned that Cobarn had bought the badges from the cathedral shop, she was keen to question him again. But this time she said she'd take Jamilla. The feminine touch for a ladies' man, she said with a grin.

Joe left her to it. His news about the badges meant that this time Emily would forget the social niceties. Cobarn was a suspect and would be treated as such. No more tact. No more tiptoeing around. Especially since news had come in to suggest that his alibi for Perdita's murder might not be as cast iron as it had first appeared. Councillor Rowlands had driven him home in the fog all right . . . but there were long stretches of the evening when nobody had seen him. After saying he had to make an urgent phone call, he'd vanished soon after ten fifteen. It was hard to calculate how long he'd been away, but it had seemed like a long time. Possibly an hour or more. The trouble with functions is that people circulate and join different groups during the course of the evening. Nobody could be quite sure whether Cobarn went AWOL or was just networking elsewhere.

Joe had taken a photograph of the chalk drawing on the tower with his mobile phone, and he showed it to Emily.

'I don't know when it appeared. I pass that tower on the way to work, and I don't think it was there yesterday. Although I can't be sure,' he admitted. His walks to work were generally quick and purposeful. He could have passed the tower a hundred times and never glanced in its direction.

'Think it's connected to the murder?'

'Do you?'

Emily shrugged. 'There might be CCTV,' she said hopefully. 'I'll put someone on it right away.'

'And we should check on all cathedral employees. It's the only outlet for those badges.'

'That's a lot of people.'

'We'll start with the shop. I'll arrange it.'

'If Cobarn can't account for one of the twenty he bought, you might not have to.'

Joe didn't reply. Somehow he couldn't see Cobarn going to the trouble of inserting the badge into the victim's mouth. Unless it was to muddy the waters. 'I'm going to pay another visit to the theatre. I want to speak to Perdita's colleagues again.'

'It's coming up to five, and the performance isn't till seven thirty,' Emily reminded him. 'They probably won't all be there.'

'Well, if the understudy's had to take over, they'll probably be having extra rehearsals. Anyway, I want to catch them off their guard. We haven't asked them to provide proper alibis yet. Perdita was killed after the performance. We have to find out what they all did.'

'All we know is that she was probably moved around eleven thirty. I still can't understand why the killer did that.'

'To delay discovery? Come Saturday morning that undercroft would have been like Piccadilly station. Or it might have been for symbolic reasons. The body was posed as a penitent in front of the altar.'

'Wonder what sins she had to repent?'

'That's what we have to find out.'

'Pity the CCTV's no use. All they've got off the footage so far is fog.'

'He chose the right night,' said Joe.

Emily didn't answer. She went off in search of Jamilla, leaving him to deal with the actors. He thought there was a good chance they'd be putting the finishing touches to their performance, especially as the understudy was still raw. In his days training to be a priest he'd observed a group who were putting on a production of the Eborby Mystery Plays in a church he was attached to. He remembered how obsessive they'd been about each and every detail. He'd admired their commitment.

He set off for the centre of the city. There was no sign of the fog now, and the dry Saturday afternoon had brought the tourists out in force. Eborby didn't have a tourist season; they came all year with their cameras and coach parties. He wondered whether *The Devils* had attracted big audiences. It wasn't the usual light-hearted tourist fare that the Playhouse put on. But the new director in charge was said to favour the 'challenging'.

He passed the cathedral again. There was no queue at the south door now. It was time for evensong, so only the faithful were making their way in for the service. But there was still a crowd milling around outside: elderly coach parties; visitors in Eborby for the day, killing time until their train journey back home; groups of young foreign students with golden limbs and a sense of effortless chic. And in the flagged square in front of the great church young men in costume handed out flyers advertising ghost tours, Viking tours, Roman tours . . . any tour of the city you cared to imagine.

Suddenly, Joe spotted a familiar figure weaving through the crowd, looking around nervously as though she was afraid she was being followed. Today Debby Telerhaye was wearing jeans with trainers and a black parka coat. She spotted Joe and raised a hand in tentative greeting, as though she was unsure whether to approach him.

He made up her mind for her. He walked over to her and asked how she was. 'Recovered from last night?'

'Yeah.' Her eyes darted around nervously. Something or someone was worrying her.

'We'd like to speak to you – ask some more questions.' He spoke gently. She seemed frightened enough without the police making it worse. 'Is tomorrow OK?'

She nodded.

'Have you heard that we found a body?'

She stared at him in astonishment. This was clearly news to her. 'No,' she said, her voice hoarse with shock. 'So I was right? I wasn't seeing things?'

'One of my colleagues has been trying to contact you.'

'I've been out all day.'

Joe looked her in the eye. 'You seem nervous. Are you sure everything's OK?'

Debby didn't answer immediately. Instead, she asked if they could walk. There was someone she didn't want to see.

Joe couldn't resist asking the question. 'Who?'

'My mum's boyfriend. I saw him in the square, and I'm trying to avoid him. He's bad news.'

Joe tried to think of the best way to phrase the next question. 'Debby, I was talking to my boss, DCI Thwaite. She used to work in Leeds, and when I mentioned your name she wondered whether you were related to a Peter Telerhaye – a young lad who went missing ten years ago.'

Debby froze. 'He was my brother,' she said, turning her face away.

'I'm sorry.'

'Look, can we go?'

Joe began to walk with her and sneaked a look at his watch. Time was getting on, and he wanted to talk to Perdita's fellow actors before they began preparing in earnest for that evening's performance. 'Sorry, Debby, I've got to be somewhere. Will you be all right getting home on your own?'

''Course I will.'

'I'll see you tomorrow then. About eleven?'

She nodded.

They had turned off down the narrow street which led to Boothgate Bar when Joe asked his next question. 'Can you see your mum's boyfriend? Is he following you?'

Debby shook her head. 'He's working . . . or he calls it working.'

'What does he do?'

'He's a pavement artist. And he has a stall in the market – flogs jewellery. He describes himself as an artist and craftsman, but he's just a wanker. You promise you'll come?' she said, anxious.

Joe stopped and met her gaze. 'I promise,' he said. Then he watched her scurry away like a frightened animal.

When Joe entered the theatre foyer, the first thing he noticed was that all publicity photographs of Perdita Elmet had been replaced with pictures of her understudy, Charlotte. The haste seemed almost indecent.

Charlotte's face suited a nun's veil. There was something

spiritual about that face, and Joe found himself thinking that she'd make a convincing Mother Superior, even if she did seem a little young for the role. And, from the little he'd seen of her, he was sure she'd be good at conveying her character's hysterical obsession as well. In fact, he wondered why she hadn't been given the part in the first place. Perhaps there were behind the scenes politics he wasn't aware of. But if that was the case, he wanted to know.

It was the first time he'd met the woman who was directing *The Devils*. Her name was Louisa Van Sturten but, despite her name, she was as Yorkshire as they came. At first she reminded him a little of Emily, only Louisa wore a long ethnic skirt, had unruly brown hair reaching halfway down her back and, unlike Emily, there was a slightly unworldly air behind her capability. This was the woman who liked her productions to be challenging, he reminded himself. He recalled that even her version of *The Importance of Being Earnest* had been set in a prison.

'I've been expecting someone to come and question us again,' she began as Joe sat down in her tiny backstage office. The place was cluttered with sketches of the set and costumes and copies of the script annotated with copious pencilled notes.

'It's been a terrible shock to everyone,' she said. 'We did wonder about cancelling the show, but everyone was sure that Perdita would have wanted us to carry on. She was a professional, after all.'

Joe had the impression that this was the highest eulogy the director could give to the dead woman.

'Of course, I can speak for the whole company when I say we'll do anything we can to help find the sick bastard who did this. I take it you haven't caught him yet?' There was a suggestion of criticism in the question.

'We're following a number of leads.'

'I don't know whether anyone told you, but we've had a bit of trouble with this production. Things going missing. Props, bits of costume, that sort of thing. They'd disappear and then turn up later in strange places. One time a piece of scenery was found slashed and had to be mended before the performance. Nothing serious, but a nuisance all the same.'

'Did you mention this to the officer who was taking statements?'

'I didn't think it was relevant.'

'Any idea who's doing it?'

She shook her head. 'It's obviously someone here in the theatre, but I can't think who it could be.'

'If anything else strange happens, you will let me know.'

'Of course. But I can't see how it could be connected with Perdita's murder.'

Joe took the photograph of the badge from his pocket. 'I know the whole company's already been questioned, but I'd like to show you this. Does it mean anything to you?'

She looked at it carefully, and he thought he saw a brief glint of recognition in her eyes. But she shook her head. 'No. Why?'

'It was found in the victim's mouth. We think her killer put it there.'

Louisa flinched, but a second later she regained her composure and studied it again, her brow furrowed with concentration. Then she looked up. 'I think I've seen something similar before, but I can't think where it was.' She shook her head. 'I'll give it some thought and let you know if I remember.'

'I know you've probably been through all this before, but where were you after the performance last night?'

'I went straight home. I was tired.'

'Anyone confirm that?'

She looked irritated. 'I've already told the officer who came to interview us. My brother was there when I got in. He's been staying with me for a while. He flew off to Hong Kong for a month first thing this morning, so you'll have to wait till he's back to confirm my alibi.' She said the final word with heavy irony.

'Did you know Perdita before the production?'

'No. She auditioned and got the part. We've never worked together before.'

'Did you like her?'

She turned her head away. 'Ours was a professional relationship.'

'You haven't answered the question.'

'And I don't intend to.'

There was an awkward pause.

'I'd like to have another word with Perdita's flatmate, if she's in?'

Louisa looked at her watch. 'I saw her a few minutes ago in her dressing room, but she said she was planning to nip out. There's plenty of time before the half,' she said. 'If I were you I'd go and get your questions asked now.'

He took the hint and went off in search of Hen. She'd shared a flat with the victim. If anyone could throw light on her life, it would be her.

But Hen wasn't there. Instead, he found Charlotte. She was slouched on a threadbare sofa in the dressing room she now shared with Hen, engrossed in the book she was reading. When Joe knocked on the open door she told him to come in, and as he entered she set the book aside, straightened her back and drew her fingers through her fine blond hair. She looked nervous, but so did most people when the police come visiting.

When he asked for Hen she looked relieved and told him she'd gone out for something to eat. She could never last till after the performance. She herself, she explained, was always too nervous to eat before she went on. She kept her eyes on his, a half smile on her face, as if she was eager to please, and her words came out in a rush.

Joe lowered himself into the armchair opposite her. 'You worked with Perdita before.'

'Yes. I told you when you were last here.' She sounded a little impatient. 'But I didn't have much to do with her outside work. In fact, she didn't have much to do with anyone. Even Hen hardly knew her, and they were sharing a flat. She kept herself to herself. Some people are like that. They value their privacy.'

'What did you think of her?'

'What do you mean?' she asked, suddenly wary.

'You must have formed an opinion. Did you like her?'

'Yes, of course. She was lovely.' The answer sounded sincere, but Joe reminded himself of her profession.

'Can you think of anyone who might have had a grudge against her?'

Charlotte shook her head.

'Did she have any boyfriends in Leeds?'

There was a slight hesitation before she replied. 'Like I said, she was a very private person.'

Joe showed her the photograph of the badge of Saint Galert, but she shook her head quickly and said she'd never seen it before, almost as though she found the sight of it distasteful.

Joe decided that he might as well ask her some more questions now that he was there. 'Was Perdita afraid of something? Did she ever complain that she was being stalked by anyone, for instance?'

'Not that I know of.' She looked as if she was about to say something else, but she bit her lip.

'Hen mentioned that Jonas saw this grey lady. Was Perdita worried about that?'

This struck a chord. Charlotte's expression suddenly changed, and she looked positively eager. 'It's supposed to mean a death in the company. I know people laugh, but . . . Well, it happened, didn't it?'

Joe said nothing. He knew actors were a superstitious bunch, hooked on rituals and omens to ward off failure. Not whistling backstage; never wearing green; and never mentioning a certain Scottish Play. And most theatres had some sort of resident ghost. Apart from the grey lady, he'd heard that the Playhouse was also haunted by the ghost of a Victorian leading man who'd hanged himself in his dressing room. He wondered which room it was, but he hardly liked to ask.

'Did it worry you?'

Charlotte looked at him, her eyes wide. 'Wouldn't you be worried?'

Joe didn't answer. This was getting too personal.

'I think it upset Jonas because he's been behaving oddly since it happened.'

'How do you mean, oddly?'

The question seemed to fluster her. 'I'm not sure. He's just different. More serious.'

'What about Hen and Perdita?'

'Perdita didn't say much, but Hen's been uneasy about it. I know that for sure. She even brought in her rosary beads.' She pointed to a set of wooden beads draped on a hook at the side of the illuminated mirror that ran along the far wall. 'She says she hasn't been to Mass for ages, but she didn't want to take any chances. And with the play being about . . .'

'I see.' He hadn't had Hen down as the nervous type, but perhaps Jonas's sighting of the alleged grey lady bothered her more than she'd made out. Hen had told him that it had been Perdita who'd been scared. But, according to Charlotte, it was the other way round. Or perhaps it hadn't been a ghost that had scared Perdita Elmet. Perhaps she'd been afraid of something or someone far more earthly.

'Louisa said strange things have been happening. Props and costumes going missing. Scenery slashed.'

'Yeah. It's been little spiteful things, like it's someone with a grudge. But nobody's been hurt or anything like that. Louisa's questioned all the backstage staff, but everyone denies knowing anything about it.'

'How easy is it to walk in here from outside?'

'Pretty easy. Think it's someone who's taken exception to the play?'

Joe didn't answer. 'How's it going . . . taking over the part?'

Joe saw her cheeks colour slightly and a satisfied look appear on her face. 'OK so far. Louisa seems pleased, anyway.'

'How did Louisa get on with Perdita?'

A flicker of alarm passed across Charlotte's face. 'They had their differences, but . . .'

'How do you mean?'

'Well, Perdita didn't always agree with Louisa's notes. She used to ignore what she said sometimes, and Louisa got angry. But it was sorted out in the end. We've had some good reviews.'

Joe smiled. 'I'm sure you have. Are your family coming to see you in your new role?'

'There's just me and my brother, and he's too busy to make it.' Charlotte lowered her eyes.

'That's a pity. Any idea when Hen'll be back?'

'She'll be here before the half if you want to come back. Or I can give her a message.'

Joe took his card from his pocket and handed it to her. Her hand shook a little as she took it.

'Can you ask her to give me a call,' he said.

On his way out he visited the box office and tried to buy a

ticket for that evening's performance. But the spotty youth in the booth told him the performance was a sell out. Murder was good for business.

Hen Butler had lied. She'd told Charlotte she was going out, but in reality she'd wanted to be on her own. Since Perdita's disappearance she hadn't felt like making small talk – and small talk was all she got from Charlotte, her new dressing room companion.

It wasn't that she didn't like the girl – there was nothing much to dislike – but she found her hard work. Charlotte lived in her own private world and, like Perdita before her, it was hard to guess what was on her mind. She suspected there were depths to Charlotte's nature that she couldn't quite fathom. Secrets, maybe – or some tragedy in her past that set her apart somehow. All she knew about her was that she had a brother, but he'd never put in an appearance at the theatre. She had the impression that he had a high-powered job that meant his free time wasn't his own. Perhaps she should ask. Perhaps she should make an effort to get to know her better. But, all in all, she'd rather be with Jonas.

It was after six o'clock – over an hour to go to the half. Jonas had gone into town earlier, and she'd wanted to go with him, but he'd shot off before she had a chance to join him. She liked being with Jonas – more than liked.

History was an excuse to share something with him, and she often talked to him about the history of the theatre. Like her he was fascinated with the fact that it had been built on the site of a huge monastic complex which had served as a hospital in the middle ages – a place of healing, staffed by nuns – until it had been brutally destroyed in the reign of Henry VIII.

She knew little was left of the original buildings; just the old undercroft in the Museum Gardens. Most of the foundations lay beneath the modern streets, only to be dug up by eager archaeologists in the case of any roadworks or redevelopment. But some of the ruins still stood in the basement of the theatre, in the area used to store scenery and props. She had never been down there, but now she was curious. She'd always been attracted to historic ruins, and she had been waiting for an opportunity to see what was down there. And, besides, it would give her something to tell Jonas when he returned; an excuse to go to his dressing room for a chat. It was certainly better than going out. Perdita had ventured out, and she was dead.

She hesitated for a moment, remembering Jonas's sighting of the grey lady. If it wasn't for Perdita's death, she would have dismissed it as a bit of excitement; a story to send a thrill through your soul when it was retold on a dark night. But there had been a death, and the thought made her nervous as she made her way down the corridor and opened the metal door that led to the scenery store in the basement.

Sometimes the backstage people were here, busying themselves in preparation for the evening performance, but now everything was quiet and the basement lay in darkness. As she stood at the top of the concrete staircase she gazed down into a pool of shadows and blackness. She felt for the light switch, and when she flicked it on the place was bathed in light, revealing a bizarre scene filled with the abandoned remnants of previous productions. Papier mâché statues; painted scenes of gardens and interiors; even a wooden mock up of a vintage car. She walked down the steps slowly, looking around.

At first she couldn't see the ruins, then she spotted a wall at one end of the huge room. It was around four feet high, pale stone, similar to the cathedral, and at its centre was the base of what looked like a gothic window. More walls protruded a couple of feet from the ground, and as she drew closer she could make out the outline of rooms: small rooms, around nine feet square. She wondered if this was where the nuns had lived all those hundreds of years ago. Or had these cell-like chambers been storerooms, something mundane?

She wandered through the props towards the ruins, her ears alert for anything unusual. The adrenalin of fear coursed through her body, making her feel alert, alive. This was fear without real danger. If there was danger, it would be outside.

The fluorescent lights above her buzzed and flickered. There were shadowy corners down there where their pale light didn't reach, and in one of them Hen could see a vague shape, an impression of a human figure robed in black, its face a blank grey mask, as though it was made of fog. It reminded her of a nun.

It was no use telling herself it was probably some prop from a previous production that her imagination had transformed into a ghostly apparition. She retraced her steps, half walking, half running, her heart pounding as she stumbled towards the stairs. She tripped over the edge of a piece of scenery, which almost sent her flying, then, as she righted herself, she heard a sound. A barely audible sob followed by another, more earthly sound: a thud, as if something had fallen on to the ground. As she looked over her shoulder she saw a movement. A dark shape rising slowly behind the medieval wall. A man shrouded in shadows.

Too frightened to scream, she dashed forward and reached the staircase, bruising her shin as it came into contact with the concrete steps. She ignored the pain and kept going until she got to the door and safety.

ELEVEN

It was eight thirty on Sunday morning, and it would be a working day for Joe. No rest. No lie in with the Sunday papers. He zipped up his leather jacket against the chill and thrust his hands into his pockets. It was an old jacket, soft with wear, but he found it comfortable, so he'd never bothered buying a more respectable replacement.

One of the advantages of living in the shadow of the city walls was that he was able to walk to work. The hospital was also within walking distance, so he could get some fresh air into his lungs before Perdita Elmet's post-mortem. Not that the air seemed particularly fresh as he walked down Boothgate towards the hospital. The fog had come down again, but not as thickly as it had on the night of Perdita Elmet's murder. But Joe still found it oppressive, weighing down on the city like an evil miasma.

As he walked, his phone rang, and he answered it, presuming it would be Emily or another member of the investigation team. But the caller's number was unfamiliar.

'Is that Inspector Plantagenet?'

It was a woman's voice, and it took him a few seconds to

place it as belonging to Louisa Van Sturten, the director of *The Devils*.

'Louisa. What can I do for you?'

'Sorry for ringing you so early on a Sunday.'

He assured her that Sunday was a day like any other during a murder inquiry.

'I've remembered where I've seen that picture before. It was outside the cathedral – one of those pavement artists was drawing something similar.'

'Thanks, I'll look into it,' Joe said and ended the call. It might be nothing, but it was worth checking. He suddenly recalled that Debby Telerhaye had told him that her mother's hated boyfriend was a pavement artist. Eborby had quite a few of them, using their creative talents to extract money from the tourists, but if he was the one, then Louisa had created a tentative link to the girl who'd first found Perdita Elmet's body. Joe wasn't sure what that meant. He wasn't sure of anything just at that moment.

Walking back to the cathedral wouldn't take long, so he decided to make a detour. It took less than five minutes to reach the square. In the early Sunday fog it was almost empty, apart from a gaggle of hardy worshippers heading for Holy Communion. The tourists were still in bed or enjoying their hotel breakfasts, so those who made their livings from them were absent too. But it hadn't rained overnight, so the pavement artists' work was still there, executed in coloured chalk on the pale stone flags. A scene from the Sistine Chapel ceiling here and a portrait of Elvis there; an eclectic mix. Joe could see more artworks near the cathedral's west door, and when he ambled over he saw that Louisa hadn't been mistaken. It was identical, down to the Latin inscription round the central image.

He called the station to get someone down there. If the artist returned to the square he wanted to question him – or her. And if he didn't come back, he reckoned someone might know who he was and how to find him.

Meanwhile, he set off for the hospital again, speeding his steps this time because he was afraid of being late and getting on the wrong side of Sally Sharpe. He liked Sally, and, besides, he'd always had a healthy respect for a woman who could wield a scalpel.

When he reached the mortuary he found that Emily had arrived before him, solemn faced and looking the worse for wear without her customary layer of make-up. Sally, in contrast, looked fresh and alert. But she had ten years on Emily, something Joe wouldn't have dreamed of pointing out if he valued his life.

'Did you see Cobarn?' Joe asked.

'In the end I asked Jamilla to pay him a visit. He said he'd bought the badges for visiting dignitaries. Said they usually appreciated a slice of Eborby's history. PR he called it. He claims he's already given a few away and the rest are in his office on Pottergate. Jamilla asked for details of the people he'd given them to, but he said he couldn't remember.'

'Convenient,' said Joe. The news was disappointing. And it certainly didn't let Cobarn off the hook.

He told Emily about the pavement art, but she seemed sceptical. Saint Galert was a common image around Eborby; the city's pet saint. But it was worth looking into all the same.

During the post-mortem, Sally kept up a commentary as she sliced into Perdita's flesh, observing that the dead woman was a healthy specimen. She had died from asphyxia, almost certainly strangled with the scarf that had been found twisted around her neck.

Emily watched in silence, as did Joe, who stared at Perdita's body as Sally went about her work. The dead woman must have been vibrant and beautiful in life, he thought. Perhaps that was why she'd died. In his experience so many women attract the wrong man; someone who abuses them or treats them as a possession. Perdita looked the sort who could inspire obsession. And obsession can lead to murder.

He saw Sally freeze for a second and glance at her assistant. She turned to face the screen, where Joe and Emily stood shielded from the action by the glass. Her usual expression of professional neutrality had vanished. She looked as if something had disturbed her.

'She was pregnant,' she said quietly. 'About three months. A boy.'

After a few moments of shocked silence, Emily spoke. 'We need to find the father.' Her words sounded businesslike.

'With DNA it shouldn't be difficult, providing he's on our

radar,' said Joe. He knew they were both thinking of Alvin Cobarn, but neither said the name.

'What can you tell us about the killer?' Joe asked. 'Would they have needed a lot of strength?'

'That depends. There's no sign of skin under her fingernails, so it doesn't look as if she tried to defend herself or put up any sort of fight.'

Joe and Emily exchanged looks. This fitted with the absence of any signs of a struggle in the undercroft.

'Could she have been drugged?'

'Won't know that until we get the tox results back,' said Sally apologetically. 'So if she was drugged, anyone could have done it; a woman, or someone physically weaker than the victim?'

'Possibly,' Sally said. She was never one to commit herself to certainties.

For the first five minutes of Joe and Emily's walk back to the police station, neither of them spoke as they absorbed the news of Perdita's pregnancy.

It was Emily who broke the silence. 'Wonder if she wanted to keep it.'

Joe didn't know the answer to that one. 'Have we any idea how long she's been involved with Cobarn?'

'He said he only met her six weeks ago.'

'Think he was lying?'

'That remains to be seen. Where was she before she came to Eborby for this production?'

'Leeds.'

'Cobarn's law firm has an office in Leeds. Wonder how much time he spends there.'

'You mean he could have known Perdita for longer than he admitted?'

'We need to question him again. Preferably without the wife there.' She paused. 'Sally said a woman could have done it, didn't she?'

'You mean the wife?'

Emily smiled. 'Why not? Hell hath no fury and all that.'

'Perhaps Perdita didn't have to be drugged. Perhaps her attacker was someone she didn't think was a danger and she was taken by surprise.'

Before Emily could answer, Joe's phone rang, and he was surprised to hear Hen Butler's voice. She asked him if they could meet for coffee. After a brief consultation with Emily he said yes. He'd meet her in the theatre cafe in fifteen minutes.

'Don't do anything I wouldn't do,' said Emily. 'And don't forget we're having another word with Alvin Cobarn.'

'I won't,' said Joe as they parted outside the theatre.

He saw Emily looking with distaste at the posters decorating the building's exterior. 'I've seen the film,' she said. 'Not the way I'd choose to spend an evening off, but each to their own, eh?'

'The seats are sold out.'

'People like a good murder,' she observed before disappearing down the road.

Joe found Hen Butler in the cafe, a half-drunk latte in front of her. She watched him approach with anxious eyes, and as he sat down opposite her she gave a nervous smile.

Joe felt he needed a dose of caffeine, so he ordered a coffee, strong and black. Then he waited for Hen to speak.

'Something happened yesterday,' she began. 'I don't know whether it has anything to do with Perdita's death, but you asked us to tell you if anything was bothering us.'

'What happened?'

'I had some time to kill before the performance last night, so I went down into the basement. I've heard there are some medieval ruins down there – the remains of the convent that used to stand on this site. I wanted to see them.'

'Interested in that sort of thing, are you?'

She nodded. 'Believe it or not, my degree's in archaeology.'

'What made you take up acting?'

'I couldn't get the kind of job I wanted in archaeology, so I went to drama school. I'd really got into it by then, and I decided to take the risk. At least I'm working, so it's paid off.' She gave him a weak smile.

Joe looked at her face. If this was her second career, she must be older than she appeared; mid thirties, perhaps. When they'd first met he'd thought her pretty but rather bland, but now that impression was banished. She was probably tougher than she looked, and he suspected that the little girl lost act had been for

Jonas's benefit. He'd sensed an attraction there; maybe a desperate need for love. Hen was still sharing temporary accommodation with strangers when most of her contemporaries would be settled. Perhaps she'd come to a time in her life when she wanted more.

'Anyway,' she continued, 'I was down there looking at the foundations when I heard a noise and saw a figure rising up from behind the old wall, and . . . There was someone down there. Hiding.'

'Can you describe this person?'

'It was dark in that corner, and I didn't fancy hanging round to find out. But I had the impression it was a man.'

'Did he say anything? Threaten you in any way?'

'I got out before he had the chance. He gave me a hell of a shock.'

'Have you told anyone else about this?'

'I told Louisa, and she sent a couple of the backstage crew down. They didn't find anything . . . apart from a chewing gum packet, and that might have been there already.' She hesitated. 'Things have been happening at the theatre. Things going missing, and . . .'

'So I've heard. It could be someone playing tricks. Maybe someone with a grudge against the theatre. Can you think of anyone?'

Hen shook her head. She still looked worried, and Joe asked her if something else was wrong.

'This is going to sound stupid,' she said.

'What is?'

'Before I saw the intruder, I thought I saw something else, and there was this noise like a sob. Very quiet.'

'Could it have been the man?'

'No. It sounded like a woman. But I could have been mistaken.'

'What did you see?'

She didn't answer straight away, as if the answer needed some thought. 'It was a vague misty shape without a face. I thought it looked like a nun, which is ridiculous, isn't it?' She didn't sound convinced. 'Then I saw the man and ran for it. If it hadn't been for him I would have gone over to investigate.'

'It obviously worried you?'

She smiled bravely. 'It was in a shadowy corner, and I couldn't see very well. It was probably a prop from an old production. I was probably letting my imagination run away with me.'

During the long silence that followed, Joe's coffee arrived. He took a sip and put down his cup, waiting for Hen to speak again.

His patience was rewarded thirty seconds later. 'Perdita said she saw a nun the day before she died.'

'I thought it was Jonas who saw her.'

'He did, but so did Perdita. According to theatre superstition she's supposed to be seen before a death. The nun was walled up for getting pregnant, you know.'

'You believe the story?'

She looked away. 'Well, she was seen, and Perdita died.'

Joe made a decision. The fact would become public knowledge soon anyway, so he reckoned it would do no harm. 'Did you know Perdita was pregnant?'

Hen's mouth fell open. 'She kept that bloody quiet. Do you know who the father was?'

'Not yet.'

'That councillor was the only man I ever saw her with,' she said, with a raise of her plucked eyebrows.

'Don't worry, we've spoken to him.'

'Do you think that's why she was killed? Did she threaten to make their affair public and go to his wife?'

'It's the oldest story in the book,' said Joe. 'But we're not jumping to conclusions at the moment.'

Hen looked at him enquiringly. 'Are you married?'

Joe lowered his eyes. 'Widowed. You and Jonas . . .?'

'Jonas only had eyes for Perdita,' she said with a hint of bitterness. 'I told him she was involved with a married man, but it didn't make any difference. Jonas is one of the good guys. He didn't deserve to be messed around like that.'

'Were you jealous of his feelings for her?'

She appeared to consider the answer carefully. 'He would have realized what she was like sooner or later.'

'And you'd have been there to pick up the pieces?'

'Maybe,' she said with a distant smile playing on her lips, as though she was picturing the scene in her mind.

'What about Charlotte? How did she feel about Perdita?'

'Difficult to know. Charlotte's a bit of an enigma. But I think they got on OK.'

'They worked together in Leeds.'

'In this game you work with a lot of people, but it doesn't mean you stay bosom buddies once the production's over.' She leaned across the table, her eyes fixed on his. 'Look, Perdita's dead, and I'm sure there's something bad going on – something connected to the theatre. I don't think any of us are safe.'

The intensity of her words surprised him. He could only reassure her, tell her to call him if she was worried.

He finished his coffee and left. When he looked at his watch he saw that it was ten to eleven. He'd told Debby Telerhaye he'd call round to see her that morning at eleven. Her mother's partner could be the pavement artist he was looking for, so it would do no harm to have a word with him while he was there. It would save a lot of time if he was already on their radar.

He was walking out of the theatre's front entrance when he saw a woman on the pavement opposite. She was slim with unruly auburn curls, and his heart lurched. If it wasn't Maddy, the woman he'd lived with until she'd abandoned him to go down to work in London, she was her double.

Maddy Owen had been the first woman he'd become seriously involved with since Kaitlin's death, and this had made her special somehow. More special than all those empty couplings and meaningless dates before and since. They'd parted amicably; gone their separate ways and all those other clichés that people used to hide the pain of parting. He wondered whether to run after the woman, to call her name, but she was disappearing rapidly into the distance. Besides, he'd probably been mistaken.

He remembered the route to Debby's house from Friday night. When he arrived the door was opened by a plump woman with shoulder-length mousy hair who wore a bright-pink track suit that did nothing to flatter her figure. At first she looked irritated at the intrusion, but when he showed her his ID and asked if he could speak to Debby she opened the door meekly and allowed him in.

The woman had the defeated look of a victim. He'd seen that

look before on women who were on the receiving end of domestic violence but, according to Emily, she'd known unbearable tragedy in her life. Her son had gone missing and had never been found.

He asked her gently if everything was all right.

'Why shouldn't it be?' she snapped.

He wished he'd kept quiet. 'I brought Debby home on Friday night, and I saw her yesterday in Eborby,' he explained. 'I said I'd probably have some more questions for her. I take it she's told you that she found the body of a woman in the city centre.'

The woman looked at him blankly.

'I know it's been a terrible shock for her, but I need a word.'

'She's never said anything about it.'

Joe could sense the pain behind the words. Her daughter hadn't bothered to confide in her, even about such a momentous experience.

'I understand your partner's a pavement artist.'

Joe saw panic in her eyes. 'So?'

'I'd like to speak to him as well. Just routine.'

'He's out. Won't be back till this evening.'

Joe heard a noise, and when he looked up he saw Debby standing at the top of the stairs looking down on them.

'It's OK, Mum,' she said, as though she was taking charge. 'Show him into the living room. I'll be down in a second.'

Joe followed Mrs Telerhaye, not knowing what to say. Small talk is hard when you're faced with someone who's endured an ordeal like losing a child. Emily's words rang through his head. The son, Peter, had gone missing and had never been found. He knew that a medium had somehow been involved, but Perdita's murder had left him with no time to delve into the details. He gave Mrs Telerhaye what he hoped was a sympathetic smile and sat down on a sleek black leather sofa that would have looked more at home in a swanky loft apartment than the Telerhayes' shabby front room.

He only had to wait a minute or so before Debby entered the room. She sat down in an armchair facing him and waited.

'I'm sorry, Debby, but now we've found a body you're going to have to make a proper statement. But I'd like a chat with you first, if that's OK.'

'Where did you find it?'

'In the ruins of the abbey church. A couple of hundred yards away from the undercroft.'

'That means that whoever killed her must have moved her.'

'We're working on the assumption the killer wanted to delay the discovery of the body for some reason.'

'How did she die?'

'She was strangled.'

'Who was she?'

'Her name was Perdita Elmet. She was an actor at the Playhouse. Please think back to Friday night. Did you see anyone hanging around?'

'It was hard to see anything in all that fog. Was she killed in the undercroft? Do you think I disturbed the murderer?'

'There was no evidence of a struggle, so he might have dumped her there and had second thoughts when you came along and he realized how public it was.'

Debby stared ahead, as if she was trying to take in this new information. 'So he might have been there? He might have been watching me from the fog?'

'It's possible. Can you remember anything else?'

She shook her head.

Joe leaned forward. 'Think. Please.'

She stood and walked over to the window, staring out at the street outside. After a minute she sat down again. 'I didn't see anything, but I had a feeling someone was there.'

'You said you saw a shape. Said it looked like a nun.'

He saw her cheeks flush, as if she was embarrassed. 'I'd had a bit to drink. I might have imagined it.'

'You seemed pretty sure at the time.'

She shrugged her shoulders. 'I thought I heard something, but I can't be sure.'

'What?'

'At the time I thought it was a sigh . . . but it could have been a creak, like a dodgy wheel or a gate opening. There were all sorts of strange noises in that fog, so it could have come from anywhere. Sorry.'

'You said you went into the undercroft to hide from someone who was following you. Any idea who it was?'

'Don't know. Someone from the pub who saw us leave, maybe.' She didn't sound convincing.

'I think you have your suspicions. Care to share them with me? It doesn't matter if you're wrong.'

She gave the door a wary glance, as though she was afraid that someone might be listening. 'I thought it might have been Sinclair,' she said, lowering her voice. 'He's the only person it could be. He's a creep.' She shuddered, and Joe felt sorry for her, trapped in that house with a grieving mother and a man she feared.

He took the picture of the pilgrim badge from his pocket and passed it to her. 'You said Sinclair's a pavement artist. Ever seen him draw anything like this?'

She studied the picture. 'Maybe. What is it?'

'It's Saint Galert. A local saint with a shrine in the cathedral. This is a copy of a badge that was bought by pilgrims who came here to Eborby in the middle ages. It was found on the body.' He had photographed the drawing he'd seen on the tower. He took out his phone and found the image before passing it to Debby. 'Does this look like Sinclair's work?'

She studied it with a frown of concentration. 'I don't know. Where was it?'

'On the side of that tower by Wendover Bridge.'

'I've never known him do graffiti. Only pictures on pavements.' She sniffed. 'He wouldn't do anything that wouldn't bring in some cash from the tourists.'

'If Sinclair turns up, can you let me know? I'd like to speak to him.'

'OK.'

He handed her his card. When she took it she stared at it for a moment and stuffed it into the pocket of her jeans. Then she focused her eyes on Joe again. 'I went to see Carlo Natale yesterday.'

'Who?'

'He was the medium who came forward to *help* my mum when Peter went missing.' The word *help* was said with heavy irony.

'He's taking part in some psychic fair at the Pavilion Hall. I saw his name on a poster, and I couldn't resist going. I needed to see if he was like I remembered.'

'And was he?'

'Worse. There were all these old women hanging on his every word. Made me want to be sick.'

'I take it he didn't do much good when your brother disappeared.'

'Worse than that. He got in the way. Kept directing the search in the wrong direction, saying that Peter was near water. The police dragged every pond, river and canal around, but they never found anything.'

'So the police must have had some faith in him?' Joe said, trying to keep the surprise out of his voice.

'They were stupid. Natale was a con man, out for what he could get. Publicity and all that. Every time the police drew a blank he turned it round. Said they weren't interpreting his readings properly.'

'You think he interfered with the investigation?'

She nodded. 'He said Peter was in this barn near Whitby. The police went there and found one of his shoes, but there was no sign of Peter.' She hesitated. 'The place had been cleaned thoroughly, and they said Peter had probably been held there. But after that there was nothing.'

'You can't have been very old at the time. You seem to remember it well.'

'My mum talked about nothing else while I was growing up, and she's kept a book of press cuttings. I often find her going through it even now – although Sinclair doesn't like it.'

'What did Natale say when you went to see him?'

'He pretended not to recognize me, but I know he did. I could see it in his eyes. Then he spouted some crap about Peter being dead and how he still wants to help us find his body. I haven't told mum. I don't think she's strong enough to . . . I told him to stay away.'

'Did you think he'd try to make contact?'

'I thought there was a risk, yeah. I wanted to make sure he didn't try anything. Like I said, Mum couldn't take it.'

'Do you still see your dad?'

Debby shook her head. 'He met someone else about a year after Peter disappeared. He lives in France now. Sometimes gets in touch on Facebook, but . . .'

'You don't fancy going to stay with him?' Joe asked, thinking that life with her father would probably be preferable to living in that dour house with her mother and Sinclair.

She bowed her head. 'He's got a new family. New wife and two young boys,' she said, as though this fact explained it all. Joe suddenly felt desperately sad for her.

He stood up. 'I'll have to send someone round to take a formal statement. It's nothing to worry about. Just routine. In the meantime, if you remember anything else or want someone to talk to . . .'

'You should question him, you know.'

'Who?'

'Carlo Natale,' she answered. 'He's evil. He's capable of anything.'

TWELVE

When Joe returned to the incident room he found Emily addressing the team. They were listening with rapt attention, and he guessed there had been a new development.

When she'd finished, Joe followed her into her office, and she brought him up to date. They'd found CCTV footage from a pub a few doors down from the flat Perdita Elmet shared with Hen Butler. At five on Friday – the evening of Perdita's death – a car had parked outside the girls' flat, just in range of the camera. It was a large black Lexus and, as the fog had only been a thin veil of mist at that time of the evening, the registration number was quite readable. When it had been checked by one of the uniformed PCs who were working on the case, the name of the registered owner turned out to be all too familiar. The car belonged to Alvin Cobarn.

Cobarn claimed that he'd last seen the victim the previous Wednesday, but now it seemed he was lying. The camera clearly showed Cobarn going back to the car ten minutes later with a young woman. With Perdita Elmet. She climbed into the passenger seat, and the car drove off.

'What about number-plate recognition? We need to know where they went.'

'We're working on it,' said Emily. She sounded tired. 'But later the fog really came down, which rendered the cameras all but useless.'

'Cobarn lied to us.'

'I know,' said Emily with a sigh. 'I think we should go and have another word.'

'Why not bring him in? Interview him under caution?'

'He might be more relaxed at home, more likely to slip up.'

Joe knew Emily had a point, but he still thought that piling on the pressure would produce faster results. However, if Emily's way didn't work, they always had the formal route to fall back on.

'No time like the present,' said Emily as she reached for her coat.

'Do we call and tell him we're on our way?'

Emily grinned. 'Nah. Let's surprise him.'

They drove out to Pickby and found Alvin Cobarn at home, wearing his Sunday uniform of chinos and open-neck checked shirt and perusing the *Sunday Telegraph*'s myriad supplements.

When his wife showed them into the room he stood up, reminding Joe of a hunted creature at bay. He looked like a man with a guilty conscience.

Mrs Cobarn hovered in the doorway for a moment then left, shutting the door behind her, meek as a Victorian parlour maid. Joe thought she was the first wife he'd encountered who didn't want chapter and verse about what was going on with her own husband in her own home, and his instincts told him something was amiss. He wondered if she was listening outside the door. If she was, it was none of his business.

'Sorry to bother you on a Sunday,' Emily lied smoothly. 'But we need to ask you a few more questions.'

'Fire away,' he said with false bonhomie. He was playing the innocent, the helpful citizen. But he wasn't as good at acting as the cast of *The Devils*. Joe could see the panic behind the smile.

'Have you remembered who you gave those Saint Galert badges to yet?'

He looked surprised. Whatever question he'd been expecting, it wasn't this one. 'No.'

'How many have you got left?'

'Hard to say. They're in a drawer in my office. You don't want me to . . .?'

'I'm sure it can wait until Monday,' Emily said, giving Joe a look. 'When did you last see Perdita Elmet?' she asked sweetly.

'Wednesday night.' The answer came quickly, as though he'd rehearsed it over and over again.

'Are you sure?' said Joe.

'Of course.'

'What would you say if we told you we had CCTV footage of you taken late on Friday afternoon? You parked outside Perdita Elmet's flat, then you went inside and came out ten minutes later. Perdita was with you. You both got into the car and drove off.'

Cobarn had been sitting on the sofa. He stood up and walked to the French window, as though he hadn't heard them. He stared out at the well-manicured garden, hands in pockets.

'Well?' said Emily.

There was no reaction. Joe caught Emily's eye, and she shook her head. They'd wait.

It seemed an age before he turned back to face them.

'OK. I went to see her. She was talking about finishing our relationship. She said she was getting sick of sneaking around behind my wife's back. She wanted marriage and children. The whole package. She said she knew it was something I couldn't give her. She said we shouldn't see each other any more.'

'How did you feel about that?' said Emily softly.

Cobarn shrugged his shoulders. 'I wasn't happy. We hadn't been seeing each other long, but I liked her.'

'Liked rather than loved?' said Joe.

'Yes. Liked. I wasn't in love with her.'

The cynical thought crossed Joe's mind that the only person Cobarn had probably ever fallen in love with was himself. Even now he was glancing into the mirror that hung on the far wall, as though gauging what impression he was making.

'But you put your marriage at risk to be with her,' Emily pointed out, matter-of-factly.

'My wife had no idea. The last thing I wanted was to hurt her. She's not been well.'

'What's the matter with her?' Emily sounded genuinely concerned.

'We're not sure. She's been for tests, but nothing's conclusive.'

'Must be difficult for you. Is that why you were tempted?'

The look Cobarn gave Emily suggested that he considered the question impertinent. 'It's something I'd rather not discuss.'

'So you picked Perdita up just after five and went off with her ten minutes later. Where did you go?'

'For a drink. She had something to eat – noodles, if you must know – but I knew I was eating later, so . . .'

'She was cutting it a bit fine for the theatre, wasn't she?'

'She didn't have to be there till half an hour before curtain up. She had plenty of time.'

'What time did you part?'

'I left the pub around six fifteen. As far as I knew she was planning to nip home then go straight on to the theatre.'

'Where did you go for your drink?'

'The Three Tuns. It's not far from her flat and, according to Perdita, none of the cast ever went there.'

'Anyone see you?'

'It was packed, but I doubt if anyone noticed us. There's a certain anonymity in crowds, don't you think?'

'Did you know Perdita was pregnant?'

Cobarn's eyes widened. 'What?' It was clear that the news had come as a surprise.

'Were you the father?' Joe asked.

'No. I mean . . . How far gone . . .?'

'Our pathologist reckoned three months.'

'Then it wasn't me,' Cobarn said unconvincingly. 'I've only known her six weeks.' He shook his head. 'I had no idea. Honestly.'

'She was living in Leeds before she came here to join the Playhouse company. Your law firm has an office in Leeds, I believe. Are you sure you didn't meet her there?'

'Absolutely sure.'

'Would you be willing to come to the station and give us a sample of your DNA?' said Emily. 'It's a simple procedure. Just a mouth swab.'

Cobarn hesitated. He looked like a man who'd been backed into a corner by a couple of snarling pit bull terriers. 'If I'm going to come with you to the police station I want a solicitor. I'm going to call one of the partners in my practice.'

'Of course,' said Emily. 'Do you want to make the call now so he can meet you there?'

The answer was a nod. He took his mobile phone from his pocket and spoke to someone called Susan. Few words were exchanged, almost as though she'd been expecting the call.

It was time to go, and as Joe approached the door he heard a scuffling outside and soft footsteps creeping over the parquet floor outside in the hall.

Mrs Cobarn had been listening, and Joe guessed she'd heard every word.

How do you create a ghost?

Perry knew there were many ways. You could kill, and your victim's sudden death would create a restless spirit with unfinished business on this earth. Or you could reawaken a soul who had left the world long ago, summon them back to their old haunts. Haunts – that was a good one. He'd use that when he came to describe his work. Haunts was clever. He felt pleased with himself.

'You OK, Fred? Anything you want? Beer? Fag? Joint?' He smiled to himself as he gazed down at the mummified corpse lying in the niche. He'd have liked to sit Fred on a chair so he could be a proper companion, but he knew that if he touched him his desiccated flesh would crumble to dust. Anyway, it might have spooked Big Sister, and as she was paying most of the bills he didn't want to irritate her too much.

He took a swig of beer and stood up. He needed to get back to work, so he began to gather his materials together. He'd do a stint as a living statue to bring in the dosh, then after that, when darkness fell, he'd begin his serious work. He'd create another ghost, another spirit for Eborby's supernatural portfolio.

He wheeled the cart from its place beside the front door and began to pack it with his stuff. The white monk's robe that served as his costume; the box he stood on; the bowl he used to collect the money. And the other things: his ghost making equipment.

Before he could finish he heard a knock on the door, and he froze, wondering whether to answer. But his curiosity overrode his caution, so he unlocked the heavy oak door. He was surprised to see Debby, the girl he'd met the previous day. He didn't know whether her visit was altogether welcome, but he invited her in all the same.

'Want a beer?' he asked.

As she stepped inside he saw her eyes stray to the back of the room: to Fred's resting place.

'Why not?'

He passed her one of the bottles that were standing on the table along with a bottle opener in the shape of a bat. The top came off with a hiss, and froth spilled down the side.

Debby lifted it to her lips and found it was warm, but she drank it all the same. 'What's in the cart?' She peered to see. It was a pull along cart: a large wooden crate on pneumatic pram wheels with a thick rope handle. It would hold quite a bit.

'Stuff for my work.'

'Art stuff?'

'That, and all my living statue gear. I made it – the cart, I mean.'

Debby didn't answer.

'Is this a social visit, or . . .?'

Debby sat down, took another swig of beer and wiped her mouth with the back of her hand. There was something about Perry that made her want to confide in him. And she needed to talk about Carlo Natale. She'd spoken to the policeman, but he was a policeman, bound to take the official line and advise her against taking the law into her own hands. But Perry might see things differently, have suggestions that a policeman couldn't countenance.

Before she knew it she'd told Perry all about Natale and the figure she'd seen in the undercroft. She'd needed to talk, and as the words tumbled out she'd watched his face. But she'd seen no reaction.

'Well, what do you think?' she said when she'd finished.

'I think you should be very careful,' he said quietly as he handed her another bottle. 'After our mum died, bad things happened. Or, rather, a bad person happened.'

His statement intrigued her, and she wanted to know more. 'What do you mean?'

'Never mind,' he said. 'Forget it.'

THIRTEEN

Alvin Cobarn had come to the police station like a lamb, Emily observed to the assembled investigation team. Joe, who was sitting at the edge of the room listening, hardly liked to point out that the man hadn't had much choice.

Soon, Emily said, they'd know for sure whether he'd been the father of Perdita Elmet's baby. She still seemed to think it likely, in spite of his protestations that he'd only known the dead woman for six weeks. Joe wasn't quite so certain.

Inquiries had been made in Leeds, but so far no evidence had been found that Cobarn had ever had any contact with Perdita there. However, one of the secretaries in his Leeds office had mentioned that he was very fond of the theatre. Joe had asked for the people at the theatre where Perdita had appeared to be questioned. He had a feeling that if they identified her baby's father, they might make some progress. Perdita clearly had a past, and he suspected that the solution lay there.

The delay in obtaining information frustrated him, and he felt he should be doing something. He was still waiting for Debby to call to say that Sinclair had turned up. But on a Sunday afternoon, with the tourists out in force, he was bound to be back at his post outside the cathedral.

He walked into Emily's office to tell her what he planned to do. At first she looked dubious, but eventually she agreed that he should go and satisfy the itch of curiosity – as long as he was back within the hour. More CCTV footage was being trawled through, and Perdita's phone calls were being analysed. Perdita's neighbours were being interviewed in the hope of finding witnesses, so, hopefully, there would soon be a stack of statements to follow up.

As he left the office, Jamilla Dal looked up from her computer and smiled. He liked Jamilla. She was a good officer, astute and with a instinct for a lie. When he finally tracked down Sinclair Doulton he'd ask her to sit in on the interview.

It was good to get some fresh air, even though the October clouds were masking the sun, turning the sky a uniform grey. That morning's early mist had lifted. But he knew it could descend again at any time, creeping around the city, turning the familiar streets into a surreal and frightening landscape. Joe hated the fog. The fog hides all kinds of sins.

He was walking fast, as he always did. It was a habit he'd had since childhood; always in a hurry over something, his mother used to say. But now, with Emily's instructions echoing in his head, it came in useful.

The cathedral square had been plunged into its usual Sunday chaos, and Joe could see one pavement artist working away near to a cafe at the far side, a good position to catch the passing customers.

He watched the artist for a few moments. He'd seen the man before and, if this was Sinclair, he wasn't at all how he'd imagined. He was a young man with a beard and dreadlocks. Joe walked over to him. 'Are you Sinclair Doulton?' he asked, squatting down so that he was on the man's level.

The artist continued working on an image of the cathedral. It was accurate, every shadow and detail picked out in shades of chalk. He was a good draughtsman, and Joe wondered if this was the only way he used his talents.

'Nope,' the artist said without taking his eyes off what he was doing. 'He's not here today. In fact, he wasn't here yesterday either.'

He didn't sound too sorry about the situation, and Joe imagined he was glad of the chance of a weekend's work without a rival to dilute his takings.

'There was a picture of Saint Galert over there by the lamp post. Was it yours?'

'No. That was one of Sinclair's.'

'Know where I can find him?'

'Sorry. I don't have much to do with him . . . even though we're in the same line of work.' Something about the way he said it told Joe that Sinclair wasn't exactly popular. 'You could try the market tomorrow. I've heard he has a stall there on Mondays.'

Joe thanked him, and as he walked away he turned to look at

the cathedral. The morning services were over, and the tourists had started to pile in again. He made his way back to the station over Wendover Bridge. He could still make out the chalked shape on the tower wall but, with the moisture in the air, it had almost vanished, like a ghost fading into the shadows.

Back at the incident room there was an air of excitement, and Emily appeared at the door of her office and beckoned him in. 'You'll never guess what turned up on some later CCTV footage taken on the victim's street,' she began, her eyes aglow with enthusiasm. 'I've had someone checking the registration numbers of every car that drove past after Perdita and Cobarn left the scene. Around six thirty the fog started to thicken, but you can still just about make out the numbers. A car drove past very slowly about quarter to seven, as though it was looking for a parking space.'

'Or the driver was being cautious in the fog.'

Emily ignored Joe's misgivings and carried on. 'It's registered to a Regina Cobarn. Alvin Cobarn's wife.'

There was a long silence while Joe took this in. 'You think she was calling on Perdita to confront her about the affair?'

'We never spoke to her when we saw Cobarn, but maybe it's time we did. Perdita's flat's out of the range of the camera. I wonder if she intended to tackle her when she came home.'

'Possibly. And if Mrs Cobarn didn't manage to see her, then she might have waited for her after the performance and . . .'

'Some time between Perdita leaving the theatre at ten thirty, and Debby seeing her dead at around eleven fifteen, Perdita met her killer.'

'You've seen Mrs Cobarn. Does she look capable of strangling someone and moving a body?'

'Not unless she had help. I'll ask someone to check on her family and associates. If she has a vengeful relative, or . . .' She didn't finish the sentence. 'I'm going to have her brought in.'

'What about her husband?'

Emily let out a long sigh. 'I sent someone over to his office to check on those badges. He has fifteen left, just lying in a drawer where anyone could help themselves. He thinks he's probably given out about four or five. It's all very vague. And it's not enough to hold him. I'm going to have to let him go.'

'And pick up the wife. One in, one out,' Joe said with a grin.

'She was a woman scorned, Joe. And you know what they say about them.'

As it turned out, Regina Cobarn wasn't at home when they went round. Or she wasn't answering the door. The officers who'd taken Alvin Cobarn back in a patrol car reported that the house was locked up and empty when they arrived.

Cobarn had looked worried. His wife going off like that without telling him was out of character, he said. They'd left him to it, assuring him that she'd probably been upset by his arrest and taken refuge with a friend. He'd replied that she had no friends.

Joe returned home at eight. The fog was coming down again, but it was nothing like as thick as it had been on the night of Perdita's murder. Had the killer taken advantage of the conditions, he wondered. Had it been an opportunist crime, a terrible impulse? Or had it been planned for a long time? He wished the results of the DNA test would hurry up. If Cobarn was the unborn baby's father, it meant that he was lying and he was back in the frame again. Joe knew science was only instant in TV shows and he'd have to be patient, but he felt like a teenager awaiting an important exam result. He wouldn't be able to relax until he knew.

He unlocked the door to his apartment and stepped into the silence. He flicked on the light switch and held his breath. Listening for intruders was a habit he'd developed. No doubt a psychologist would have told him that it was a sign of anxiety, maybe of post-traumatic stress after his shooting and his colleague's death. But that had been a long time ago, and besides, none of the psychologists he'd seen after the tragedy had been the slightest bit of use.

He poured himself a beer – a bottle of Black Sheep, his favourite – and switched on the TV. It was a cop show set in some bleak, brooding landscape, so he switched it off again. He had enough of that sort of thing at work.

He rummaged through his CDs – he still hadn't come to terms with the iPad – and selected a Thomas Tallis mass. As he sank back into the chair listening to the soaring voices, he closed his eyes. His weekend had been filled with work, leaving no time to think. No time to remember Kaitlin and her death. Perhaps that was a good thing, he thought. But it still left him with a heavy feeling of guilt like a tight knot in his stomach.

He finished the first bottle and opened another. Emily would have disapproved if she could have seen him. She'd have said drinking alone was the first step on the downward path. But she had a husband and a family around her, so what did she know?

He hadn't eaten, but he didn't feel hungry. He stood up, walked to the cupboard and took out a box of photographs. Sometimes he didn't look at it from one month to the next, but tonight he felt a compulsion to open it, to release the past. There she was. Kaitlin. She'd been beautiful. And troubled. She'd been singing in the choir that visited his church, and he'd thought she was the loveliest creature he'd ever seen. He abandoned his vocation, and they'd married. But shortly after their wedding they'd quarrelled when he'd revealed things about himself that shocked her. Her sister, Kirsten, had returned later to accuse him of murdering her. He'd tried to persuade her that he was innocent, that her accusation had been born of a guilty conscience, but he knew he'd failed to convince her, and he dreaded her threatened return. One day, perhaps she'd come back and stir up trouble for him, but in the meantime he had to carry on.

He felt his eyes sting and saw a tear drop on to a picture of Kaitlin smiling in her wedding dress. That sort of happiness could never have lasted. There had been too many secrets in his life. Too much darkness.

The doorbell rang, tearing through the peace, and his heart began to pound. He wasn't expecting anyone. Then he took a deep, calming breath, telling himself it was probably one of his neighbours. Or somebody selling something. He placed the box of photographs back in the cupboard carefully before answering the door.

'Hello, Joe.'

The sight of Maddy Owen robbed him of speech for a few seconds. He'd convinced himself that it couldn't have been her he saw the other day near the theatre. He'd assumed she was still down in London enjoying her new life. But here she was standing in his doorway, wearing a tentative smile, as though she wasn't sure of her reception. 'I thought I saw you near the theatre, but . . .'

'Can I come in?'

He stood aside, and as she passed her arm brushed his. He could smell her perfume, and he suddenly felt numb.

'I hope I haven't disturbed you.'

'Not at all,' he said automatically. 'It must be almost a year since I heard from you. I thought . . . What are you doing here?'

'London didn't work out. The job was good but . . . I've come back to Eborby.'

'You've got a job up here?'

'Deputy Director of the Museum. Promotion.' She took a deep breath. 'My sister died in Cambodia six months ago.'

He leaned towards her, sensing her pain. He'd never met her sister, who'd been living abroad since university, but the news still came as a shock. 'I'm so sorry,' were the only words that came into his mind. But whatever he'd said would have been inadequate.

'My parents need me up here. They're devastated. Besides, I'd had enough of London. The man I was seeing turned out to be a bastard. He was involved with someone else, someone I thought was a friend, so . . . It was just time to come home.'

Joe flopped down into the chair, and she sat down opposite. It wasn't that he wasn't pleased to see her, but he could see hope in her eyes and he wasn't sure how he felt about taking up where they'd left off. It needed some thought. 'Want a drink?' he said.

'Have you eaten?'

He shook his head.

'Let's go out, and then we can have a proper talk.'

All of a sudden Joe felt hungry, so he nodded in agreement.

Half an hour later they were sitting in what had been their favourite trattoria on Gallowgate. The place hadn't changed much, and neither had the staff. The waiter greeted them as if he was sure he'd seen them before but couldn't quite remember when. It had been a while.

Once their meals were in front of them, the small talk turned to something deeper.

'I'm so sorry about your sister,' Joe repeated, feeling that something so momentous shouldn't go unmentioned. 'What was she doing in Cambodia?'

'Aid work. That's what she was like – always wanting to save the world.' She gave a weak, distant smile, as though recalling happy memories. 'She was killed in a motorbike accident.' She looked up from the spaghetti she was attempting to twirl around her fork without much success. 'She always was the adventurous one. It would have been selfish of me to stay in London. My parents are in pieces. Even after six months the grief's still raw. I don't suppose you ever get over losing a child, do you?'

Joe knew that Maddy's parents lived in a small stone-built village twelve miles north of the city. It was a picture postcard village with a green, an ancient church and an admirable pub, and it was somewhere he'd enjoyed visiting with her when they'd been together, although he'd always had a vague impression that her parents didn't quite approve of their relationship. 'I can understand that,' he said. 'Are you staying with them?'

'No. I've taken a small flat on Aldgate. I didn't want to be too far away.' She bowed her head. 'You know what it's like.'

Joe had met many grieving parents, both as a policeman and before that as a trainee priest, and they all shared one thing in common – the pain would stay with them for ever.

'That's why my mum turned to Carlo. I was sceptical at first, but he's brought them so much comfort. I've sat in on some of the sessions. He's remarkable.'

Joe stared at her. 'You're talking about Carlo Natale?'

'You know of him?'

'Yes. His name's come up in an inquiry I'm working on.'

'How do you mean?'

He could see the worry in her eyes, concern that her mother's lifeline was about to be exposed as a fraud, that their whole fragile facade of comfort was about to be shattered. He took pity on her. 'A witness mentioned him, that's all.'

'And?'

'I think this witness had a bad experience. But that doesn't mean to say . . .'

'People like Carlo will always attract people who are trying to disprove his work. But I know it's real,' she said with brittle confidence. 'He's told us things about Simone that nobody but the family knew.'

'I believe he's appearing at the Pavilion Hall; some kind of psychic fair.'

'That's right. I'm taking one of my new colleagues to see him tomorrow after work. She's just lost her mother, so . . .'

'I see.'

She returned her attention to her meal, eating with concentration as though she was hungry. Or perhaps she'd detected the cynicism in his voice and was wary of the way the conversation was going. He didn't want to shatter her hopes, but he couldn't help remembering Debby's statement that Natale was a con man who'd interfered with the investigation into a child's disappearance.

His instinct was to warn Maddy. But he'd wait for the right moment.

Jonas was glad the performance was over. The role of Urbain Grandier was exhausting, with its harrowing scenes of madness, torture and execution, and each night when he hurried to his dressing room to remove his gory make-up he found he needed at least half an hour to return to the outside world. He could see how the part could drive an actor mad if he started living it too deeply; how the scenes of agony and insanity could start to possess you. But he wouldn't let that happen.

When he had changed, he liked to go to the pub to reconnect with normality. He had always tried to persuade Perdita to go with him, but she'd rarely taken him up on the invitation. Unlike Hen, who was always keen to volunteer. But Hen hadn't been the focus of his interest. He'd done his best to conceal his attraction to Perdita because he'd sensed there had been someone else. But he'd been prepared to wait, even though it had taken all his acting abilities and all his self control.

He sat in front of the mirror and slapped make-up removal cream on to his face before snatching a fistful of tissues from the box beside him. As soon as his face was cleansed of the blood he'd daubed on for the final gruelling scene, he heard his dressing room door burst open.

He swung round in his seat and saw Charlotte standing there, still in her nun's habit but minus the veil. As he stood up, she screamed. Then she collapsed in a heap of black cloth on to the ground.

FOURTEEN

Seven o'clock in the morning was too early for Joe, especially as he'd stayed up late the night before, drinking alone and going over every detail of the evening he'd spent with Maddy. She hadn't gone back with him to the flat. They'd parted awkwardly outside the restaurant with vague promises to get together again soon. She'd sounded keener than he'd felt.

The feeble morning sun was trying to burn away what was left of the night mist as he walked to the station. When he arrived in the incident room Emily was already in her office, and she summoned him to join her. From the expression on her face, he could tell she had news.

'Cobarn's wife's in hospital.'

'What's wrong with her?'

Emily picked up a pen and turned it over and over in her fingers. 'She was found by the river by a dog walker last night. She'd tried to slash her wrists with a kitchen knife. Lucky she was found when she was.'

Joe sank down into the chair facing Emily's desk. 'Think it's an admission of guilt?'

'Who knows? She won't be the first wronged wife who's got rid of her husband's mistress, and I dare say she won't be the last.'

'She didn't look the type.'

'Come on, Joe, you've been in this job long enough to know that sometimes there isn't a "type". Fancy having a word?'

Joe shook his head. 'Maybe we should wait. It could be construed as harassment.'

Emily rolled her eyes. 'I nearly forgot that Cobarn's a lawyer. Not that we should treat him any differently from any other suspect.'

'I don't see how she could have moved Perdita's body on her own,' said Joe.

'Maybe she killed her and panicked. Rung her husband, and he helped her cover up what she'd done.'

'What about the position of the body? She was arranged like a penitent.'

'To Regina Cobarn, pinching her husband must have seemed like a whopping great sin.'

'Any thoughts on the badge in her mouth?'

'Might have been done to confuse us. The serial-killer touch.'

'One body doesn't make a serial killer,' Joe pointed out.

The phone on Emily's desk rang. When she'd finished speaking, she gave a weary sigh.

'That was Jonas Ventnor. One of the actresses was attacked in her dressing room last night.'

'Who?'

'Charlotte Ruskin. Perdita Elmet's replacement. She wasn't hurt, but the attacker gave her a fright. Jonas thought we should know.'

'Is Charlotte at the theatre?'

'Yes. They've all gone in for an early run through; ironing out some glitches, was how Jonas put it. I think he's expecting us to go round. Do you want to do it while I see what's going on at the hospital?'

Joe nodded. He was frustrated with their lack of progress. Perdita, the victim, still seemed unsettlingly nebulous. The team had so far had no luck tracing her relatives, and the only formal identification in her flat were a passport, a couple of credit cards maxed up to their limit and a few unhealthy bank statements. These had all been in the name of Pauline Elmet, and Joe wasn't particularly surprised that she'd chosen a Shakespearean alias to pursue her theatrical career. Research so far had shown that she'd worked at a number of theatres all over the north, spending several months in Leeds before transferring to the Playhouse. Nobody they'd spoken to at the other theatres had known much about her past, although someone thought she'd attended a drama school in London. This was being checked, but Joe wasn't sure whether it would shed any light on her ultimate fate.

The walk to the Playhouse gave him a feeling of déjà vu. He wondered whether the answer to their puzzle lay in the relationships and rivalries of the cast. Or was the answer even simpler? Had she died because of her affair with Cobarn? As he crossed

Wendover Bridge, he looked at the tower and saw that the chalked shape had virtually disappeared.

By now he knew his way backstage. When he found there was nobody in the auditorium apart from a couple of cleaners, he made straight for Jonas's dressing room. The door was open, and Jonas stood as he walked in.

'Where's Charlotte?'

'In her dressing room with Hen. Last night she was shaken, but she seems a lot better this morning. Maybe I was hasty in reporting it, but with Perdita . . .'

'I understand,' said Joe. 'You did the right thing.'

'Are you any nearer finding out who killed her? Only, I asked when I rang earlier, but the officer said he couldn't tell me.'

'We've been talking to the man she was having an affair with, but I can't say more than that. Did you know about him?'

'Hen told me. Did he do it?' Joe saw that he'd clenched his fists, as though he saw Cobarn in his mind's eye and was preparing to land an imaginary punch.

'I can't comment. Sorry.'

Joe left him and made for Charlotte's dressing room. He found her sipping coffee with Hen in attendance.

'Jonas called us to say you'd been attacked,' Joe began.

Charlotte gazed at him with wide blue eyes. She possessed the kind of vulnerability that made Joe's heart beat a little faster. He tried to envisage her as Sister Jeanne, the crazed Mother Superior . . . and failed. Hen would surely have been more suited to the part, but what did he know about the workings of the theatre?

Hen sat down beside Charlotte and put a protective arm around her shoulder. 'I told her she should report it last night, but she wouldn't.'

'I didn't want to make a fuss. Besides, I wasn't really attacked. I just found a man in here when the performance was over, and he started coming towards me. I fainted and hit my head – lost consciousness for a few moments. By the time I'd come round he'd gone.'

'I had to call a taxi to take her home. I wasn't going to have her going off on her own,' said Hen.

'Where were you when this happened?' Joe asked Hen.

'With Jon, who's playing Cardinal Richelieu. We got talking about Perdita, and—'

'Can you describe the man you saw?' Joe asked Charlotte. 'I take it you didn't recognize him?'

'I've never seen him before in my life. He was tall, about five eleven. And he had dark hair; short and slicked back with one of those widow's peaks where the hair forms a point in the centre of the forehead. He was wearing Victorian dress; a tail coat and a high collar. It must have been a costume from a previous production, but why . . .?'

'I think someone was playing a trick, trying to frighten her,' said Hen, tightening her grip on the other woman's shoulder.

'It's possible,' said Joe. 'Are you OK now, Charlotte?'

Charlotte gave a brave nod.

Now he was with her it seemed the perfect opportunity to ask some questions. 'Did you know Perdita was three months pregnant?'

Charlotte shook her head, avoiding his eyes.

'When you worked with her in Leeds, were you aware of any relationships she had?'

'I've already told you, I didn't know her that well.'

'So you don't know if she was involved with a man called Alvin Cobarn?'

Another shake of the head, more vigorous this time.

He was getting nowhere, so he left the room, retracing his steps down the shabby backstage corridor. Somebody had given Perdita's replacement a fright, but he wasn't sure what, if anything, it meant.

When he reached the auditorium he heard a voice calling his name. He turned to see Louisa, the director, marching towards him armed with a clipboard which lent her an air of authority.

'I take it you've been speaking to Charlotte about our little incident.'

'What do you know about it?'

'Only what Charlotte said. That list of past employees I was asked for is ready, by the way. Do you want to come to my office to pick it up?'

When Joe was handed the list he scanned it quickly for familiar names. One in particular stood out, as though it had been inscribed in huge red letters. He pointed to the name. 'What can you tell me about this man?'

Louisa pressed her lips together with disapproval. 'He worked on the scenery for the last production. He was a good artist, but we had to dismiss him. He was lazy, always skiving off somewhere, leaving the place unlocked. He was a liability.'

'How did he take his dismissal?'

'Not well. He made all sorts of threats. He wasn't a nice man.'

'Any chance he might still have keys to the theatre?'

'He could have taken copies,' Louisa answered. She suddenly looked worried. But it wasn't Joe's job to reassure her.

He thanked her and left the building. Sinclair Doulton had worked there, and he had a grudge against the place. Finding him was a priority.

FIFTEEN

Emily received Joe's news enthusiastically. And when he told her that Sinclair had a stall at the market on Mondays, she asked what they were waiting for and grabbed her coat.

'Did you get to the hospital to see Regina Cobarn?' he said as they were walking out of the police station.

'Yes, not that it did me much good. The ward sister said that she wasn't up to receiving visitors, especially the police.'

'Was her husband there?'

'No. Which is strange, don't you think?'

Joe said nothing. In his experience people often didn't behave as you'd expect. Perhaps, he thought, his abandonment of his wife in her hour of need was just a symptom of a marriage that had long ago rotted and died.

'I'll try and hurry up those DNA results. I want to know if Cobarn was the father of Perdita's baby.'

'And if he wasn't . . .?'

'Then we find out who was. She was working in Leeds until this production, and I've got an old colleague there making enquiries. If she had a secret lover, he won't stay secret for long,' she said with confidence.

They made their way through the narrow streets, now packed with visitors ambling slowly while they absorbed the atmosphere of the medieval city, oblivious to the autumn chill. It was coming up to lunchtime, and the watery sun had brought them out in force, some gazing in shop windows and others scanning the menus outside cafes and restaurants with hungry eyes.

As they walked down Boargate, the traffic-free main tourist street, Joe spotted a living statue in the centre of the road. A monk, entirely monochrome grey-white, who lifted a hand in blessing each time somebody threw a contribution into the bowl at the foot of the small grey platform he stood on. Joe nudged Emily to draw her attention to the performer, but she ignored him and hurried on. It might be clever, but she'd seen his sort countless times before in Eborby. It was just another way of parting the tourists from their cash.

Joe caught up with her, and they wove through the crowd until they reached the wide expanse of Queen's Square, where they took a short cut down one of the alleys that led off the square to the market. Joe watched Emily make her way through the stalls, apparently taking an interest in the goods on sale. But he knew she was looking for the same thing as he was.

The only thing they knew about Sinclair Doulton's stall was that it sold jewellery, but there were a dozen or so stalls selling cheap beads and watches. Doulton hadn't got a criminal record, so all they had was a vague description: wiry and average height with reddish hair and tattooed arms. Joe spotted several men around who might fit the bill, but only one who was manning a stall selling jewellery of any kind.

The goods for sale on his stall were more imaginative than its rivals. Some of the necklaces looked handmade. Colourful beads, chunky bracelets and pendants on leather thongs. There were bags, too, made of brightly coloured remnants. Joe had expected tat, and he was pleasantly surprised.

'Think that's our man?' said Emily.

'It'll do no harm to ask,' Joe replied, fishing in his pocket for his warrant card.

Joe tried to look casual as they approached the stall. The last thing he wanted was to put the man on his guard. Or, worse still, panic him so that he made a run for it, losing himself in the crowd and necessitating a manhunt.

But Emily lacked his innate caution. She marched up to the stall and held up her warrant card like a shield. 'Sinclair Doulton?'

'Yes, love. What can I do you for?' The man reminded Joe of a weasel, and there was a cockiness, a suggestion in his voice that an encounter with the police didn't faze him. Or maybe it was an act, a show of bravado.

'Is this one of your pictures?' Joe produced his photograph of the graffiti on the tower.

Sinclair Doulton studied it with a frown of concentration on his face and passed it back. 'Not mine. I'm a pavement artist. I do pavements and only pavements,' he said, as if explaining to a rather dim child.

'Do you recognize the medallion the figure's holding?'

Sinclair suddenly looked wary. 'Why?'

'Just answer the question,' said Emily.

'It's Saint Galert. Why do you want to know?'

'You drew something like it outside the cathedral,' said Joe.

'It's local, isn't it? One of the symbols of Eborby. Thought it might appeal.'

'Have you ever bought a badge like this from the cathedral shop?'

There was no mistaking the momentary flash of panic in the man's eyes as Joe gave him a photograph of the badge found in Perdita Elmet's mouth.

Doulton handed it back as though it was contaminated and shook his head.

Joe caught Emily's eye. They both knew he was lying.

Doulton glanced at the stall, as if something there was worrying him. Joe followed his eyes.

'Nice necklaces,' he said, pointing to some leather thongs hanging at the back of the stall. There were three, all identical, all easily recognizable. Suspended from the thin strips of leather was a Saint Galert badge, the same as the one found on Perdita Elmet.

He leaned over and unhooked one, and as he handed it to Emily, the corners of her mouth twitched upwards in a smile of triumph.

'You said you'd never bought any of these badges from the cathedral shop, and now we find you've got three of the things. How did you get hold of them?'

'I got them from a mate.' The words sounded defensive, but Joe could detect something else. Fear.

'You see,' Emily began sweetly, turning the necklace over in her fingers, 'the staff at the cathedral told us that they were the sole stockists of these things. Where did this mate of yours get them from?'

Sinclair Doulton looked worried now. 'He never said. He gets me bits and pieces for my jewellery from time to time. I never think to ask where it comes from.'

'We'll need his name,' said Joe, getting out his notebook to make it look official.

'I don't know his name. He's just a lad I see sometimes in the Swan. I wouldn't say I really know him. Look, what is this?' he asked with fresh aggression. Someone had obviously told him once that attack is the best form of defence. But they were wrong.

'We'd like you to come down to the station with us,' said Joe, before taking out his mobile and requesting a patrol car to bring in a suspect.

Doulton looked around, as if seeking a means of escape. Then he seemed to bow to the inevitable. 'OK, but you're wasting your time. I don't even know what all this is about.'

'It's about the murder of a woman called Perdita Elmet,' said Emily. 'She was an actor at the Playhouse. She was found dead in the abbey ruins on Saturday morning.'

'Never heard of her.'

'You used to work at the Playhouse, didn't you?'

'What if I did?'

'You got the sack. You must feel a lot of resentment towards the place.'

He shrugged. 'It was one of those things. Anyway, I was glad to get out, 'cause they were all a bunch of pretentious wankers, especially that Louisa, the director. She's downright weird. I could tell you things about her . . . And for the record, I never knew anyone called Perdita whatsit, so why should I kill her?'

Somehow Joe wasn't convinced. After bagging the Saint Galert necklaces, he allowed Doulton to ask a neighbouring stallholder to take over. The overweight young woman, who had been straining to hear what was going on, agreed, no doubt hoping her curiosity would be satisfied on his return.

When they reached the interview room, Joe was a little surprised that Doulton didn't ask to contact Mrs Telerhaye to let her know where he was. Emily had told him her name was Julie, but he always thought of her as Mrs Telerhaye, the mother of Debby and the missing Peter, almost as if she had no existence of her own.

They sat facing Doulton over the table where the tape was running. Doulton was lounging back in his chair, arms folded. To the casual observer he looked completely relaxed. Joe knew it was a facade, and he wondered how long he'd be able to keep it up.

'Where were you on Friday night?' Emily began.

'I went out for a drink.'

'Who with?'

'On my own. Fancied getting out of the house.'

'Where did you go?'

'The Swan.'

'Anyone see you?'

'Doubt it. Place was packed.'

'It was foggy. Nasty night to be out and about.'

'So? I'm a big boy.' He gave Emily a suggestive wink, and she turned her head away in disgust.

'Have you ever met Perdita Elmet?' Joe asked, pushing Perdita's publicity photograph across the table to the suspect.

'I've told you once. I've never seen her.' Doulton studied the picture with a smirk. 'But I wish I had. Tasty.'

'Do you still have contact with anyone you worked with at the theatre?'

'No. Like I said, they're all a load of wankers.'

'Even the backstage staff?'

'I'm an artist. I painted the scenery and made props, and I was bloody good at it. Most of that lot were just there to provide muscle and shift stuff around. Thick as shit, some of them.'

'Did you have much to do with the actors?' Joe asked.

'Not much. They kept themselves to themselves. Never invited the likes of me to the pub after the performance or their last-night parties.'

'You resented that?'

'Why should I?'

Joe could think of many reasons, mainly the injured pride of a self-styled artist who's treated as an odd-job man by a crowd of egos as insecure as his own. 'Have you still got the keys to the backstage area?'

'No,' Doulton said quickly. 'I handed them in when I left.'

'You didn't take copies?' Emily asked.

Doulton shook his head, avoiding their gaze.

'Your partner's daughter thought you were following her on Friday night,' Joe said. 'Were you?'

Doulton snorted. 'The silly cow's paranoid. It's her age.'

'You haven't answered the question.'

'She's always saying I'm following her, but it's all in her head. I've told Julie she needs to see someone.'

'You're saying she's unstable?'

'I'm saying that all that business with her brother drove her a bit barmy. I wouldn't take any notice of what she says.'

Joe looked at Emily. That was the first impression he'd had of Debby, but it had turned out to be wrong. She had seen a body. If he was to give his opinion now, he'd have said she was a credible witness: damaged, maybe, but credible. 'And you still can't tell us anything about this man who supplied you with the Saint Galert badges?'

Another shake of the head. 'He's a bloke in a pub. Young lad. We didn't swap life stories or exchange phone numbers,' he said sarcastically.

'Describe him.'

'Tallish. Blond. Thin. That's it, really.'

'I don't think he exists.'

'Think what you like. You can't prove anything.'

Emily gave a theatrical sigh. 'You harass and follow your partner's vulnerable daughter; you're found in possession of badges identical to one found on the body of a murder victim; and you were dismissed from a job at the theatre where the victim worked, so you have a reason to resent anyone connected to the place. You're denying any involvement, but you can't come up with a believable alibi. You see our dilemma, Mr Doulton.'

The man didn't answer. The cockiness was fading now, and the worry was starting to show through.

They had until the morning, and then they'd have to decide whether to question him further or release him. At least for a while, Joe thought, Debby Telerhaye wouldn't have to share a roof with the man she hated. She'd have a peaceful night.

The man turned up at Eborby police station at six o'clock on the dot and told the civilian officer on the front desk that he wanted to see somebody about his sister's murder. When he gave the name of his dead sister as Pauline Elmet, the officer rang straight up to the CID office.

Emily had been about to head for home to spend some time with her husband and children. Sinclair Doulton was safely tucked up in his cell, and his house was being searched, so there was little more they could do until the following day. But it turned out that the DCI's plans for an evening of peaceful domesticity had been shattered.

Joe had only just arrived home when he received the call from work. *Come back in. There's been a development.* He felt hungry and annoyed. He'd been intending to give Maddy a call, maybe go for a drink and try to find out more about Carlo Natale. The case of Peter Telerhaye was cold, but he was still curious. That would have to wait, though.

He found Emily pacing up and down her office like a restless prisoner. As soon as he walked in, her eyes lit up with relief.

'I've been waiting for you,' she said. 'I thought you should be in on the interview.'

'Why? What's happened?'

'Perdita Elmet's brother's turned up. Says his name's Simon Elmet and that he lives in Nottingham. He's been away for the weekend in Brighton, so he's only just heard about it on the news.'

'Where is he?'

'Waiting in one of the interview rooms downstairs. The family liaison officer's been giving him a cup of tea and a bit of TLC.' She grabbed her handbag from her desk, the capacious bag that she always said contained her whole life. She slung it over her shoulder and marched out. Joe followed.

The man waiting for them in the interview room was in his early thirties, tall and slim with neat fair hair and a well-scrubbed look. His open-necked striped shirt was crisply ironed, as were his beige trousers. He had the look of a professional man off duty, and he wore a slight frown of concern on his blandly handsome face.

Emily introduced herself and shook his hand, wearing an expression of efficient sympathy. Joe did likewise, and the young female FLO slipped tactfully out of the room.

'Mr Elmet. Thanks for coming in,' Emily began. She glanced at Joe. 'Sorry to have to ask this, but can you prove you're who you say you are?' There had been times when cranks had tried to become involved in investigations by claiming to be relatives. There had even, long ago, been a journalist who'd done something similar. Emily wasn't taking chances.

Simon Elmet took his wallet from the jacket draped over the back of his chair. He opened it and passed it to Emily. Inside was a photograph of Simon with a young woman. It had been taken a good few years ago, but there was no doubt that his companion was the woman they knew as Perdita. There were also bank cards and a driving licence in the name of Simon Elmet, as much proof of identity as most law-abiding people carry with them.

Emily gave him a reassuring smile and returned the wallet. 'Thank you, Mr Elmet. Sorry, but we have to check.'

'I understand,' he said, returning his wallet to its pocket.

'We're very sorry about your sister. It must be a shock for you. Do your parents know yet?'

'No. They're in Australia for a few months visiting my elder sister. I suppose they'll all have to be—'

'We can deal with that if you prefer,' Emily said quickly, as if she was keen to relieve the man of the inevitable burden.

'Thanks, but it'd be better coming from me.'

The awkward silence that followed was broken by Joe's first question. 'When did you last hear from Pauline?'

'It must have been about five months ago. She'd been out of work for a while, and she phoned my parents to say she'd got a job at a theatre in Leeds.'

'Did they go and see her performances?'

'No. They live down in Cornwall, and my dad doesn't drive much these days. I'm afraid she didn't have much contact with the family.'

'Nottingham's not that far from Leeds. Did you visit her much while she was in Yorkshire?'

'I only saw her the once. To tell you the truth, Pauline and I weren't close.'

'Why was that?' Emily asked.

He bowed his head. Joe could see his face had reddened with embarrassment. 'If you must know, she was trouble. There were a number of undesirable men when she was a teenager. Then there was her stage career. Like most people in the acting profession she had long periods out of work, but instead of taking temporary jobs like the others, she was always asking my parents for money. They're not well-off enough to fund her indefinitely, so I had to insist that they stopped the handouts and let her stand on her own two feet.' He sighed. 'It created ill feeling between us.'

'Tell us about the last time you saw her.'

'I was up in Leeds on business, and we met for a pizza. She was full of herself as usual, going on about her brilliant career and how she'd got this fantastic new boyfriend. Pinched him off someone else, which was typical.'

'And that was the last time you saw her?'

'Yes. A few days later we had an argument over the phone, and I haven't heard from her since.' He looked Emily in the eye. 'My little sister was the black sheep of the family, but her death's still come as a shock.'

'What did she say about the man? Do you know his name?'

'She might have told me, but I wasn't taking much notice. Sorry.' He paused, as if he'd just remembered something. 'A colleague of mine was in Leeds on business. He saw her in a posh restaurant with a middle-aged bloke, all lovey-dovey.'

'When was this?'

'Must have been a week or so after I saw her.'

Emily leaned forward. 'Can you describe the man she was with?'

'All my colleague said was that he was middle-aged and looked as if he was worth a bob or two. Smooth was the word he used.'

Joe caught Emily's eye. If he'd been a betting man he'd have laid odds on the mystery man being Alvin Cobarn. 'We'd like to speak to this colleague of yours. Can we have his contact details?'

There was a moment of hesitation before Elmet delved in his jacket pocket again and brought out his mobile phone. He gave a name and a number, which Emily noted down, but Joe sensed he was uneasy about the transaction.

They asked Elmet if he'd be willing to view his sister's body, and he agreed with barely disguised reluctance. He was staying at a bed and breakfast place off Boothgate, he said. He'd see to everything tomorrow.

Elmet was clearly anxious to leave, so Emily terminated the interview, and as they watched him walk off into the night the fog started to descend again. Joe hoped it wouldn't worsen. He felt uneasy when he couldn't see what was going on around him.

When he returned to the incident room he typed Simon Elmet's name into his computer. He often wondered why his first reaction to his fellow citizens these days was to wonder whether there was something criminal lurking in their past. He hadn't been like that in his days training as a priest; in fact, he'd been the opposite, obliged by his chosen calling to think the best of everyone. His years in the police had made him cynical. And it wasn't something he was particularly proud of.

He hadn't really been expecting to find anything, and he was surprised when Elmet's picture appeared on the screen.

And he was even more surprised to learn that three years ago Simon Elmet had served two months in prison for attacking a man in a London nightclub.

SIXTEEN

Emily's reaction to Joe's news was muted excitement. Simon Elmet had a history of violence. And that violence had been associated with his sister. From their interview it had been difficult to imagine Simon in the role of protective brother defending his sister from an unwanted admirer but, according to the records, that was more or less what happened.

He had known his victim, a business colleague, and apparently there had been some ill feeling between the two men for a while. However, things had only boiled over when the drunken victim had made suggestive remarks about Perdita before embarking on what could only be described as a clumsy sexual assault. Simon Elmet had lost control, punched the man and hit him in the face with a bottle. It sounded to Joe as if months of simmering resentment had preceded the attack. The incident with Perdita had probably been the trigger, but it still suggested that Simon's feelings for his sister ran deeper than he'd admitted. And that he was a man who was likely to lose control.

Emily asked for his claim that he'd spent the weekend in Brighton to be checked out. But that, like contacting his friend who'd seen Perdita with a man in Leeds, could wait until tomorrow. Sinclair Doulton was still being held, and they'd question him again once the search of his house was completed, so, after calling the hospital to get the latest update on Regina Cobarn's condition and being told that she still hadn't regained consciousness, she instructed Joe to get home. They'd make an early start in the morning.

The fog had thickened in the half hour since they'd seen Elmet off the premises, and as Joe walked back to the flat his footsteps echoed in the dense grey air. It was hard to gauge distance in such conditions. What was near sounded far away and vice versa, so maybe Debby had been wrong when she thought she was being followed that Friday night. As he walked on, landmarks loomed out of the mist. The library. The cathedral. Canons Bar, the towering city gate he passed under each day. The familiar buildings looked different, strange islands in a sea of white cloud, and the effect was disorientating. He speeded up, anxious to get home, and as he neared the flat his mobile started to ring.

'Hi.'

He recognized Maddy's voice at once.

'Are you at home?'

'Just getting there,' he said. 'I've been working late.'

'The murder?'

'That's right.'

For a few seconds there was an awkward silence.

'Have you eaten?'

Joe had to admit that he hadn't. And he was hungry. He suggested they meet at the Italian again in half an hour. It was an unimaginative choice, but it was easy, and a pizza would fill the space in his stomach perfectly. And besides, Maddy had been due to take her colleague to see Carlo Natale after work that day, and he was curious to discover what had happened. Natale's link with Debby Telerhaye's missing brother had been at the back of his mind. He knew he should be concentrating on the murder of Perdita Elmet, but Debby was there nagging away . . . like his conscience.

'Are you OK in this fog?' he asked. 'Do you want me to pick you up?' He wasn't sure whether he asked the question out of gallantry or whether he just wanted to see where she was living now.

'I'll be fine,' she said. She sounded amused at his concern. He didn't argue.

Half an hour later they were sitting at a cosy table in the corner of the trattoria on Gallowgate again. The staff had given them the most intimate spot and served them with knowing smiles. It's said that all the world loves a lover, and Joe had no desire to disillusion them. Let them think what they want – he was there to eat and to gain information.

They were halfway through their main course when Joe introduced the subject of Carlo Natale. 'How did you get on at the psychic fair today? You were taking a friend to see Carlo Natale, weren't you?'

She nodded and put down her fork. 'I know it's easy to be sceptical, but he's amazing,' she said with breathless eagerness. 'He knows everything. He told Jen her mother's whole life story and told her she didn't mind about her selling her house. Jen was worried about that, you see. That house meant such a lot to her mum because her dad built it, and—'

'So she went away happy?'

'I wouldn't describe it as happy . . . but she said she certainly feels more at peace.'

'And what do you think?' He watched her face. The Maddy

he knew had never been the gullible type. If anything, she had always possessed an edge of cynicism.

'I think he's the real deal, Joe. I don't see how he couldn't be. How could he know all that stuff?'

'Research.'

'Oh, come on. He knows things nobody outside of close families could possibly know. You can't get that sort of stuff off the Internet.'

'Facebook. It's amazing what people put on. Their most intimate secrets laid bare.'

'We're not talking about the Facebook generation here.' She picked up her fork again and began to prod at her food.

'Promise you'll be careful, that's all.'

'Aren't I always,' she said lightly before changing the subject.

He'd wanted to warn her off Natale in stronger terms, but she turned the conversation round with such skill that he found himself discussing their respective jobs for the rest of the evening.

When they left the restaurant, the fog had thickened still further. Joe insisted on walking Maddy home in spite of her protests, but he wasn't sure if he'd go into her new flat for a drink if he was invited. He wasn't sure how he felt at all. They'd known each other so intimately once, but now, after their prolonged separation, they almost seemed like strangers.

But he was pleased when she linked her arm through his. It was hardly far, just a couple of hundred yards, but they began to walk slowly, almost as if they wanted to prolong the moment.

As they passed close to the entrance to Singmass Close, Joe spotted something drawn on the wall of the shop just inside the archway on the side opposite the restaurant. There was something vaguely familiar about the image, and he stopped suddenly, disentangled his arm from Maddy's and darted towards the archway.

It was illuminated directly by the nearby street light, so even in the swirling fog he could make out a life sized man in Victorian dress skilfully executed on the brickwork in chalk. Joe gazed at it for a while before taking a picture with his phone. As he examined it closer he spotted something in the figure's hand which looked very like the Saint Galert badge that had been found on Perdita Elmet's body. His heart beat faster as he took another close up.

'What is it?' Maddy said at last.

'I wish I knew,' was his reply.

Joe walked Maddy to the front door of her new flat on Aldgate, a modern building tastefully in scale with its old surroundings. He refused her offer of coffee, using an early start as an excuse. She'd looked disappointed when they'd parted with a chaste kiss, and as he'd walked away he'd felt a stab of regret. But he put it from his mind, and when he got home he fell into a deep, exhausted sleep.

As soon as he arrived in the incident room the next morning he told Emily about the drawing on the wall, but she didn't take much interest, saying that she had more urgent things to deal with. But Joe was remembering the claim of Perdita's understudy, Charlotte Ruskin, that she was attacked by a man in Victorian dress; a man who fitted the description of the chalked figure on the wall. Or, rather, it hadn't been an attack: when questioned about the incident, she'd admitted that he hadn't actually touched her, only given her a nasty fright. Even so, Joe wanted to get to the bottom of it.

A team had been sent to search Sinclair Doulton's place while the suspect himself sat helplessly in one of the cells in the basement of the station. If there'd been anything incriminating to find at his home, his arrest meant that he hadn't had a chance to dispose of it.

The results of the search came in sooner than Joe had expected. Three more badges had turned up in the shed at the bottom of the small garden where he created his jewellery and a set of keys had been found on a key ring helpfully bearing a handwritten label marked *theatre*. After further investigation, it was confirmed that they were copies of the keys he'd had access to when he worked backstage at the Playhouse. When Emily was told about these discoveries, she looked triumphant. With any luck, she said, the case might soon be wrapped up.

Joe suspected that Debby Telerhaye's account of Doulton's behaviour might have coloured his opinion, so he'd been trying hard to keep an open mind. However, when he'd come face to face with the man in the interview room, this had been difficult.

Now it was time to have another go. They had the suspect brought up from the cells, knowing time was against them and soon they'd have to either charge or release him.

Before they began the questioning, while he and Emily were alone in her office, there was something he wanted to ask her. After talking to Maddy the previous night, it seemed urgent. He'd sensed danger. Something out of kilter. He might be wrong, but he felt he couldn't take the risk.

Emily started going through the messages and paperwork that had come in overnight. Joe watched her for a few seconds before speaking.

'Maddy's back in Eborby.'

Emily looked up. 'That's good.' She must have picked up on his uncertainty because she added, 'Isn't it?'

Joe didn't acknowledge the question because he didn't know the answer. 'Her sister died six months ago.'

'I'm sorry to hear that,' Emily said automatically.

'Her mother's been consulting a psychic.'

Emily raised her head, suddenly alert. 'And?'

'It's Carlo Natale. Same one Peter Telerhaye's mum called in.'

'Well, he wasn't much good. Peter's never been found.'

'I know. But I'm concerned that Maddy's being drawn in. She took a bereaved colleague to see him at that psychic fair in the Pavilion Hall yesterday.'

'People deal with grief in all sorts of different ways. You should know that.'

'You implied Natale was bad news. What exactly did he do?'

She considered the question for a few seconds. 'He muscled in and started to control the situation. He became the family's spokesman, and he wouldn't even let the family liaison officer do her job because she had a negative aura, whatever that means. The SIO at the time thought he was on some sort of power trip.'

'Think it could have been something more sinister?'

Emily shrugged her shoulders. 'I was only a humble DC then, assigned to routine paperwork, so I didn't have much to do with him, but you might have something there. From what I gathered he was a master of diversion. Smoke and mirrors.'

'Could he have had something to do with Peter's disappearance?'

'To be honest, I don't know what to think. All I know is that there was a bad feeling about him in the incident room. But there was nothing that could be proved. I could be wrong.'

'I don't think Debby Telerhaye thinks you are.'

'Poor Debby must have been traumatized by the whole thing. I wouldn't give too much credence to anything she says.'

'I think her suspicions might be correct.' Suddenly, he felt fiercely protective of the girl who'd faced such terror in the fog. 'What if it hadn't been Sinclair who'd been following her?'

'You're not saying Carlo Natale was stalking her, are you? If you are, I think you're getting into the realms of fantasy, Joe, I really do. And I'd take anything she says with a hefty pinch of salt. I wouldn't be surprised if she was attention-seeking. For years her mother's been focused on her missing son, and I bet poor little Debby never got a look in.' She stood up. 'I'm going to have another word with Sinclair. I bet he won't be so cocky now we've found those theatre keys.'

'I'd like to find the man who sold him the badges.'

'If he exists. And we need to speak to Simon Elmet – find out the truth behind his conviction. He could be lying when he told us he hasn't seen his sister for months.'

'Mind if I skip the interview with Doulton?'

She looked mildly disappointed. 'OK. I'll get Jamilla to sit in.'

'I'll see if anything's come up on Simon Elmet's alibi for the time of his sister's death. And we also need to speak to that friend of his who's supposed to have seen Perdita in Leeds with a man.'

'I'll leave you to arrange that then,' Emily said. 'And you're right. I don't think we can rule Elmet out just yet.'

Joe didn't answer. There was something else he wanted to do after he'd got the interview with Elmet out of the way. He feared for Debby Telerhaye. And he wasn't absolutely convinced that it was Sinclair Doulton who posed the threat.

SEVENTEEN

Simon Elmet hadn't been lying. He had spent the weekend in Brighton with a married woman in a discreet hotel not far from the seafront. However, this didn't necessarily mean he had an alibi. He'd taken Friday off work and he hadn't met his lady friend and checked into their hotel until six o'clock on Saturday evening. It had been a single night of passion; all the time she could afford, according to Simon, without arousing the suspicion of her husband.

Joe worked out that he could have travelled to Eborby from Nottingham on Friday and made it to Brighton in plenty of time for his clandestine tryst. But why, he asked himself, would he have wanted to kill his estranged sister?

The two men met in the National Trust cafe on Vicars Green; a neutral venue, less threatening than the police station, and Joe bought the coffees, hoping to put his companion at his ease.

'Why didn't you tell us about your conviction?' he asked as Elmet shovelled a spoonful of sugar into his Americano.

Elmet's hand stopped in mid air, and some sugar grains tumbled on to the wooden table. 'It was three years ago, and I didn't think it was relevant. I used to have a temper back then, but prison changed me. A shock to the system, isn't that what they say?'

'You were fighting over Perdita . . . sorry, Pauline?'

Elmet stared into his coffee cup for a while before answering. 'The man I attacked was a bastard. I'm partner in an architect's practice, and he'd done things that could have ruined us. Pauline was just the catalyst. My other partners sacked him after the . . . incident. And they welcomed me back after I'd served my sentence. I think that says it all, doesn't it?'

Joe didn't reply. It was always possible that friendships and alliances had overcome a sense of justice.

'Was one of these partners the colleague who saw Pauline with the man in Leeds?'

Elmet nodded, and Joe realized why he'd seemed reluctant to

hand over the witness's details. He'd have been afraid he'd say something about the assault.

'Anyway,' Elmet continued, 'we were down in London for a meeting, and we ended up in a nightclub. Pauline had a job down there, and she turned up – I must have mentioned I'd be there. Anyway, this man started pawing her, talking about her as if she was a prostitute, and when I saw him treating her like that it was the final straw. I saw red. Lost control. I'm not proud of what I did, but I'd had a bit to drink, and the old inhibitions . . .'

'How did Pauline react?'

'She was angry. She told me she could handle it and that I was an idiot.'

'How did you feel about that?' Joe spoke softly, using the skills that had become second nature during his seminary years.

'I was hurt. Wouldn't you be? But I'd never have hurt her. I swear.'

Joe saw a film of tears glaze his eyes. 'Where were you on Friday night?'

'In my flat in Nottingham. I watched TV for a bit, then I read for the rest of the evening. Work's been hectic recently, and I took a couple of days off. I knew I was meeting Suzie at the weekend, so I took it easy. Chilled out.'

'Any witnesses?'

Elmet shook his head. 'Only Oscar Wilde. I decided to plod my way through his complete works.'

'*Yet each man kills the thing he loves*,' quoted Joe. 'Did you kill Pauline? Did she do or say something you didn't like, and you lost that temper of yours?'

He shook his head again, more vigorously this time. 'Absolutely not. And I attended anger-management classes in prison. They worked.'

'Does the name Alvin Cobarn mean anything to you?'

'No. Who is he?' said Elmet before draining his cup.

'Pauline's lover.' He almost left it at that but, as he knew Elmet would find out sooner or later, he decided to tell him the truth. 'She was pregnant,' he said gently. 'Three months.'

Joe watched Elmet's reaction to the revelation and saw the man's fists tighten and a flash of anger appear in his eyes. Or it could have been grief. 'I'm sorry to have to break it like that, but . . .'

He was unprepared for the sudden sob, heralding a torrent of tears; noisy, messy tears setting mucous cascading down the man's chin. Joe looked round, unsure what to do. Everyone in the cafe had looked up from their cakes and scones. Some looked away immediately with British embarrassment, but others continued to stare.

He put a guiding hand on Elmet's elbow and led him out into the street. He was reluctant to let him return alone to an anonymous B and B, and his own flat wasn't far away, so he offered to take him there, even though he knew that, professionally, it probably wasn't the wisest thing to do.

Elmet allowed Joe to lead the way, saying he was sorry to make a fuss and assuring him that he'd be fine in a minute. As Joe opened his front door and stood aside to let Elmet in, he asked if there was anything he wanted, but Elmet said no. All he wanted was to be left alone for a while. He needed to come to terms with what Joe had told him. Then a look of horror passed across his face as he remembered that he hadn't broken the news to his family in Australia yet.

For the second time Joe offered to take that particular burden off his shoulders, and this time Elmet accepted.

Joe took a bottle of single malt from the sideboard and poured Elmet a glass. The man flopped down on to the sofa and took it gratefully with both hands, drinking the golden liquid down fast. He took a deep breath and held the glass out for more.

Joe looked at his watch. The hour he'd allowed for a quick coffee and an informal chat had turned into an hour and a half. 'Look, I've got to go out.' He glanced at the whisky bottle. It was half full. 'Will you be all right?'

'Yeah. If I can just . . .'

Joe put his hand on his shoulder. 'I don't like to leave you like this, but . . .'

'You go on. I'll be fine.'

'Just let yourself out when you're ready.'

Joe hovered by the doorway, undecided. But what harm could it do? The worse that could happen would be that Elmet would finish the bottle.

He left him to it.

* * *

Emily was pleased that Sinclair Doulton was in a confessional mood. He admitted that he'd had copies made of the theatre keys, giving his motive as: 'I thought they might come in useful.' When she'd probed further, he'd admitted that he'd been in there from time to time, but he swore on his mother's life that he hadn't done anything to harm anyone.

He'd given a girl who'd wandered into the basement a bit of a fright, and he'd messed with a few props, but that was about it. He made his actions sound innocent, almost playful. But Emily couldn't help wondering what his real intentions had been. Had he been spying on the female actors? Or planning a bit of petty pilfering? Whatever he'd been doing there, she was sure it was something nefarious, and she managed to persuade the powers that be to give her more time to question him. His connection with the theatre where the victim worked had swayed it, but she knew time was limited and she had to make the most of her opportunity.

Half her team had been assigned to digging out all the available dirt on Sinclair Doulton, while the other half were doing the same with Alvin Cobarn.

She'd expected Joe back by now, and she was impatient to talk to him. Simon Elmet's colleague had been contacted, and he remembered seeing Perdita with a man about a year ago. Being an architect, the witness had an eye for detail, and he'd given a good description. The trouble was, the description he'd given didn't, by any stretch of the imagination, match that of Alvin Cobarn. Which meant there could well be another suspect in the mix. The thought of an extra complication was making her head ache, and she'd taken two paracetamol tablets with her morning coffee.

If they could find Perdita's new mystery man, they might get somewhere.

Joe felt unhappy about leaving Simon Elmet alone, but it couldn't be helped. The man didn't look the type who'd trash the flat, but you never knew. He was strung up, unpredictable. In times of pressure those prison anger-management classes might not be as effective as the authorities hoped. And Elmet was a man under stress. His sister had just been brutally murdered, and he hadn't been ruled out as a suspect.

It was past lunchtime, and Joe's stomach was starting to growl. He told himself that what he planned wouldn't take long. The heart of Eborby was relatively compact and, with most of the streets narrow and pedestrianized, it was easier to navigate by foot than by car. The modern monstrosity that was the Pavilion Hall stood just outside the city walls, so it wasn't far if you knew the short cuts.

Last night Joe had looked up the programme for the psychic fair on the Internet. According to the website, Carlo Natale was the main attraction, and he was making regular appearances over the course of the event. His failure to locate Peter Telerhaye clearly hadn't marred his career.

When he reached his destination, Joe paid the admission fee because he wished to be there anonymously. Showing his warrant card and demanding access would have drawn attention that he didn't want. He was there to observe.

Luckily, he'd timed it well. He arrived just as Natale was finishing his turn in the temporary theatre set up at the end of the hall. He saw the man take a self-satisfied bow before plunging into the audience, shaking the hands of elderly women with adoring eyes, kissing the odd wrinkled cheek now and then. At first glance this didn't seem the kind of set-up where Maddy would fit in, but obviously he was wrong. Like her mother, she'd become hooked. And, like a true convert, she was trying to bring others into the fold. He studied the audience more carefully and saw younger people in the crowd. And there were men, but they were a small minority.

His heart lurched when he spotted a familiar face watching Natale. No wondrous smiles, no rapturous applause; instead, Debby Telerhaye was staring at Natale as if she was trying to see into his soul. Unblinking, focused and full of hatred, it was a stare that would have shaken most people. But as he acknowledged his disciples, Natale seemed unaware of this sliver of dissent.

Until Debby stood up and shouted over the ovation. 'Where's Peter? What have you done with him?'

As soon as she'd spoken she turned and ran out. Joe tried to follow but he was held up by a couple of elderly ladies walking with sticks.

He rushed out into the main hall and looked round for Debby. At last he spotted her in the crowd, and he pushed and excused-me'd his way towards her.

He needed to tell her she might be putting herself in danger. But it was too late. After a few seconds there was no sign of her. She'd gone.

EIGHTEEN

When Debby had asked her question at the end of the performance, Natale had disappeared behind the curtain, anxious to avoid a confrontation – which, in her mind, meant that he was a coward as well as a crook. After that she'd left the Pavilion Hall, adrenalin pumping through her body, feeling lost. She had no lectures that afternoon, but the last thing she wanted was to spend it with her mother, who'd been in tears since they'd come for Sinclair. It was wearing being the prop for a fragile parent, and she needed a break.

She'd run out of money for idle shopping, so wandering through Eborby was the only option. Fortunately, she never tired of exploring the city. Every time she looked up she saw something different, a new aspect of the familiar: an unusual window or a slice of architectural history she'd never noticed before. She walked down Boargate, barging her way through the wandering tourists without apology. They'd think her rude, but it didn't matter because she'd never see them again.

A living statue stood on a small dais in the centre of the thoroughfare, and Debby stared. It was a tall man in eighteenth-century dress who looked like a mauve Mozart: mauve clothes, mauve face, mauve hair, mauve everything. Each donation was acknowledged with a deep bow and an elaborate flourish of his thin arms. Perry had said he dressed as a monk, so it couldn't be him. Besides, this Mozart was far too tall.

She walked on to the cathedral, intending to sit a while in Vicars Green. She liked it there, on the small patch of grass in front of the close of ancient houses. On fine days in the summertime, students lounged on the steps beneath the Roman pillar in the centre of the grass, but today it would be deserted. She'd have the place to herself, a chance to think about her next move.

When she reached the cathedral square, habit caused her body to tense as she scanned the scene for signs of Sinclair. In recent months the square had been associated in her mind with her mother's hated boyfriend and, even though she knew he was still being questioned by the police, the reaction was automatic. She hated how he spoiled it for her. How he'd spoiled everything since he moved in.

She slowed her pace to look up at the cathedral towers, jutting upwards into the leaden sky. She'd never ventured inside. If she entered the amazing church and was disappointed at what she found, she was afraid that it might lose its magic.

But somebody she knew was going in, hurrying in through the south door, bypassing the queue of tourists waiting to gawp at the cathedral's interior. Perry was dressed in a long denim coat and washed-out jeans, and his hair looked neatly combed. The sight of him entering that place seemed incongruous somehow. It was somewhere he shouldn't be. But he was.

She shivered. The damp, chill leftovers of the previous night's fog still hung in the air, and she wished it would clear once and for all. She sat down on a vacant bench opposite the cathedral entrance. When Perry came out, she'd ask him what he was doing there. And if it had anything to do with his art. Or his ghosts.

Only, he never came out, and after a while she gave up and went home.

The bandages made Regina Cobarn's hands feel clumsy, as if somebody had frozen her arms with anaesthetic and cut off her fingers. Her head felt numb too, stuffed with cotton wool and razor blades. She would have cried if she'd had the strength.

She opened her eyes. Her husband was there. He'd turned up, but she didn't know why. He was a liar, a destroyer. For years she'd ignored his sins, but once the police became involved, she'd had to face the truth, and she'd found that impossible to endure. Alvin knew how she'd suffered when their only child had been born dead; he knew how eggshell-brittle her existence was. But he'd still hurt her by sleeping with that cheap little actress. His actions had pierced her heart, and she'd died inside.

He was bending over her, almost as though he was about to kiss her. The Judas kiss of betrayal, his duplicity masked in smooth words of concern.

She turned her head away, but the action was painful. Then she heard the words, 'I'm so sorry,' her husband's voice muffled, as though he was speaking under water.

She wanted him to go. She wanted to speak to the police. She was married to a murderer, and she needed protection.

Once he had gone she asked the fat blonde nurse, the only one who'd shown her any sympathy, to call the police station for her. She needed to tell someone.

After the performance, Jonas Ventnor stood in front of the mirror in his bloodstained shift. The stage blood had stiffened the fabric so much that it was becoming increasingly difficult to get the thing on and off. It chafed beneath his arms and on his naked nipples as he moved around, and he was glad that the evening's performance was over.

The auditorium had been packed since Perdita's murder. It was prurient curiosity, he supposed; the same mentality that made public executions such a crowd-pleaser in days gone by. The applause had been muted though, as though the play had disappointed in some way. He wondered what they'd expected to see.

He sat down in the swivel chair in front of the mirror and looked at his face, hideous with the effects of an agonizing execution: a portrait of suffering; of gore, sweat and bruising. After taking a long drink from the water bottle on the counter, he took a deep breath and reached for the make-up removal cream. To his annoyance the jar was empty, but he delved into his bag and found a new one. He placed it on the counter and slumped forward, putting his head in his hands. He was exhausted. He'd felt that way since Perdita went missing. He'd harboured hopes that his attraction to her would be reciprocated and had watched her like a lovesick schoolboy, even though she'd given him no encouragement.

He knew he'd become a little obsessed with her, perhaps because of her coolness rather than in spite of it. She'd been a beautiful, mysterious challenge. He'd dreamed of making love to her, of their limbs entwined as their lips met in the communion of passion. These dreams had continued since her death, only now he woke up sweating as he realized that much desired body was cold as marble and he was kissing the icy lips of a corpse. He was glad he was living alone, glad that there was no flatmate there to hear him weep.

He was starting to hate this theatre with its talk of death, ghosts and bad luck. Even Hen had succumbed to the atmosphere, and he'd never thought she was the over-imaginative, hysterical sort. She still hung around, and he knew she wanted him. But all his feelings were for Perdita, and he had started to wonder if Hen had been jealous. But he couldn't imagine her losing control. She was no murderer, he was sure of that.

His thoughts turned to Charlotte and her claim that she was attacked by a man in Victorian dress. He had little doubt that the incident had been a product of her over-fertile mind. There was something unstable about Charlotte which he found unnerving, so he avoided her whenever possible. He'd asked her what Perdita had been like when they'd worked together in Leeds, though, unable to let his obsession drop. Charlotte had replied in unconvincing platitudes: Perdita had been lovely, great.

Anyway, he had a TV part in the New Year, and next week he was auditioning for an Alan Ayckbourn play in Sheffield. He hoped he'd get the part so he could leave this place with its unhappy associations for good. He took another drink. His head was starting to ache, as if it was filled with cotton wool.

He heard a soft knock on his door, and he stood up, feeling a little dizzy. His towelling dressing gown was draped on the back of the shabby sofa, but he guessed his visitor would be Hen, who was used to seeing him in costume, so he left it where it was. Since Perdita's death she'd taken to coming to his dressing room to ask if he wanted to go for a post-performance drink. He'd always refused, politely, but in spite of him telling her earlier that he was going straight home, it looked as if she hadn't got the message.

He shouted, 'Come in,' and the door began to open very slowly. What was the silly cow playing at? 'Come on, Hen, stop messing about.' He wasn't in the mood for games.

Eventually, the door opened fully to reveal his visitor, who stood there for a second before stepping into the room.

'Hello,' Jonas said warily. 'What can I do for you?'

His visitor stared at him with blank eyes and said nothing.

NINETEEN

When Joe had returned to his flat the previous evening, he'd half expected Simon Elmet to be there, possibly drunk. But instead he'd found the place neat and hardly any of the whisky gone, leaving Joe to conclude that the man had self control and that he might have gone back to his B and B as planned. Joe had tried to call him, but there was no reply.

As the evening had worn on he'd half expected to hear from Maddy, but his phone hadn't rung. Perhaps, he thought, she'd been comforting her parents. Or the colleague who'd lost her mother.

He had the uncomfortable feeling that Maddy was on the brink of something, maybe an involvement with Carlo Natale and his particular form of spurious comfort. Why was it, he thought, that people scoffed at the time-honoured solace of the church and flocked to any money-grabbing charlatan who offered an alternative form of hope? He'd seen the rapturous expressions of the women hanging on Carlo Natale's every word. He had to acknowledge that the performance had been clever. But he knew that's what it was – a performance.

The next morning all trace of the lingering fog had vanished, and Joe walked to work early. But at nine thirty their routine enquiries were disrupted when a call came in to the incident room. Another body had been found. This time it was at the theatre, and the victim had undergone a violent attack prior to death. He had been found hanging, half kneeling, half standing, from a clothes rail in one of the dressing rooms.

The team was already at the Playhouse when Joe and Emily arrived. They were admitted through the stage door, where a young constable stood on guard. Emily had a motherly word with the lad while Joe watched, impatient to get on.

All they'd been told was that the corpse was male, and during the journey there in the patrol car, Emily had speculated on the likely identity of the victim. She claimed she was giving good odds on it being one of the army of backstage staff. But once they reached the crime scene it turned out that she was wrong.

Joe recognized Jonas Ventnor right away. He was still dangling there, his once handsome face distorted and discoloured, and Joe's first instinct was to lift him down, to give him some dignity in death. However, he knew better than to touch anything before the forensic team and Sally Sharpe had completed their work.

He edged closer to get a better view of the body. It seemed that the initial report was right. The dead actor was covered in blood, and it looked as though he'd undergone a savage beating. The attack had indeed been violent and uncontrolled, and Joe found it difficult to believe that the killer of Perdita Elmet had been responsible for this second outrage. But when he looked at the victim's gaping mouth, he saw something that made him think again. A pilgrim badge lay on the protruding tongue, as though it had been placed there carefully after death. He nudged Emily and pointed to the badge.

'It's the same killer. But why? What did the poor sod do to deserve this?' she said, almost in a whisper.

'There's a lot of blood on the body but none round about,' he said, looking around the room.

'He must have been killed somewhere else and moved. That's what he did with Perdita Elmet.'

'I don't think so,' said Joe. 'Take a closer look.'

Emily peered at the body, and after a while a grim smile appeared on her lips. 'It's make-up and stage blood. If we'd actually taken the trouble to go and see the play, we might have realized earlier. We won't know if he has any injuries until all this lot's washed off in the mortuary. Maybe we can't rule out suicide after all. Maybe he killed Perdita out of thwarted passion and couldn't live with what he'd done. The badge might be some sort of sign.'

Joe shook his head. 'He had an alibi for Perdita's murder. He went for a drink with another actor after the performance and didn't leave till midnight.' He thought for a moment. 'I think the ligature around his neck is the belt belonging to that dressing gown over there on the sofa, which means, if it isn't suicide, our killer uses anything to hand. Perdita's scarf, Jonas's dressing gown belt.'

'Do you think that's relevant?'

'I don't know.' He scanned the room again. 'No sign of a struggle, and Jonas was a fit, healthy young man. I can't see anyone being able to strangle him without him putting up a fight.'

'No indication that Perdita defended herself either. We haven't got the tox report back yet, but I bet they'll find she was drugged.' She nodded towards the corpse. 'Him too. No sign of a drink, or . . .?'

'Perhaps the killer cleared up after himself,' said Joe. 'He's cool and organized. He takes his time. We've been working on the assumption that this was about Perdita and her relationships, but if this turns out to be murder, it changes everything.'

'You could be right. Maybe it's something to do with the play itself. *The Devils*. It's been controversial in its time, hasn't it?'

'I suppose so. But by modern standards . . .' He didn't bother finishing the sentence. He didn't have to. 'Of course, it could be someone with a grudge against the theatre . . . or actors in general. Sinclair Doulton fits that particular bill. And we released him yesterday.'

'There was no evidence against him.' There was a hint of defensiveness in Emily's reply.

'We still don't know how he got hold of those badges.'

'We brought in the necklaces from the stall and the badges we found at his house.'

'Doesn't mean he hasn't got more tucked away.'

Their thoughts were interrupted by Sally Sharpe's arrival.

'You're keeping me busy,' were her first admonishing words.

'Sorry, Sal. We'd like you to tell us if it's suicide or not.'

They watched as Sally went about her work. Once the scene was recorded on camera and video she asked for the body to be taken down. It was only then she could make a proper examination of Jonas Ventnor's neck. She loosened the ligature carefully, took the badge from the mouth and placed it in an evidence bag. Then after a while she looked up, her eyes focused on Joe.

'I think he's been dead about twelve hours or so but, as you know, these things are never exact.' She looked worried. 'I can't be a hundred per cent sure until the post-mortem, but the position of the bruising seems about right for hanging. There's a tall stool behind the body. If he tied the ligature round his neck then threw himself forward, he would have strangled himself. I think that's what happened. But I could be wrong,' she added, like the mumbled disclaimer at the end of a TV advert.

'Suicide, then?'

'I'm not so sure. If he was drugged, someone could have led him over to the stool, got him to sit, then given him an almighty shove. And there's the badge. It's the same as the one found in Perdita Elmet's mouth, so there must be a connection.'

'Well, the theatre's the common denominator,' Emily said.

Joe thought for a few seconds. 'If he died around twelve hours ago, it must have been shortly after last night's performance, so we need to interview all the cast and backstage staff as soon as possible. We have to find out who saw him last.'

Emily looked exasperated. 'Why isn't there any CCTV in this bloody theatre?'

Joe knew the question was rhetorical, but he shared her frustration. 'His phone's over there by the mirror.' He turned to the officer by the door. 'Bag it up and send it off to get his calls analysed, will you? You never know, his killer might have called him to arrange a meeting after the show.'

Once the young man had left, Emily turned to Joe. 'I want Sinclair Doulton brought in again. We need to know where he was last night.'

'You think he celebrated his release by murdering Ventnor?'

'We can't rule it out.'

'Maybe Ventnor knew something he didn't share with us and had to be silenced.'

'Whatever the motive, I want Doulton. I don't care how much fuss his bloody solicitor kicks up, he's coming in.'

In the face of her determination Joe knew that expressing any doubts or disagreement would be futile. Her phone rang, and when she'd finished the call, she turned to Joe. 'Regina Cobarn's come round. She asked one of the nurses to ring the station to say she wants to speak to us. Says it's urgent.'

'Do you want to go or shall I?'

Emily considered the question. 'You go when we've finished here.'

It was Joe's phone that rang this time. And the news the caller on the other end of the line had to convey was totally unexpected.

'That was Sunny,' he said, staring at the phone. 'I don't quite believe this.'

'What?'

'They've got the DNA results on the baby Perdita Elmet was carrying.'

'And?'

'It's not a match for Alvin Cobarn. He's not the father. But they've got a match to a sample from someone who was convicted of drink driving two years ago.' He raised his head and saw the impatience in Emily's eyes, as though she was longing to grab hold of his jacket lapels and shake the revelation out of him.

'It's someone whose name came up in the Peter Telerhaye enquiry. It's Carlo Natale. He was the father of Perdita Elmet's baby.'

TWENTY

The actors and staff at the theatre were being interviewed again. So far they'd all expressed shock and disbelief, saying what a good bloke Jonas had been. A good bloke and a brilliant actor who'd been destined for great things. It was the sort of eulogy that Emily and Joe had heard so many times before, but somehow, in that theatrical setting, it seemed even more convincing than usual.

With two members of the cast dead in tragic and suspicious circumstances, that evening's performance had been cancelled. However, Louisa Van Sturten had insisted that the production would resume the following night. It was what Perdita and Jonas would have wanted, she'd stated piously.

The majority of the cast and backstage crew had given credible alibis for the estimated time of Jonas's death. They'd either been in the pub together or at home, with varying degrees of verification. A few of the assistant stage managers and lighting people lived alone, as did Louisa, who lived with a relative who was currently away on business, and therefore had no alibi. However, most of the actors, apart from Hen Butler, whose flatmate's demise now meant that she lived a solitary existence by default, had someone to vouch for them.

Hen was particularly distressed at Jonas's death, but Joe reminded himself that pretence was how she earned her living. He had chosen Perdita over her, rejected the affection she'd offered. She said she'd asked Jonas earlier that evening if he fancied a drink, but he'd refused, saying he was going straight home. There had been something guarded about her statement, Joe reckoned. She couldn't be ruled out as a suspect.

Nobody in the theatre had been told it might be another case of murder, so most assumed it was suicide or an accident. One sound engineer even suggested it might have been some sort of auto-erotic experiment gone wrong. They hadn't attempted to enlighten him. A bit of temporary ignorance might work to their advantage.

Everything at the theatre was under control by the time Joe made for the hospital. Emily ran an efficient operation, and as well as dealing with the theatre staff, she'd arranged for Sinclair Doulton to be picked up again.

It seemed that the stage door hadn't been locked until half an hour after the performance ended, so anybody could have slipped in unseen. They'd confiscated Doulton's keys last night, but he wouldn't necessarily have needed them.

No unfamiliar fingerprints had been found either, just the cast's, and it seemed that they were in the habit of visiting each other's dressing rooms during rehearsals to borrow items, compare notes and exchange gossip. And if the killer was an outsider, he could easily have worn gloves.

Emily had sent a patrol car over to the Pavilion Hall to pick up Carlo Natale and bring him in for questioning. With the DNA results, they now realized that Simon Elmet's colleague's description of the man seen with Perdita in Leeds fitted Natale perfectly. As Joe waited for the clairvoyant to turn up at the station, he was annoyed with himself for not making the connection before.

His heart sank when the patrol reported back that Natale wasn't there and nobody knew where he was staying. All they had was a contact number, a mobile phone they tried several times with no success. If they wanted to speak to him they'd have to exercise patience and wait for him to turn up. But neither Joe nor Emily felt very patient where Natale was concerned.

The death of Jonas Ventnor had distracted Joe from his intended interview with Regina Cobarn. But she'd been seen near Perdita's flat on the night of her murder, and she'd tried to kill herself. Even though she had the perfect alibi for the time of Jonas's death, Joe still wanted to speak to her.

It was just before midday when he arrived at the hospital. He never felt comfortable in hospitals. He had spent a long time incarcerated in the Royal Liverpool after his shooting, and the smell and the sight of blue linoleum and swing doors brought back painful memories. For a while he had hovered between life and death. But when life chose him, he'd had to endure the agony of realizing his partner, Kevin, hadn't survived the attack. Joe had experienced the guilt of the survivor . . . and he'd wondered why he'd been spared when he would have been glad to have died in Kevin's place. Kevin had had a wife and daughter . . . whereas Joe had lost Kaitlin by then. Kevin had had more to live for, and his death had seemed so unjust. But Joe had learned long ago that life is rarely fair.

He found Regina Cobarn in a side ward on her own. Perhaps, he thought, they hadn't wanted to put an attempted suicide in with the other recovering patients. He found a staff nurse, who told him that she'd be ready to go home the next day. Her lips pursed with disapproval as she said the words, and he could almost read her mind. Regina Cobarn's action had been selfish, and she'd made herself an unnecessary burden on the health service. Joe, who understood despair, wasn't so sure.

Regina was still ash pale, and her bloodshot eyes appeared to have sunken into her skull. When he walked in and she turned her head to look at him, he thought those eyes looked half dead.

Joe drew up a chair and sat down, watching the woman's face, establishing eye contact and hoping she'd sense his sympathy. 'How are you feeling?' he asked. The question was hardly original, but it was the first that popped into his head.

'OK, I suppose.'

'We had a call at the station to say you wanted to speak to us about something. We were told it was urgent.'

She took a deep, rasping breath. 'Yes. It's my husband. It's Alvin.'

'What about him?'

'He killed that girl . . . the one he was having an affair with.'

'Perdita Elmet?'

'That's right.'

'What makes you think that?'

'Because when he came back home from that Traders' Association dinner he had a shower. He never has a shower at that time.'

'He told us he went to see Perdita early that evening, but he denied seeing her after the performance. You don't believe him?'

'He's lying. When you've been married as long as we have, you can tell.'

Joe didn't speak for a few moments. His next question would be an awkward one, and he was thinking how to phrase it best.

'Your car was caught on CCTV near Perdita's flat, just before a quarter to seven on the night she died. Did you go there to visit her?'

'Yes.' She swallowed hard. 'I went there, but she wasn't in. It was a stupid thing to do, but I went there on impulse. I wanted to talk to her, to try and persuade her not to wreck my marriage. I should have known she'd be on her way to the theatre then, but I wasn't thinking straight. Looking back, I'm glad I didn't find her in. I would only have made a fool of myself.'

'We have reason to believe she was killed shortly after she left the theatre that night. Your husband was out, so you have no alibi. You could have followed her when she left the Playhouse. And if you did, you could have killed her.'

The woman's eyes filled with tears. 'I swear I could never do anything like that.'

'Is there anyone who might be angry enough to do it for you?'

'Of course not.'

'No relatives you're close to?'

'I'm an only child.' She paused. 'And I've never been that close to anyone apart from my husband. Nobody would kill for me, Inspector. Not even the man I married.'

'Do you really think your husband killed Perdita Elmet?'

'He left home around five, and I never saw him again until almost one in the morning. He could easily have arranged to sneak out of the dinner and meet her again that night. He's always saying those functions are boring. Why did he stay so long?'

Joe knew she could be right. There had been a long period during that evening at the Traders' Association dinner when nobody had seen him. It would have been easy for him to slip out. 'Did your husband visit you last night?'

'Yes. He came after work.' She didn't sound too delighted about his attentiveness.

'What time did he leave?'

'About eight. Why?'

Joe reached over and touched the restless fingers which were peeping from the white bandage. Alvin Cobarn was still on their suspect list.

There was too much going on in Debby's life at that moment for her to be able to concentrate on some stupid Shakespeare play and some lame novel by someone she'd never even heard of until the beginning of that term. She sloped off from college at break time to go wandering again. Wandering helped her to think.

Sinclair had been taken in for questioning again which, in her opinion, meant that he'd killed that girl in the undercroft. She wondered if he'd killed her by mistake and if she herself had been the real target. She knew he'd been longing to get rid of her and have her mother and the house to himself, and she was sure he'd been following her in the fog. But would he go as far as murder? She thought he probably would. Sinclair was capable of anything.

Her mother's judgement must have been so damaged by what happened with Peter that she was no longer able to recognize self-serving wickedness when she met it, which meant she was vulnerable. Just as she had been to Carlo Natale. And Natale was back in town, lurking like a waiting spider in his web.

Her restless mind turned to Perry. She hadn't seen him since he'd disappeared into the cathedral yesterday. She could hardly see him as the devout type, so perhaps his visit had something to do with his art: or perhaps there were more mysteries about him she had yet to uncover. Maybe he had a deep spiritual side. After all, anyone who created ghosts had to be spiritual, she reckoned. Sort of.

She wondered whether Perry would be at his strange home or whether he was out doing his living statue act. Now that she was at a loose end, having decided to give her English lecture a miss, she thought there was no harm in finding out. She'd surprise him.

She slung her bag over her shoulder and set off. She'd never met anyone like Perry before, and she was attracted to the fact that he was different, arty. He was the sort who wasn't governed by a need to get some boring job, to toe the line just like everyone else. There was an excitement about him, maybe even a danger. Who else would keep a mummified corpse in his house, treating it like a piece of home decor . . . or a household pet?

Last time she'd been at his place he'd offered her a beer, and she'd enjoyed sitting there with him, swigging from the bottle as a camaraderie developed between them. She was looking forward to their next meeting. Confronting Carlo Natale had given her new confidence. Besides, life was short, and it was time she started living.

However, when Perry opened his door he didn't look particularly pleased to see her. He had obviously been eating because he had crumbs of toast on his chin and his jaws were still moving, chewing what was left of his food. He stood in the door, barring her way.

'Hi,' she said brightly. 'Mind if I come in?'

'I'm expecting my sister back any minute.'

'I won't get in the way. How's Fred?' She hoped that her positivity would break down his defences but he didn't move.

'He's as well as can be expected.' He moved to close the door. 'See you around, eh?'

She suddenly felt bold. 'Why don't you want me to meet your sister?'

'She doesn't like strangers.'

'A stranger is only a friend you haven't met yet.' She couldn't remember where she'd heard this cliché, but she thought it sounded good in the circumstances.

He yawned and rolled his eyes. 'Whatever.'

'That medium I told you about – I got the impression you knew him.'

'Well, I don't.' He closed the door a little further.

'I haven't got your mobile number.' She didn't want the encounter to end. She didn't want to have to go back to the house where her mother would be sitting, exuding melancholy.

'Give me yours. I'll call you.'

He took his phone from his pocket, and she snatched it eagerly, keyed in her number and handed it back to him.

He didn't thank her. Instead, he shut the door in her face, and she stood staring at the wooden barrier for a while. If she merely found him interesting before this meeting, his dismissive manner made her keener. Maybe she was falling in love, she thought. She'd always liked boys who were different, who didn't follow the crowd. He was playing it cool at the moment, but she was sure she could get him to realize her true worth in time. For the first time in her life, Debby Telerhaye's heart fluttered at the thought of being close to another human being.

She walked slowly to the end of the street, unsure what to do. What he'd said about his sister had piqued her curiosity, and she suddenly wanted to see her, to find out what she was like, this girl who was afraid of strangers.

She stood on the street corner in front of a house which had served as a corner shop in years gone by, but now stained curtains dangled at its grubby plate-glass windows. She intended to hang round for five minutes and then go if the sister didn't put in an appearance. For a moment she contemplated returning to college, but she dismissed the idea. She'd make for town and hang round the shops; maybe she'd nick some make-up like she had the other week.

Five minutes passed, and there was no sign of anybody who might be Perry's sister. She wondered if he'd made her up to put her off. After all, there had been no evidence of a female in residence when she'd last been there.

She was about to abandon her vigil when she saw the door open, and Perry shot out, closing it behind him and checking it was properly shut. He wore a long sleeved T-shirt and no coat, even though the air was chill and damp. And he carried a rucksack, which he slung over one shoulder.

Debby knew he hadn't seen her, and she couldn't resist the temptation to follow him at a safe distance. She wanted to know where he was going. And what he was hiding from her.

He walked purposefully, and she was relieved when he didn't look round. If he'd seen her, she hardly liked to contemplate the embarrassment she'd feel. She hung back, putting a good distance between them. This sort of thing sounded so easy in books and films, but in reality it was hard being inconspicuous.

She felt more confident when they reached Gallowgate. There were more people here, shopping in the pound shops and wandering in and out of the charity shops. She could blend in with the crowd here, become just another shopper. She stood outside a clothes shop opposite the ancient churchyard of Saint Saviours and pretended to gaze in the window. He was still in view, and she saw him stop outside a small half-timbered pub with bright orange notices advertising karaoke and quiz nights displayed in its leaded windows.

He looked around before entering the pub, and she stepped quickly into the shop doorway. He hadn't looked like a man heading for a relaxing drink, and she wondered whether he was meeting someone in there.

It was one thing going drinking with some of the others from college at a weekend, but going into an ordinary pub on her own was a no-no. Besides, this particular pub, she'd heard from a lad on her course, had a bit of a reputation.

As she was pondering her next move, she saw a familiar figure striding down the street towards her. It was Sinclair. Just her luck.

She stepped further into the doorway and held her breath, praying he wouldn't see her. She saw him glance at his watch, as if he was late for an appointment, and she turned to look in the shop window, wondering whether to seek refuge inside. But it was the sort of expensive place where the assistants were all over you, so she abandoned that particular plan. There was a charity shop next door, but that meant she had to break cover. She pressed herself into the doorway and watched as he drew closer.

She mustn't panic. If he saw her, she'd have to play it cool. But as she peeped round the corner of the shop window she saw him disappearing into the pub Perry had just entered.

He was bound to be in there for some time. She shot out of her hiding place and began to walk in the opposite direction. She'd had a narrow escape.

After buying their drinks at the bar – Perry a bottled lager and Sinclair a scotch – Perry led the way to a dark corner, far from the little leaded windows. The darkness seemed right, somehow. Darkness hid innumerable sins.

Once they were seated, Perry hoisted his rucksack on to his knee. It wasn't heavy. What he had to offer didn't weigh a lot.

Sinclair looked uncomfortable. Perry could see a change in him. His usual cockiness had vanished, and there was a haunted look in his eyes.

'Something wrong?'

'I've been hauled in by the filth twice – questioned for hours.'

'What about?' Perry asked, suddenly wary.

'Some girl who got herself murdered. They had to let me go sharpish second time, though. I demanded a solicitor. I know how the bastards work,' he added self righteously. 'Now some guy's died at the theatre where I used to work, so it wouldn't surprise me if they came sniffing round again.'

Perry smirked. 'Is that the theatre that gave you the push?'

'Piss off. It was artistic differences.' Sinclair took a drink. 'What have you got for me today?'

Perry sighed and opened his rucksack, his eyes scanning the room to make sure they weren't being watched. 'I've got some good stuff. Unusual.' He edged away from Sinclair and placed some items from the rucksack on the red plastic bench between them.

'How much?'

'Fifty?'

'You're joking.' He pointed to a packet of badges. Saint Galert. 'And you can keep those. I've had the cops round asking about them. Saw the bloody necklaces on my stall and took me in.'

Perry's eyes widened in alarm. 'Why?'

'Something to do with that murder. I don't want anything to do with them . . . not if they're going to get me into bother. Where do you get them from, anyway?'

'It's all legit.' Perry's lie was automatic. 'I'll take them back, then. You can have the rest of the stuff for forty.'

'Thirty-five.'

Perry wanted to make him sweat, show that he was in charge. It was a long time before he answered, but eventually he nodded. 'Deal.'

'You never drew that nun on the tower by the river, did you? Only, the police thought I'd done it and kept me in a bleeding cell overnight.' He leaned towards Perry, grinning like a death's head. Perry could smell his sour breath. This wasn't going well. 'Maybe I should tell them about you. I saw you drawing on the wall by Singmass Close the other night.'

Perry felt the blood drain from his face. 'I've had enough of this.' He shoved the badges back in his rucksack and stood up. 'I'm not the only one with secrets. I know all about you from Debby.'

Sinclair stared open mouthed as Perry stalked out of the pub.

TWENTY-ONE

On his way back to the station, Joe went over Regina Cobarn's words in his mind. But when he shared his thoughts with Emily, she observed that women whose husbands were unable to keep their trousers on were capable of making up all sorts of fantasies to extract their revenge.

However, after uttering this caveat she sent someone over to find out what Cobarn had done after he'd left the hospital. Cobarn too had suffered a sort of betrayal. Perdita had been carrying another man's child, and perhaps this had touched a raw nerve. And perhaps Jonas had died because he'd known more about the whole affair than he'd admitted – or even because Cobarn believed he was the unborn baby's father. Emily agreed with Joe that Cobarn couldn't be ruled out.

Since his visit to the hospital, Joe had been stuck in the incident room, going over every aspect of Jonas Ventnor's life. He discovered that Ventnor's parents lived in Surrey and that he had a sister and two brothers. He had always been well-liked, and his career was going well; he'd even won a small part in a TV soap, starting in January. Apart from the death of Perdita Elmet, no cloud had overshadowed Jonas's life, and he'd been behaving quite normally on the evening he died.

The consensus of opinion from his theatre colleagues was that he'd had no reason to kill himself. They hadn't yet been told that his death was being treated as a possible case of murder, and the longer they were in ignorance, the more they'd be off their guard.

Joe still favoured Sinclair Doulton as a suspect. On his first arrest, he'd made do with the duty solicitor, but the second time he'd chosen one of his own. She was young and keen, and she'd curtailed the interview as soon as the questioning became awkward. She looked expensive: Joe wondered how he could afford her. Apart from Doulton's lack of an alibi, there was no solid evidence against him, so they'd had to let him go. The solicitor had been delighted with her own cleverness and, forgetting professional etiquette, she'd whispered, 'Better luck next time,' in Joe's ear as she'd left. He didn't like her. But she obviously loved herself.

They still hadn't spoken to Carlo Natale and, according to the programme, he wasn't due at the psychic fair again until tomorrow. Joe was confident that he'd soon turn up, but Emily, more pessimistic, reckoned he'd probably decided to do a runner when he'd found out about Perdita. Somehow, neither could imagine the pair of them together. But the DNA evidence was conclusive. Carlo Natale had been the father of Perdita's child.

They'd also discovered that Carlo Natale wasn't his real name. He had been born Charles Nuttall to a Sheffield steel worker and had adopted his more exotic identity when his career as a psychic medium began.

Simon Elmet was now back in Nottingham, and Joe rang him to ask whether he'd heard Natale's name before. When Simon answered he sounded much better and said that Natale's name might have been the one his sister mentioned, but he couldn't be certain.

Trying to sound casual, Joe asked him what he'd been doing at the time of Jonas's death, and Simon replied that he'd decided to go home instead of spending another night in his B and B in Eborby. He'd caught the train and arrived in Nottingham around nine that evening. But he lived alone and had met nobody, so he had no witnesses. He was sorry he couldn't be more help. Joe said he'd tried to call him and had got no reply. But Simon explained that his battery had run down and, with the upset of his sister's death, he'd forgotten to pack his charger. Joe believed him, although he wasn't sure if Emily would.

As Emily was busy organizing overtime rotas, she asked Joe to attend Jonas's post-mortem. This suited him because there were things he wanted to ask Sally. Nothing definite; just ideas and possibilities that were swirling through his head.

He left the incident room early because he wanted to take a detour. He walked into the town and past the cathedral and Vicars Green until he came to Gallowgate, where he and Maddy had eaten the night before. It disturbed him to think that while the life was being squeezed out of Jonas Ventnor, they had been enjoying a meal. But the world is like that; life and death, sin and goodness living side by side like neighbours.

When he reached the entrance to Singmass Close he focused on the wall beneath the archway. The life-sized image of a man in Victorian dress was still there. He could see it better in the daylight, and he saw that it was well-executed. Professional. Sinclair Doulton was a talented artist, whatever other failings he had as a human being. He could have done this easily. And chalk was his medium of choice.

Suddenly, he wanted another word with Charlotte, Perdita's understudy. She'd seen a man dressed in nineteenth-century costume in the theatre, a man very like the one depicted in the wall drawing with black slicked hair forming a widow's peak on his forehead. Had someone borrowed a costume from the theatre wardrobe to play a trick on her? He needed to find out.

He looked around for any convenient CCTV cameras. He saw none, but then the artist, whoever it was, had probably been careful, just as he'd been at the tower when he'd drawn the nun. And besides, cameras had proved useless in that all-concealing fog.

He realized that if he didn't hurry he'd be late for the post-mortem, which wouldn't endear him to Sally Sharpe. At least Sally dealt with cold facts, not fancies and ghosts, and at that moment he found this quite appealing. He reached the hospital with three minutes to spare and made his way to the mortuary. On his way in he passed a body bag being wheeled in on a trolley. Habit made him bow his head as the technician vanished, oblivious, through a pair of plastic swing doors.

The full post-mortem confirmed Sally's first assumptions. This wasn't so much a case of hanging than of slow strangulation. Jonas Ventnor had been strangled with the belt of his dressing gown, but he didn't appear to have put up a fight. He had yielded to death peacefully.

'I think he might have been drugged,' Sally said. 'I've ordered a full tox screen, but it would help to know what we were looking for.'

'Any sign of a needle mark?'

She shook her head.

'Something he drank?'

'Possibly.'

'Several members of the cast said he always kept a bottle of water in his dressing room for after the performance. But there was no sign of it.'

'You think the killer spiked it and took it away after the murder?'

'It's possible. I ordered a search, but nothing's been found.'

She looked up from the open cadaver. 'If it was something like Rohypnol or GHB it might not show up in blood samples. More chance with urine, so I'll send off samples of both.'

'I knew I could rely on you, Sal.'

'Nice to be appreciated.'

'How's the engagement?'

She smiled ruefully. 'Long.'

It was hard to interpret her meaning, and Joe thought it best not to enquire further.

She left her assistant to finish off and, once she had discarded her protective gown and gloves, she led Joe to her office. The post had arrived while she'd been occupied with Jonas Ventnor, and she sifted through the envelopes, discarding the majority as unimportant.

But there was one she descended on like a hungry vulture, tearing it open with eager fingers. 'I think this might be what we're waiting for,' she said as she began reading. 'I fast-tracked the samples from Perdita Elmet, and these are the results.' She read through the papers quickly. 'There's a lot of technical stuff, but basically they found traces of Rohypnol. Lucky.'

'Not for her. It's the date rape drug, isn't it?'

'Yes, but there were no signs of sexual interference. It would have rendered her semi conscious, completely helpless and unable to fight back. Her killer had her at his mercy, which is a horrible thought. The only upside is that she probably wouldn't have realized what was going on.'

'It explains why she didn't try to defend herself.' He thought for a moment. 'Could a woman have done it?'

'It's possible. Mind you, the killer had to move her body from the undercroft to the abbey, so . . .' She tilted her head to one side. 'If it was a man, it wasn't someone who gets his enjoyment from the victim putting up a fight.'

'I don't think it's sexual at all,' said Joe.

'Personal then? Something to do with her private life?'

'That's the theory we're working on, but we're not getting very far. We could have someone with a grudge against the theatre. Or perhaps Jonas was killed because he knew too much.'

Sally didn't answer. That was Joe's territory.

Debby went home, hoping that as Sinclair was out and about he wouldn't be back for a while. She'd been startled to see him coming out of the pub with Perry, bidding him a gruff goodbye as if the two men were acquainted but didn't like each other very much. Her opinion of Perry had changed in an instant. If he consorted with the likes of Sinclair then her nascent dream of being muse to a fascinating and unpredictable artist had vanished.

Her phone rang. It was her mate Sarah, asking if she wanted to go out that night. There was a male stripper on at the Maypole Inn, and it would be a laugh. It had been Sarah who'd left her to walk home on her own that night when she'd found the body, and she couldn't say she really liked her. But at that moment she'd do anything to avoid spending an evening under the same roof as Sinclair.

She said yes. She'd meet her at nine.

When Joe returned to the incident room he found Emily waiting, pacing up and down between the desks as though she was longing to share important news. Before he could tell her about the Rohypnol she waved a list in front of him.

'It's Jonas Ventnor's phone calls. He received one from Alvin Cobarn before the performance. Lasted two minutes. Think he was arranging to meet after the show?'

'It's possible.'

'Cobarn's own wife's convinced of his guilt, which surely has to count for something.'

'Sally had some news of her own,' Joe said. 'The results of some toxicology tests came back while I was there. Perdita Elmet was drugged with Rohypnol before she was strangled.'

Emily nodded slowly. 'It explains why there were no signs of a struggle in the undercroft.'

'And it indicates that the whole thing was carefully planned. And she probably knew her killer.'

'Not necessarily. Someone could slip the stuff into a drink while the victim's not looking. We don't know exactly what Perdita was doing after the performance that evening. She told her colleagues she was meeting someone. She might have gone into a bar.'

'The water bottle Jonas Ventnor normally kept in his dressing room's missing. That could have been drugged as well. Sally's sent samples from his body off for analysis. If he was drugged the killer could have walked him over to that stool, sat him down, tied the belt around his neck and shoved him off so that he'd be strangled slowly. Not nice.'

Emily said nothing for a few seconds. When she spoke there was a new determination in her voice. 'We have two common denominators – the theatre and Alvin Cobarn. I want him brought in again. And I want his house searched. If he's using Rohypnol on his victims, he's keeping it somewhere.'

Joe had to agree. When a man's wife accuses him of murder, they had to take notice. But he still wasn't absolutely convinced.

He had an uneasy feeling that there were things going on that he didn't fully understand.

'I went and had a look at that drawing on the wall by Singmass Close I told you about. The Victorian man.'

'What about it?'

'One of the cast of *The Devils* – Charlotte Ruskin – saw a man answering that description before Jonas's death. And a nun was seen in the theatre by Jonas before Perdita's murder. Then a picture of a nun appeared on the tower by Wendover Bridge.'

Emily took a deep breath. 'What are you getting at, Joe?'

'The theatre's reputedly haunted by two ghosts, whose appearance is said to be a portent of disaster. The first one's a nun who was walled up in the convent that once stood on the site, and the second's an actor who hung himself in a dressing room in the nineteenth century. I'm sure there's a connection with the deaths, but I can't for the life of me think what it could be.'

Emily greeted this with a smile that came dangerously close to a sneer. 'You're not saying they were killed by these ghosts? Come on, Joe . . .'

'What I'm saying is that the killer knows these stories and thinks it'll muddy the waters.'

'Alvin Cobarn's very involved with that theatre, so he's probably aware of the stories.'

'As is everyone who buys one of these "haunted Eborby" books from the tourist shops.'

Emily ignored his words. 'Let's pay him another visit. A courtesy call to ask how his wife is.'

'We should phone first . . . ask him to explain the call to Jonas.'

'I want to see his face, Joe. I want to know whether he's lying.'

'It's hard to tell with Cobarn.'

'True, but this time he'll be nervous. And if we turn up unannounced he won't be ready for us.'

'Weren't you told to tread carefully?'

'Sod that, Joe. Just because he puts "councillor" in front of his name, he doesn't scare me.'

Joe knew there could be no arguing with Emily once she'd made up her mind. He went with her to see Cobarn as she asked.

As it was working hours, they found him in his office. His

secretary was quick to offer them tea, so she obviously wasn't aware of the situation. Or perhaps her hospitality to visitors was just a habit she'd developed over the years of smoothing nervous clients. Emily accepted her offer with a: 'Thanks, love. Two teas. Milk, no sugar.'

Cobarn emerged from his office to greet them with a 'what the hell is it now?' expression on his face. But he hid his annoyance from his secretary and invited them in with scrupulous politeness.

'This is too much,' he hissed once they were alone. 'You realize that this amounts to harassment?'

Emily's handbag sat on her lap like a defensive shield. She delved into it, pulled out the list of the phone calls received by Jonas Ventnor and handed it over. 'Recognize any of these numbers, Mr Cobarn?'

'Yes. Why?'

Joe heard a challenge in his voice.

'You rang Jonas Ventnor shortly before he was due to go on stage on the night he died. Why?'

Cobarn had been looking tense, fidgeting with a paper clip. He put it down on the desk in front of him and visibly relaxed. 'I was inviting him to a function. The Arts Committee are having a reception to entertain dignitaries from our twin town in France. I'd spoken to Jonas on quite a few occasions and found him a very . . .' He searched for the right word. 'Personable young man. And he once mentioned to me that he spoke fluent French, so I thought he'd be the perfect person to represent our theatre. I was going to invite Louisa Van Sturten, the director, as well, but I couldn't get hold of her.' He looked smug. 'You can check my calls to confirm this if you like.'

'You didn't arrange to meet him after the performance?'

'Of course not. Why should I?'

He spoke with such confidence that Joe knew they were likely to find the missed calls to Louisa there, just as he said. But it still didn't prove that he was telling the truth about what had been said to Jonas. 'Did Jonas know about your relationship with Perdita?' he asked.

'I doubt it. We were both very discreet.'

'Her flatmate knew. She'd seen you together.'

'That was unfortunate.'

'Perdita said she was meeting someone after the performance on the night she died. Was that someone you?' said Emily.

For a while Cobarn didn't speak. Then he looked her in the eye. 'Yes. We'd arranged to meet at the pub we'd visited earlier that evening. I slipped out of the dinner and waited for her outside. It was foggy, but I didn't particularly want to go in there alone. She never turned up, so I waited for a while then walked back. At least with that dreadful fog there wasn't any danger that I'd be seen.' His lips twitched upwards into a bitter smile.

'You didn't try to ring her?'

'I've suspected for some time that my wife has been looking at my calls, so I usually rang Perdita from the office. I was careful. Look, I'm afraid I have no witnesses, so you'll have to take my word for it.'

'How is your wife?' Emily asked.

'Recovering. It's been a difficult time for us, and I'd be grateful if we could be left alone in future.' He raised his eyes. 'In fact, I'm thinking of making a formal complaint to your superior. The intrusion really has been intolerable. It drove my wife to attempt suicide.'

'Why did you have a shower when you got back home that night?'

Cobarn stared at Joe, open mouthed. 'How did you know that?'

'Just answer the question,' said Emily.

'Because I'd spilled white wine down my shirt and it was sticky. Now, if you'll excuse me.' He stood up. They were being dismissed.

Joe could sense Emily's irritation as they left the room without a word, almost colliding with the secretary, who was entering with a tray filled with fussy porcelain tea cups.

'Sorry, can't stay,' Emily said to her. 'Perhaps another time.'

Carlo Natale had heard they were looking for him, but he wasn't particularly worried. He was used to keeping one step ahead of the police who, in his experience, were singularly unimaginative and boneheaded. He'd present himself to them, a picture of cooperation, when he was ready.

And he had another problem to take care of. But he'd always

found clingy, obsessive women easy to deal with. All it took was a little magic.

In the meantime he had something to do, something he'd started a few days ago but hadn't had a chance to finish. It was something that would revive his reputation. There was a pleasing symmetry about what he had planned. A resolving of unfinished business.

TWENTY-TWO

Julie Telerhaye was drinking. She drank a lot these days, and Sinclair did nothing to discourage it. Not that he was there much any more. He seemed to spend a lot of time doing what he described as 'work', either drawing on pavements for the tourists or making and flogging cheap tat at the market.

He made his jewellery in the shed at the bottom of the garden; a place Julie and Debby weren't allowed to enter. There was valuable stuff in there, he said; equipment he didn't want anyone to touch. When the police had looked in the shed, they'd taken things away in evidence bags, as they had done when Peter had gone missing. Debby guessed this meant they'd found something suspicious, and she'd felt betrayed when they released him again. Perhaps they hadn't been trying hard enough to find the evidence that would get him out of her life permanently.

When she left the house to meet her mates in the pub at nine, her mother was lost in her own world and seemed unaware that she was going. Sinclair was nowhere to be seen, and as she sneaked from the house, she felt uncomfortable about leaving Julie on her own. But she'd made her choice when she'd hooked up with Sinclair.

She was still disappointed about Perry. She'd had hopes for their relationship but, as far as she was concerned, if he was involved with Sinclair, it was over before it had begun. Maybe she'd find someone tonight. Although, with a male stripper on the menu, the place was bound to be full of screaming women.

Her heart was pounding as she walked to the pub. A shroud of fog was descending again, giving the urban landscape the look of a London street in a Sherlock Holmes adaptation. As she reached the tall bulk of Boothgate Bar, she told herself everything would be fine, even though she could only see about ten feet ahead. Until she felt a sudden wave of panic and almost swung round to retrace her steps. But she'd come too far now. She'd have to go through with it. Even if, in her heart of hearts, she didn't particularly like or trust the other girls.

Her phone made a noise. She had a text. '*Doing anything tonight?*'

She answered. '*Out with mates.*'

'*Where?*'

She hesitated before replying. She didn't recognize the number, but she'd given hers to Perry. Her misgivings about his meeting with Sinclair vanished at the thought that he had taken the trouble to contact her. If he turned up, it was bound to raise her in her mates' estimation. Debby had a man. She texted back and put her phone away.

A night out would do her good.

Joe was still smarting at Alvin Cobarn's dismissal when he arrived home. According to the man's wife, he was guilty, but now he was hiding behind his contacts and position and trying to intimidate the police into leaving him alone. Emily, however, wasn't intimidated easily. And neither was he.

He'd picked up a Chinese takeaway on the way home because he couldn't be bothered cooking, and when he'd finished eating he looked out of the window, only to see that the fog had come down again. Joe had often wondered why the Romans had built their northern headquarters of Eboracum in a fog-prone valley: they were usually so efficient at everything else. Ever since the founding of the city, fog had been a hazard of life there. The natives grew used to it over the years, but it was still a pain, especially where driving was concerned.

His neighbour, an elderly lady who, he suspected, liked to mother him, had posted an evening paper through his front door. But one look at the headlines made him throw it down. *Police release suspect for theatre murders. Police chief admits lack of evidence.* He supposed the police chief in question was Emily.

It didn't look good, but he couldn't deny that the reporting was accurate. There was a lack of evidence. He picked up the paper and posted it into the waste-paper bin.

When the phone rang he half expected to hear Maddy's voice, but instead it was George Merryweather, sounding annoyingly cheery.

'Joe, I've been talking to the manageress of the cathedral shop. She's going to ring you tomorrow morning to report it, but I thought I'd tell you right away.'

Joe sat upright, suddenly alert. 'What is it?'

'She's done a full stock take as she promised, and there's quite a lot missing. Ten Saint Galert badges, along with other small items: medallions, crosses, Saint Christophers, rosary beads, that sort of thing. She's upset about it because she thinks one of her staff must be responsible, someone she'd trusted.'

'Has she any idea who?'

'She doesn't like to make accusations.'

'She's going to have to, George.'

'I know. Anyway, she'll be in touch tomorrow morning.'

Joe wanted to know the identity of the cathedral shop thief, but he'd have to curb his impatience. 'George, are you doing anything this evening?'

'Only feeding the cat.'

'Can I come round?'

'I'd be delighted to see you.' It was the reply Joe had hoped for.

He set off for George's house in the cathedral close. As he walked, the fog closed in around him. In the jaundiced glow of the street lamps he could see several feet ahead. But, having lived in Eborby for many years, he knew it could worsen as the evening wore on.

The cobbled cathedral close was occupied mostly by senior clerics. Joe loved George's pretty Georgian house which, although not particularly spacious, exuded an air of history, of continuity. It was furnished with shabby yet comfortable dark Victorian furniture, with splashes of colour provided by worn chintz upholstery and red velvet curtains at the windows. Those curtains were drawn now, blocking out the night and giving George's living room a cosy feel, enhanced by the glow of several table lamps scattered around the room.

George invited him to sit and took a bottle of single malt from a monumental dark oak cupboard which took up one wall of the room. Joe accepted the drink gratefully, but he wanted to keep a clear head. He needed to pick George's brains.

'What can I do for you?' George asked when the drinks were poured.

'You're an expert in the supernatural, George. This case I'm working on might be linked to the history of the theatre. I've heard a nun is supposed to haunt the place.'

'That's right. It's built on the site of a convent, and the foundations are still in the basement. I went to see them once. Quite impressive.'

'Can you tell me what you know about nun? What's the story?'

George's eyes lit up with interest. 'Now you've come to the right man. My predecessor was called in by the theatre – this was many years ago. One of the management wanted the place exorcized because strange things were happening backstage. Since this business started I've looked at his notes. All sorts of tall tales have been going round over the years. One version says that some poor girl was walled up for getting pregnant, and then there's another story that she was imprisoned for claiming she saw angels. My predecessor, Canon Selby, actually found the convent records in the cathedral archives, and there was only one recorded incident that seemed to fit the bill.'

'What was that?' Joe asked, feeling that George's revelation might prove to be important in some way.

'A nun called Sister Galert killed one of her fellow nuns by hitting her with a heavy kerb stone while they were working alone together in the convent's herb garden. She told the Abbess that a devil had appeared and struck the other nun dead because he wanted her soul. The Abbess, it appears, wasn't fooled for a moment and accused the nun of murder. You see, the killer nun had been violently jealous of her victim, who had a beautiful singing voice and was popular with the rest of the community. The victim also claimed to have seen angels and was considered particularly holy, which, no doubt, increased the killer's envy. It was also discovered that Sister Galert had made more subtle attacks on her rival previously, but had done no serious harm.'

'What happened to Sister Galert?'

'The Abbess ordered her to be locked up in a cell in the basement of the convent for the rest of her life. And as far as we know, that's what happened.'

'Hence the restless spirit.'

'That's right. Canon Selby never did do the exorcism for some reason – not sure why – so Sister Galert's probably still there. A restless spirit indeed.'

Joe sank back in the armchair. 'We haven't made it public, but we found a Saint Galert badge on each of our victims, placed in their mouths.'

George nodded slowly. 'I wondered why you were so interested in finding out whether any were missing from the shop.'

'The theatre's also supposed to be haunted by an actor who hanged himself in the nineteenth century.'

'I had heard something about that, although I'm not aware of the details. As far as I know Canon Selby was only told about the nun. But if the story's true he might also be a restless spirit, trapped in the place of his suffering, poor man. If the theatre want my services to put him to rest, I'm always available.'

Joe drained his glass. 'Ever heard of a clairvoyant called Carlo Natale?'

George shook his head. 'Can't say I have. Why?'

'His name's come up in our investigation. That's all.'

'Another drink?'

Joe looked at his watch. 'I'd better be off. Early start in the morning.'

He took his reluctant leave of George. He would have liked to stay, but he knew it would be unwise. He had enough difficulty getting out of bed in the mornings as it was. It had been easier when he'd lived with Maddy. She had always been an early riser.

The fog was denser as he walked home, listening for approaching traffic and following footsteps, and the thought that Perdita Elmet had died on a night like this kept going through his head. He found himself looking on every wall he passed for another drawing. But he hoped he wouldn't see one because he sensed that it would herald another death.

When he reached his flat he found he'd left his mobile phone on the sideboard and that there'd been a message from Maddy. She needed to see him.

He had a shower, helped himself to more scotch and put Allegri's *Miserere* on his CD player. He didn't call Maddy back. He wasn't ready.

Debby thought the stripper was gross. He looked old enough to be her father, and his oiled body was running to fat. Besides, the stuff he did with shaving foam was enough to put you off men for life.

She'd shrunk into the corner while he was gyrating around, keeping an eye on the door in case Perry turned up and hoping the stripper wouldn't single her out and grab her to do something she'd rather not contemplate. If you didn't go along with it, everyone would think you were a prude. And in that herd situation she still cared enough about the opinion of the other girls not to want to stand out.

By eleven she'd had enough. Perry hadn't turned up as she'd hoped, and she was tempted to tell the others she was going because she had a headache. The memory of last Friday night was still there in the back of her mind, but she tried to tell herself that fog cut two ways – you couldn't see an attacker but, on the other hand, they couldn't see you either. She reckoned that if she walked home quickly, she'd be fine. She'd emptied most of her vodka shots into her grateful companions' glasses, so she hadn't had much to drink. And she was wearing her flat ballerina pumps, so she'd be able to run away from trouble if necessary.

She was thirsty, so she went to the bar to buy an orange juice. As she queued she found herself standing next to a woman who was waiting to be served. When she moved away with her drink, the woman reached across to the bar, catching her drink with her elbow. It sloshed on to the floor, narrowly missing Debby's dress. Debby was about to turn and call her a clumsy cow, but the woman spoke before she could get the words out.

'Sorry. That was my fault. Let me buy you another.'

'It's OK. Honest,' she heard herself mumble, subdued by the woman's effusive apology.

'I insist. Orange juice, was it?'

Debby nodded, and a few moments later the drink was in her hand, accompanied by another apology.

She rejoined her friends for ten minutes, but she took the

disappearance of the stripper behind a curtain as an opportunity to put her headache excuse into action. Besides, it was true. She suddenly felt as if her head was filled with cotton wool, and the room was starting to go round. Surely the woman hadn't put a vodka into her orange juice? No, she'd heard her order it and, besides, why would she? Perhaps she was coming down with a bug of some kind.

She stood up, swaying slightly, and her companions grinned knowingly. She was pissed.

'I'm going.'

'You should get a cab.'

'Cabs cost too much.' She had to concentrate hard on getting her lips around the words.

With great care she left the group, ignoring their half-hearted calls to come back. She knew they didn't particularly care. Nobody cared.

When she got outside she saw the wall of fog and suddenly felt afraid.

Then she felt a hand on her shoulder, steering her forward into the dark.

TWENTY-THREE

The manageress of the cathedral shop rang the incident room at eight thirty, and Joe took the call. She repeated what George had told him the previous night, but he hadn't the heart to tell her he already knew. Besides, he had something important to ask.

'We've been given a list of cathedral employees, but we need you to tell us who has access to the missing goods.' He paused. 'Is there anyone in particular you suspect?'

There was a long silence on the other end of the line, and he could visualize the woman wrestling with her conscience. She wouldn't like to accuse anyone outright in case she was wrong. On the other hand, it was a murder enquiry, and it was her duty to help the police. He waited while she made the decision, and eventually his patience was rewarded. 'The only person I can think of is a young artist who helps out once a week. He's a nice boy,' she said, 'if a little . . . eccentric. I don't want to accuse him, but he does sometimes behave a little strangely. I've wracked my brains, and I really can't think of anyone else apart from . . .' She lowered her voice. 'There's an ex con who helps us as well, but he doesn't have access to the stock room, and we keep an eye on him, if you know what I mean. So far the arrangement's worked very well, and everyone deserves a second chance, don't they?'

'We'll need his name, just to check.'

'I don't want him to think he's not trusted.' He could hear the alarm in her voice, as though she feared she was guilty of an act of betrayal.

'I promise we'll be discreet. What about this artist?'

'As I said, he's been acting a bit oddly. And he does have access to the stock.'

'What's his name?'

'Perry Antrobus. I can give you his address if you like.'

'That would be helpful.'

'I really don't like doing this.'

'We just need to eliminate him from our enquiries,' Joe said smoothly. He really hadn't time for this woman's scruples, although he understood where she was coming from.

She provided Perry Antrobus's address and the details of the ex con, a petty thief who'd been given the opportunity to prove he was going straight. Somehow Joe hoped it wasn't him.

Emily had just returned from a meeting with the superintendent, and he could see her through the open door of her office, going through some papers. He knew from experience that behind her apparent concentration she was annoyed about something. And he could guess what it was. He'd put money on the super telling her to back off from Alvin Cobarn.

His phone rang again, and he heard a woman's voice on the other end of the line. It was Julie Telerhaye, and she was gabbling in panic. He asked her to calm down and tell him what had happened.

'Our Debby didn't come home last night. I've phoned round a few of her mates, and they said she left the pub just after eleven to walk home on her own. It was foggy, and they told her to get a cab, but . . . I keep trying her mobile, but it's switched off.'

Joe's heart began to beat faster. He would have thought that, after the fright she'd had when she found Perdita Elmet's body, she'd have taken more care.

'We'll need to speak to the friends she was with,' he said calmly. 'Have you got their contact details?'

Julie Telerhaye only had names for three of them, the ones she'd already contacted. She didn't know the others. After Joe noted the names, Julie spoke again.

'One of the girls, Chantalle, said she seemed drunk when she left. That's why I'm worried. Anything could have happened.' He could hear the hysteria rising in her voice.

'I'll get things moving here and send someone round to be with you,' he said. 'Is Sinclair there?'

'No. He didn't come home last night either.'

Joe said nothing. He hardly liked to point out that the absence of Julie's daughter and partner could well be connected. The thought made him feel slightly queasy.

As soon as the call was ended he rushed to Emily's office. They had to find Debby Telerhaye. He didn't want to contemplate what would happen if they delayed.

All patrols were on the lookout for Debby Telerhaye and Sinclair Doulton, either separately or together, and officers had been sent over to the college to interview Debby's friends. Everything had been set in motion, but Joe had a feeling of dread in the pit of his stomach as various scenarios played out in his head. All of them bad. And there was still no sign of Carlo Natale, which was starting to worry him too.

Someone had gone round to the address Perry Antrobus had given, a small terraced house in an outlying suburb. But when they got there the householder, an elderly widow, had never heard of Perry. He'd given the cathedral a false address, and Joe wondered why.

Obtaining a list of the college's staff and students was routine in cases like this, and DC Jamilla Dal had been assigned to deal with it. Just before lunchtime she hurried up to Joe with a look of triumph on her face.

'You know you're looking for a Perry Antrobus in connection with the theft of those badges? Have a look at this.' She thrust the list in front of him, pointing to one name in particular with a well-manicured fingernail. 'He works in the college's catering department. Part time. There can't be two Perry Antrobuses, can there?'

'I wouldn't have thought so. Well done, Jamilla. Nice one. What's the address?'

Jamilla showed him. It was the same one as he'd given the cathedral. Perry Antrobus didn't want to be found.

'According to the rota, he's supposed to be working there today. Want him brought in?'

'I think so, don't you?'

Joe wondered whether he should visit the college himself. Emily had called him a control freak on many occasions, when he hadn't trusted others to complete a simple task. This time he controlled his first instincts and allowed a couple of detective constables to drive over there. However, he insisted that one of them was Jamilla. He trusted her.

All Sinclair Doulton's usual haunts had been checked, but he hadn't been found. Emily was working on the theory that he had Debby, although she couldn't explain his motive for abducting her. Unless he was the killer and had her marked down as his next victim, in which case she was probably dead already. That was the only thing that made sense.

Perry Antrobus was picked up at the college canteen, and he was on his way to the station. Now that Sinclair had put himself so firmly in the frame, Emily wasn't sure how important Perry was to the investigation. But it looked as though he might have stolen the Saint Galert badges, so there was a possible link, and Joe needed to find out what it was.

There was a rehearsal that afternoon to iron out a few glitches Louisa Van Sturten had noticed in the previous night's performance. Jonas Ventnor's replacement had twice forgotten his cues, probably, Louisa said, because they'd all been under a lot of strain. By the time the run through was over, everybody seemed more confident.

Charlotte, of course, was word perfect and had been since she had stepped in to replace Perdita. In fact, Hen Butler thought her performance was superior to the dead woman's: more intense; more convincing in the scenes of madness and hysteria.

At one forty-five, Louisa said they'd call it a day. If they rehearsed any more, they'd be stale for that night's performance. Hen couldn't agree more. Sometimes she thought she ran through her lines and moves on autopilot as it was.

As she was walking towards the stage door she heard someone call her name, and she turned to see Louisa hurrying towards her.

'Have you seen Charlotte?'

'She's in our dressing room. Why?'

'There's something I want to show her.' She was carrying a folder, which she opened and held out for Hen to see. There was a picture inside, an old sepia photograph of a man in immaculate nineteenth-century dress, artistically posed with a bent finger supporting his chin. Hen had seen a photograph of Oscar Wilde striking a similar pose.

'She said she saw a man in Victorian dress that time she was attacked,' said Louisa anxiously. 'I know it sounds crazy, but I just wondered whether this could be . . .'

At that moment Charlotte appeared, and Louisa thrust the folder at her. 'Have a look at that, will you. Do you recognize him?'

Hen saw Charlotte turn pale as she swore under her breath and snatched the picture. 'That's him,' she whispered. 'Where did you get this?'

'It was in an old cupboard in my office. Someone's made an archive of programmes and pictures of past actors and productions. His name's on the bottom – Enoch Bartholomy. He died in 1894. This is the actor who committed suicide in his dressing room.'

Joe received a call from Simon Elmet, asking how the investigation was going. He asked about Jonas's death, eager to know whether it was connected to his sister's. Joe was torn between being completely honest about the Saint Galert badges and giving a semi-official non-committal reply. After all, Elmet couldn't be ruled out entirely as a suspect, especially as he had no real alibi for Jonas's murder. Once his parents were back from Australia, Simon was due to return to Eborby to make arrangements, and Joe told him that he was always available if he wanted to talk. He felt it was the least he could do for the dead woman's brother.

At three o'clock he was told that Perry Antrobus was waiting in the interview room. He had come quietly, but had said nothing apart from demanding the services of a solicitor.

In the interview room Joe found a young man in his twenties with spiky peroxide blond hair and an array of piercings. With uniform unconventionality he wore black, and there was a smirk of mild amusement on his face, as though they were laying the whole thing on for his entertainment.

Joe sat down and nodded to Perry's solicitor, a man with a crumpled suit and a world-weary expression who probably wasn't much older than his client.

After producing a plastic bag containing a Saint Galert badge from his pocket, Joe pushed it across the table. 'Recognize this?'

'We sell them at the cathedral shop.' He stared unblinkingly at Joe. His eyes were a startling blue, and he looked the picture of innocence.

'We have reason to believe you've been stealing these badges, along with other goods from the stock room. What do you have to say to that?'

'I needed them.'

'So you admit it?'

He nodded, and when Joe asked him to speak for the benefit of the tape, the solicitor bowed his head in defeat. It didn't bode well when a client was so ready to confess.

'Why did you take them?'

'I sold them to a bloke I know who makes them into jewellery. He's an artist like me – makes unusual stuff and sells it on his market stall. It goes down well with the tourists.'

'What's this man's name?' Joe asked.

'Sinclair. Don't know his surname. He does pavement drawings by the cathedral too. He's good.'

Perry went on to outline how he'd met Sinclair in a pub and got talking. Sinclair had already started making jewellery, but using the religious stuff from the cathedral shop had been Perry's idea. There was hardly any security there, he said, so taking it had been easy. They met in the pub from time to time to do the transaction. Sinclair paid quite well. 'Better than the bleeding shop,' he said with a scowl. 'Minimum wage I get there, mean bastards.'

'Don't you feel any guilt about stealing from the cathedral?' Joe asked, curious about how this young man saw the world.

'Why should I?' He said the words with an innocent certainty that made Joe realize that any counter argument was useless. 'That place stole from the poor for centuries – charging them for souvenirs of some saint who probably never existed. That's how it funded all that opulence. Theft.'

'I can't deny that,' said Joe. 'But things have changed a lot since the middle ages, Perry. Cathedrals struggle for funds these days.'

Perry gave Joe a smug grin. 'That's not my problem.'

Joe found it hard to read the young man, but he was sure of one thing: Perry was the centre of Perry's world, and he had an exaggerated opinion of his own importance in the artistic world. And arrogance like that can be dangerous. 'Why did you give a false address to the manageress at the cathedral shop?'

'I value my privacy. Besides, if she needs to contact me about shifts and all that, I can always be reached on my mobile.'

'We need your proper address. And don't even think of lying. We'll check it out before you're released.'

The solicitor opened his mouth to object, then thought better of it.

'It's just off Mungate.'

Joe produced a business card and biro from his pocket and told Perry to write the address on the back. After a moment of hesitation, he obeyed.

When he handed back the card, Joe studied it. He wasn't familiar with the street but, from the boy's demeanour, he was sure the address was right this time.

'Mind if we have a look around the property?'

'Yes, I do mind. I've got all my art stuff in there, and I don't want some plod with his size twelves treading all over it. If you want to come in, you'll have to mind your manners and get a warrant.'

This was the answer Joe had expected. He left the room for a few minutes and asked one of the team to check whether the address was genuine. When he returned he decided to try another approach. 'You work part-time in the canteen at Eborby College.'

'You're not a detective for nothing, then. I also work as a living statue. I have what's known these days as a portfolio career. Three jobs. Sounds greedy with all this unemployment, doesn't it, but I assure you I don't make a fortune out of any of them.'

Joe suddenly felt like hitting him, but he took a deep calming breath and continued. 'Do you know a girl called Debby Telerhaye? She's a student at the college.'

'It's a big place.'

Joe handed him a photograph of the missing girl. 'This is her.'

'I've seen her around.'

Joe thought the answer was too casual. 'Ever spoken to her?'

This time he stayed silent.

'She's missing. Where were you last night?'

'At home.'

'Any witnesses?'

'No. I live with my sister, but she was out for the evening. No alibi. And before you ask, I have no idea where this Debby girl is. She's probably somewhere having fun. Unlike the rest of us.' He pulled a face, which irritated Joe further. Or perhaps that was the intention.

Joe took out his phone and scrolled down to the photographs he'd taken of the two wall drawings. 'Ever seen these before?'

Perry barely looked at them. 'No. What are they?' His innocent denial didn't fool Joe for a moment. There was a slight tremble in his voice, and he avoided Joe's gaze.

'They're the two ghosts that are said to haunt the Eborby Playhouse. A nun from the time there was a convent on the site, and an actor who committed suicide in his dressing room. Did you draw them?'

'What makes you think that?'

Joe was encouraged by the lack of an outright denial. 'Did you?'

Perry looked at his solicitor. 'I'm not feeling well. I need a break.'

'Want to see a doctor?' Joe said with heavy sarcasm.

'I just need a break. And a coffee. Black no sugar.'

'I'm going to arrange for a warrant to search your premises,' Joe said as he stood up.

'Won't do you any good. There's nothing there to find.'

'Even so, we'd like to take a look.'

Perry looked away and said nothing.

'Any messages for me?' the man asked the young Spanish woman behind the Oaktree Court Hotel's grand mahogany reception desk.

'Mr Natale, isn't it?' The woman lowered her voice. 'The police have been here looking for you. They asked us to contact them as soon as you returned.' Her training and her natural tact meant that she showed no surprise or emotion.

'That's fine,' the man said smoothly. 'It'll be about an accident I witnessed. Just routine paperwork. I'll give them a call as soon as I get to my room.' He gave her a reassuring smile. 'No need for you to bother yourself. Thanks.'

The woman waited until he'd disappeared into the lift before making the call. Whatever the police had wanted, she knew it wasn't a routine matter. In fact the word 'murder' had been mentioned.

Sinclair Doulton wasn't going to take the blame. Neither was he going to pass up an opportunity to improve his lot. Knowledge is power, and the knowledge of what he'd seen on the night Perdita Elmet died was enough to put somebody in prison for a very long time. And if that person couldn't pay in one way, he'd think of some other method. Julie Telerhaye and the money she'd received from her guilt-ridden estranged husband had served their purpose. It was time to move on.

He'd stayed in a mate's empty flat instead of going back to Julie's last night. He hadn't wanted her hanging around, whingeing, because he had things to do; arrangements to make for his future. He'd arranged the meeting, and now he knew his plan couldn't fail.

The fog was still swirling around the trees when he began to walk towards the river, delighted with his own brilliance.

TWENTY-FOUR

'Carlo Natale's turned up at his hotel,' Emily announced to the team. 'I think we should pick him up and bring him in for a nice chat.' She beamed around the room. Joe had just finished interviewing Perry Antrobus, and it seemed that the experience hadn't done a lot for his mood. He'd snapped at one of the young constables, although he apologized immediately afterwards. Perry Antrobus had got to him, and Emily wondered why.

Natale had arrived in a patrol car, keeping his head down in case he was spotted by a member of his public, which was unlikely as the visibility outside was worsening and the area around the police station was virtually deserted. Once he was down in the interview room recently vacated by Perry Antrobus, he assumed a cooperative expression; the public-spirited citizen, anxious to help clear up a misunderstanding.

Joe and Emily decided to conduct the interview together. Good cop, bad cop. Emily usually preferred to play bad cop, saying that playing the villain was always more fun. That left Joe in the role of good cop. Emily reckoned that with his background, it suited him. He wasn't so sure.

'Where have you been, Mr Natale?' Joe began.

'Leeds. I had a day or two off from the psychic fair in Pavilion Hall, so I decided to go back to my flat. Besides, there was some business I had to attend to.'

'What kind of business?'

'A couple of clients to see privately.'

'We'll need their names and addresses,' said Emily, pushing a sheet of paper and a pen over the table.

'I can't remember offhand. The details'll be in my Leeds flat.'

'That's not a problem. We can send someone over there.'

Natale looked uncomfortable, and Joe knew that he was lying.

'We've been wanting to talk to you about Perdita Elmet. You know she was murdered?'

'I saw it on the news. I don't know what it has to do with me.'

'She was carrying your baby.' Emily's statement was blunt, and Joe saw Natale's mouth fall open. 'Did she tell you?'

Natale shook his head. 'We had a brief fling in Leeds, but . . . It wasn't serious. We agreed to go our separate ways.'

'Bit of a ladies' man, are you?'

Joe saw Natale's cheeks redden. 'I've never lived like a monk. I had no idea she was pregnant and no reason to want her dead. I haven't even seen her since Leeds.'

'She's not the reason you came to Eborby?'

'Certainly not. How do you know the baby's mine?'

'You gave a DNA sample when you were arrested for drink driving. You didn't come forward when you heard about her death.'

'To be honest I didn't want to get involved. Besides, I couldn't help.'

'Your psychic powers didn't tell you who did it, then?'

Natale looked away.

'Debby Telerhaye's missing,' he said, watching the man's face carefully.

Natale didn't flinch. 'That's terrible. You should be out looking for her.'

'We know all about your involvement with her brother's case.'

'I tried to help, and I was unsuccessful. Nobody regrets that more than I do.'

'I seem to remember you did more than help,' said Emily. Joe could hear the aggression in her voice. 'You interfered, sent search teams on a wild-goose chase. And you controlled the media – told Julie Telerhaye that making TV appeals would be useless and that the police had no leads. As a result she wouldn't cooperate with us and opportunities were lost.' When she leaned forward and put her face close to Natale's, Joe saw him back away. 'You were a bloody nuisance on that investigation, Mr Natale, and I've often wondered why.'

'Sometimes my channels become blocked,' Natale said smoothly. 'It was as if the spirits didn't want me to find Peter. I kept getting messages, but they proved to be dead ends. It had never happened to me before, and it's never happened since.' He bowed his head. 'I can only say how sorry I am.'

'What about Debby?'

'She turned up at the Pavilion Hall. She was angry, and I don't blame her. I wanted to contact Julie, but I didn't know where she'd moved to, and then I heard she was in Eborby so I found out her address. I intended to visit her and Julie while I was in Eborby and apologize. But I didn't. I was too much of a coward.'

'Debby thought someone was following her,' said Joe. 'Was that you?'

It was almost a minute before the psychic spoke again, his voice so quiet that it was almost inaudible. 'I admit that I did follow her a couple of times. I was trying to pluck up the courage to approach her. I needed to explain about Peter. I needed to tell her it wasn't my fault. The spirits . . .'

'Were you following her last Friday night?'

Joe had expected a denial, but instead Natale nodded. 'I'd hung around outside her house for a while, and I'd seen that Julie had a new man in tow. I didn't know how he'd react if I suddenly turned up, so I decided to approach Debby. She was only a little girl when I last saw her, and now she was a young woman. I followed her to a pub where she met up with some friends. I had a drink and watched her, standing where she couldn't see me, but once I'd had one drink I realized it was a stupid idea and I left. I knew that if I'd approached her then, looming out of the fog, I'd only have frightened her to death.'

'What time did you leave?'

'Around nine thirty. I had the impression that she was a bit nervous, as though she'd realized she was being tailed. I thought it best to give up and maybe try another time. Like I said, I didn't want to scare her. That would have been counterproductive.'

'So you bided your time until last night,' said Emily. 'What have you done with her? Where is she?'

'I wasn't in Eborby last night. And I never saw Debby Telerhaye. I swear that's the truth.'

Joe could hear panic in his voice, the panic of someone who fears they're about to be blamed for something they didn't do. But he still wasn't sure whether he believed him. 'Where were you?'

'I told you. Leeds.'

'Where were you between ten thirty and midnight last Friday – the night Perdita died?'

'I went straight back to the hotel after I'd been in the pub watching Debby, and around ten thirty the organizer of the psychic fair turned up and we had a drink. You can check.'

'We will.'

Joe saw him close his eyes. 'I feel that Debby's very near. She's still in Eborby, I'm sure of that. She's still alive but she's in great danger.'

Emily snorted. 'Up to your old tricks again, Mr Natale. I believe it was the same when Peter disappeared.'

Natale's eyes snapped open. 'Were you part of the investigation team?'

'Yes. I know exactly what you got up to.'

'I always acted in good faith,' he said. 'If I got it wrong, I'm sorry.'

His display of contrition didn't fool Joe for a moment, and he was sure it hadn't taken Emily in either. 'Why are you in Eborby, Mr Natale?' Joe asked.

'For the psychic fair.'

'Only, an officer spoke to one of the organizers,' said Emily. 'It was you who contacted them rather than the other way round, and you were quite insistent. Pushy, was the way she put it. You wanted an excuse to come here because you'd found out the Telerhayes were here.'

'Not exactly.'

'What is it you're not telling us?' Joe asked.

'OK. There was someone else in that pub that Friday night, someone who was watching Debby.'

'Who?'

'I saw him at Julie's house. I think it's her new boyfriend, but I can't tell you his name. He was definitely stalking Debby, couldn't take his eyes off her. It's him you should be talking to, not me.'

Emily decided to hold on to Natale for a while, in spite of his protestations that he had a show to do that evening and he needed to prepare himself – to get in the right frame of mind to face the ordeal of contacting the spirit world. This didn't cut much ice with Emily, who put him in the cell adjacent to the one occupied by Perry Antrobus. All they needed now was Sinclair Doulton and they'd have the full set, she observed. But, in spite of their best efforts, Sinclair was nowhere to be found.

As they made their way back to the incident room, she asked Joe whether he believed what Natale had said about Sinclair Doulton being in the pub that night, watching Debby, possibly stalking her. Joe said he wasn't sure. It could be a way of diverting their attention. On the other hand, it could be true. When they found Sinclair, they'd ask him.

Things were looking bad for Sinclair. He bore a grudge against the theatre, he was an artist who could easily have executed the ghosts on the walls, and he had access to a supply of Saint Galert badges. News had also come in from Sally that traces of Rohypnol had been found in Jonas Ventnor's body. If, as Joe suspected, his water had been spiked, that meant it had to be someone who had access to the theatre. At the moment, in Emily's opinion, Sinclair Doulton was the best suspect they had.

She asked Sunny to check Natale's alibi for Perdita's murder with the organizer of the psychic fair before asking the team to find out more about the man. If he'd so much as farted in the wrong place, she said she wanted to know about it.

Half an hour after Natale had been taken down to the cells he asked to see them again. He had something important to tell them. A matter of life and death.

Emily was tempted to make him wait. But Joe reckoned they had nothing to lose by hearing what he had to say. However, while they were deliberating, news arrived that they'd obtained a warrant to search Perry's place, so Emily busied herself with getting things organized. She wanted the team to look for anything to connect Perry to the murders or to Debby Telerhaye's disappearance. And if there were any artists' materials that might be linked with the drawings on the walls, she wanted to know.

Once that particular business was out of the way, Emily said she was ready to face Natale again.

'He's playing games with us, Joe. He likes to put on the Mystic Meg act – thinks it impresses us.'

When Natale entered the interview room again, Joe sensed something different about him. He seemed to have lost his swagger, and there was a distant look in his eyes. Joe hadn't seen him like this before, and the change surprised him, but Emily sat next to him with her arms folded, as though she was waiting for more lies and evasion.

'You asked to speak to us again,' Joe said.

Natale took a few deep breaths and closed his eyes. When he opened them he focused on Joe's face and began to speak. His voice was different, low and hypnotic. 'I've seen her.'

Joe's body tensed. 'Who?'

He closed his eyes again and placed his fingers on his temples, frowning with concentration. When he began to speak, the words came out in a rush. 'There's someone else there. Someone in black. Long robes. A nun with no face. I can feel hatred, envy eating into the soul like a worm. Wheels. Squeaking. Now she's in a church. In front of the altar. Like a star. There's dirt in her mouth. There's something around her neck. Something blue pulled tight around her white neck. Penitent. Paying for her sin.'

'Who is the nun? Can you see her?'

Natale jerked forward, burying his face in his hands.

Joe glanced at Emily and saw a faint smile playing on her lips.

'Bravo, Mr Natale. Good performance. And you've just described your ex-girlfriend's murder. How did you know about the blue scarf? We haven't released that information to the press.'

Natale raised his head, his eyes puzzled, as if he found the whole thing baffling. 'I don't know. I just saw it. The nun killed Perdita. That's all I can tell you.'

'Can you tell us where Debby is?' Joe asked.

Natale shook his head. 'These things don't come to order. If a spirit comes through . . . Look, when are you going to let me go? I have things to see to . . . urgent things.' He had begun to fidget and shift in his chair.

'What things?' Joe asked.

The man blustered for a few moments. 'I can't say. But I assure you it is important. Please.'

Emily stood up. Joe would have liked to continue the conversation, but the DCI had obviously decided it was over.

'What did you make of that?' she asked when they were on their way back to the incident room.

'Not sure. The things he told us about the nun and the scarf aren't common knowledge, and he was the father of her baby. If she was making life awkward for him, he might have decided to get rid of her, using the fog as a cover.'

'We'll let him stew for an hour or so, then we'll have another go.' She checked her watch. 'We've still got a few hours before we have to charge or release him. Let's make the most of it.'

'Think he knows where Debby is?'

'I'm sure he does.'

When they reached the incident room, Sunny stood up and strode over to then, solemn as an undertaker on duty. He'd been in touch with the psychic fair organizer, and she'd confirmed Natale's alibi for the time of Perdita's murder. Joe heard Emily swear under her breath.

'And that Perry Antrobus's place has been searched, and the lads who went there say it's downright weird,' Sunny continued. 'It's some sort of converted chapel, and there's all these gravestones on the floor and a mummified corpse in the corner. Shouldn't be allowed. Could we do him for preventing a lawful burial?'

'That depends,' said Joe.

'Did they find anything else?' Emily asked.

'Only some coloured chalks – could have been used to do those pictures on the walls. We could do him for defacing property,' he added hopefully.

'He says he lives with his sister – any sign of her?'

Sunny shook his head again. 'Not even any women's clothes. He's been lying about that and all.'

'Anything else?'

Sunny shook his head.

Emily looked disappointed. She'd had high hopes of the search, and now she seemed deflated. If they couldn't get more on Perry Antrobus, they'd have to let him go. And with his new alibi, the same went for Carlo Natale, although Joe didn't like to think about that.

Just as Emily was returning to her office, a call came through.

A body had been found in the river. Some hardy soul walking their dog in the fog had spotted it caught in some branches. A patrol car had gone down there to investigate and had called it in to CID because the dead man matched the description of someone they'd been told to look out for.

It was possible that the body belonged to Sinclair Doulton.

How had she got here? Debby had no idea. All she knew was that she could see nothing in the darkness and that she could smell something unpleasant – something that stank of decay. A pain shot through her head when she opened her eyes. She'd had hangovers before, but this was something different. Besides, she hadn't thought she'd had much to drink in that seamy pub crowded with shrieking females.

She was lying down, and when she tried to sit her head span and she flopped back again. She could see a faint shaft of grey light some way away but, other than that, everything was black. She explored with her hand and found that she was still fully dressed apart from her shoes and jacket. The thing she lay on felt like a lumpy mattress and smelled of damp, and an old blanket of some kind covered her body, harsh and chafing against her bare legs.

She tried to sit up again, and this time she succeeded. Feeling around she discovered that the mattress was lying on a stone floor, damp and icy to the touch. As her eyes started to adjust to what little light there was, she began to make out lumps and strange shapes in the gloom.

If she could make a noise someone might hear her. Unless this place was isolated. Then there would be nobody to hear her scream, however hard she tried.

TWENTY-FIVE

The fog was lifting, but it still lay heavy on the water. Joe thought it looked like a river of the dead, bearing souls to the underworld.

By his reckoning, Sinclair Doulton's body hadn't been in the water long. A section of the river bank had been sealed off and a crime scene tent erected over the body, so as not to alarm any passing member of the public while the CSIs and Sally Sharpe went about their work.

Emily and Joe stood side by side in the chill, dank air, staring down at the sodden body that oozed river water on to a plastic sheet. They both wore white crime-scene suits. Hardly the height of sartorial elegance, Emily observed, but on the other hand everyone else was wearing the same and nobody worried about what you looked like when you were examining a cadaver beside a misty river.

'Well, we can cross him off our suspect list,' said Emily.

'Unless it turns out to be suicide.'

'He didn't seem the suicidal type.'

'You never know what goes on inside someone's head,' said Joe softly.

Emily didn't reply. Instead, she edged nearer the action and began to question Sally, who was taking the dead man's temperature.

'Was it drowning?' Joe heard Emily ask.

Sally turned her head. 'There's a contusion on the head that might be suspicious. On the other hand, he could have knocked himself on something when he fell in. I won't be able to tell you any more until the post-mortem.' Her last statement sounded weary, as if she thought Emily should have known better than to ask by now.

Joe squatted down to look at Sinclair Doulton's pallid face. His eyes were still open, and he looked astonished. 'Anything found on him?' he asked a young female CSI, who was writing something on a clipboard.

'The contents of his pockets are in that tray,' she said, waving her hand towards a plastic tray filled with dripping items. 'We'll bag them up when they've dried out a bit.'

Joe could see a wallet. A mobile phone. House and car keys.

'And that was found stuck at the back of his mouth.'

She pointed to a small object lying amongst the drying items. It was a small medallion. A Saint Galert badge.

Jonas Ventnor's understudy still hadn't quite got the hang of the part. Jonas had brought a gravitas, a sense of bitter tragedy, to the role of Urbain Grandier, but his replacement's interpretation was superficial in comparison. However, Louisa Van Sturten knew she had to stick with him because there wasn't time to get anyone else to step in. She hoped, given time and increased confidence, he'd grow into the part.

But this was the least of her worries at that moment. She had a more immediate problem, one that was sitting weeping in the dressing room, getting through a rapidly diminishing box of tissues.

'Tell me exactly what happened,' Louisa said, putting a comforting arm around Charlotte Ruskin's shoulder. She'd never seen herself as the comforting type, and the situation made her feel awkward.

When she'd heard screams from Charlotte's dressing room she'd gone to investigate, along with the rest of the cast, who'd followed her down the corridor to see what the commotion was about. Hen had gone out after the morning rehearsal, so Charlotte had been alone in there, and when Louisa had opened the dressing room door, she'd seen the woman cowering, hysterical, on the floor in the corner. The director had sent the others away because Charlotte was distraught. Then she'd tried to calm her, without much success.

All Charlotte would say was that he'd hit her. There was a graze and bruising on her right cheek, and Louisa's first reaction had been to take out her phone and put in a call to the police. This was her production, and things were going badly wrong. There were superstitious souls amongst the cast, who were saying it was cursed.

'Take a deep breath.'

Charlotte obeyed, and her whole body shuddered.

'Can you tell me what happened?'

The young woman blew her nose and let the mucus-covered tissue drop from her hand. Louisa handed her another from the box.

'It was the same man I saw before. He was waiting for me. I screamed, and he hit me. Then he ran off.'

'The police are on their way, so he won't try it again. Do you need to go to the hospital?'

Charlotte shook her head vigorously. 'No.'

'Are you up to going on tonight?' Louisa did a quick calculation, wondering who she could get to take Charlotte's part, to understudy the understudy.

To her relief Charlotte looked up bravely and assured her she'd go on whatever happened. And she didn't want the police involved. She couldn't bear to relive it over and over again.

Louisa helped her up and muttered something about going to the cafe for a cup of tea. But first she told Charlotte that there was a first-aid kit in her office and she should dab something on the grazes.

'As long as you promise not to tell the police.'

Louisa didn't reply. She had no intention of cancelling her call to the police because she wanted them to sort this business out once and for all. But she didn't spell this out to Charlotte because she wanted her calm and in a fit state to play her part that evening.

Charlotte walked with her to the office, leaning on her arm like an invalid, and when they were halfway there she suddenly stopped. 'I know who attacked me,' she said. 'I know his name. And he's angry.'

'Who is it?'

'It's that man in the picture. It's Enoch Bartholomy,' she whispered. 'And he's going to kill again.'

They'd obtained more time to question Carlo Natale, which put Emily in a good mood, although she confided to Joe that this meant she'd have to miss her daughter's parents' evening. Her husband, Jeff, would have to go on his own and drag the other kids along with him. She didn't sound too pleased about the situation, but after all her years in the job she was resigned to disappointments.

As they were about to set off for the interview room, Joe received a call from Louisa Van Sturten at the theatre. Charlotte Ruskin had been attacked in her dressing room, but her attacker had fled, leaving her with a grazed cheek.

'Someone's really got it in for that production,' said Emily.

Joe paused. 'She named her attacker.'

'Who is it?'

'That actor who committed suicide in 1894. Enoch Bartholomy.'

'She's seeing things. Or making it up.'

'Not necessarily. There are lots of costumes in that place . . . and wigs and make-up. Ghosts don't attack people. Living human beings do.'

'I'll send Jamilla round to have a word.'

'It could be connected to the murders. Our three victims are all linked to the theatre.'

'Sinclair Doulton isn't.'

'He worked there, and he admitted he was there playing tricks.'

'Well, Doulton can't have attacked Charlotte.'

'But was he responsible for Debby Telerhaye's disappearance?'

Emily frowned as she realized the implications of Joe's words. 'You mean he might have been keeping her somewhere. And now he's dead, he can't go back there and feed her.'

'It's only a theory.'

'It's a possibility. I'll get someone to double check all the places he had access to. I think we should speak to Julie Telerhaye sooner rather than later. I take it she's been told he's dead?'

Joe nodded. Jamilla had already been round to break the news, and the family liaison officer was staying with Julie, at least until Debby turned up. The poor woman must be in a terrible state, Joe thought. With her partner dead and her only daughter missing, he hardly liked to think what she was going through.

When the phone on Joe's desk rang, he grabbed the receiver, hoping it would be news that some patrol had found Debby safe and well.

When he heard Maddy's voice, he felt a stab of curiosity. But her first question disappointed him. 'Is it true you've arrested Carlo Natale?'

'He's helping with our enquiries,' said Joe, realizing his answer was frustratingly vague and bound to irritate Maddy, who'd always liked things clear cut.

'What's he done?'

'I can't tell you that, Maddy. Sorry. Why are you asking?'

'I was going to the Pavilion Hall to see him tonight, only the session's been cancelled. My mother's really upset. I promised I'd find out what was going on.'

'I'm sorry,' said Joe, surprised and dismayed at the hold Natale seemed to be having over Maddy and her mother. He felt angry on their behalf if he was giving them false hope.

'Can I see you tonight?'

'I doubt if I'll be free. I'm sorry.'

'I should be with Mum, anyway,' she said after a brief silence. 'Like I said, she was desperate to see Carlo. She really thought there'd be a breakthrough tonight and we'd be able to contact my sister.'

'I'll call you tomorrow,' he said. He felt bad. But if Carlo Natale had anything to do with the murders or Debby's disappearance, it was up to him to make sure that he never harmed anyone ever again. And that included Maddy and her vulnerable mother.

It was time to talk to Natale again. Emily reckoned he'd had enough time to contemplate the error of his ways, as she put it, but Joe wasn't sure it would be that easy.

As Natale entered the interview room, he looked at his watch. 'I'm supposed to be at the Pavilion Hall in half an hour.'

'It's been cancelled,' Emily said.

Joe half expected her to add 'due to unforeseen circumstances' but she resisted the ancient joke.

Instead, she began the questioning. 'You claim to be a clairvoyant, Mr Natale. Any idea who killed Perdita Elmet and Jonas Ventnor?'

'I'm afraid not.' The words were cool, as if he suspected Emily was mocking him.

'You claimed to know what had happened to Peter Telerhaye.'

'What's that got to do with anything?'

'You see, I find that strange. The little boy disappears, and you turn up claiming to know where he is. Then you come to Eborby where his family have made a new life and, lo and behold, his sister goes missing as well.'

Natale bowed his head. 'I failed with Peter Telerhaye. I don't know why, because the messages coming through were incredibly strong. I was sure I could locate him.'

'A stone barn near Whitby surrounded by oak trees, wasn't it?'

'I don't remember.'

'That doesn't matter,' said Emily. 'It's all on record. They found the location you described. It was a derelict barn which hadn't been used for years. They found one of Peter's shoes there, and someone had gone over the upper floor with bleach, which destroyed any traces of DNA. The consensus of opinion was that Peter had been held there and someone had cleaned up after themselves. But there was no sign of Peter.'

'The fact that he'd been there means my messages were accurate. That was acknowledged at the time,' Natale said hopefully.

'Have you ever spoken to Sinclair Doulton?'

'Who?'

'Julie Telerhaye's partner – the one you claim was following Debby.'

He wrinkled his brow, as though he was pondering the question very hard. 'No. Why?'

Joe had been watching the man carefully, every nuanced expression that passed across his face. 'He's dead,' he said. 'Along with your former girlfriend Perdita and her co-star Jonas Ventnor. Sure you've never meet Jonas?'

'No.'

'Were you tempted to look Perdita up when you came to Eborby? The play she was in was well publicized, so you could easily have spotted her name. I think you came to see a performance and met up with her afterwards. If you paid for your ticket by credit card we can check.'

Natale's face coloured, and he avoided Joe's gaze. 'OK, I saw the play, but not on the night she died. Have you checked my alibi?'

Emily didn't answer. 'When did you see the play?'

'Last Tuesday. I went out of curiosity, and I found it disturbing . . . all that madness and torture. I can't say I enjoyed it.'

'In that case you saw Jonas Ventnor. He was playing the male lead – Urbain Grandier.'

'Maybe. But I didn't meet him. I came to see Perdita because I was curious to see her act – in the time we were together, she'd never allowed me to see her perform. I don't know why because she was good, even though the play wasn't really to my taste, although I believe it was based on real events.' He gave a little shudder. 'I didn't hang around to meet her afterwards. As far as we were both concerned it was over.'

'So she didn't let you know she was pregnant that evening?'

'I've told you already. I had no idea.'

'That must be hurtful,' said Emily gently.

'I haven't really had time to think about it.' The bravado had gone.

'She was seeing someone else, you know. A man called Alvin Cobarn. He's a local councillor. They met because he's on the Arts Committee.'

'Then perhaps he killed her when he found out she was pregnant with another man's child.'

'He has been questioned,' said Emily. 'He said he didn't know about the pregnancy.'

'He could have been lying. Jealousy is a strong emotion. And if the man hasn't yet had children of his own, who's to say how he'd feel about his hopes of fatherhood being raised then dashed,' said Natale. His voice had become persuasive, almost hypnotic.

'What makes you think Cobarn has no children?' said Emily sharply.

Natale's answering smile was smug and secretive, as if to say 'I have powers of knowledge that aren't given to others.' However, Joe suspected he'd made a lucky guess.

'Let's talk about the Telerhayes. Why did you want to make contact again?'

'Because I feel I can help them. Julie knew I was always there for her if she needed me, but she never got in touch.'

'And this bothered you?' said Emily. 'You like to have people in your power, don't you. You get off on it.'

He let out a long sigh. 'That's ridiculous. I knew it would be painful to see them again. When Debby turned up at the psychic fair it wasn't a happy encounter. She has many unresolved issues concerning her brother's disappearance. I think I said she was angry, and that anger was focused on me, which is hardly surprising as, in her eyes, I failed to reunite the family. It was more the police's fault than mine, of course, but the police is a nebulous organization. I'm an individual who can be blamed.'

Joe thought his words made some sense, but he said nothing.

'Besides, I have a strong feeling that Peter's now in the spirit world. The best I can do for the family is let them know he's safe and happy, to give them closure.'

The door opened, and Sunny sidled in like a man who fears

he's interrupting some clandestine tryst. He handed a note to Emily and sneaked out. She unfolded the paper, and handed it to Joe once she'd read it. Then she looked Natale in the eye.

'You say you were at your Leeds flat on the night Debby Telerhaye disappeared, is that right?'

'Yes.' Natale sounded wary.

'Are you sure? You didn't go out or spend the night with one of your lady friends?'

'I was in all evening. I didn't go out.'

Emily looked like a quiz show host asking a contestant whether the answer they'd given was their final one. 'We've been making enquiries with your neighbours, Mr Natale. A Mrs Sadler lives in the flat next door to you, is that right?'

Natale nodded.

'Mrs Sadler's in her seventies, but she's sharp and her hearing's perfect, according to the constable who spoke to her. She told him you weren't there on the night Debby went missing. She's sure of the day because there was a TV programme she was looking forward to – *Midsomer Murders*.

'She took a parcel in for you and tried knocking at your door several times during the evening, the last occasion being around ten, just after her favourite detective programme ended. Her balcony adjoins yours, and she could also see that there were no lights on.'

Natale stared ahead as though he was in a trance.

'Where were you that night, Mr Natale?'

'No comment.'

Joe leaned across the table and put his face close to Natale's. 'Where is Debby Telerhaye?'

Natale closed his eyes for a few seconds, then opened them wide. 'All I can tell you is that she's with the dead.'

'She's dead?' Emily sounded alarmed.

'No. She's with the dead. That's quite different.'

TWENTY-SIX

'What will I do without him?' Julie Telerhaye sobbed, clinging on to Jamilla Dal's sleeve.

Jamilla plucked another tissue from the box on the coffee table and handed it to Julie, making soothing noises. She'd come straight there from the theatre, where she'd spoken to the actress who'd been attacked – she knew they were all called actors these days, but somehow she always forgot. The woman had been evasive and said she didn't want to make a fuss. When she'd reported back to Emily, Emily told her not to worry. Julie Telerhaye took priority.

Jamilla had just been in contact with the station again, only to be told that there was still no news of Debby. She could only reassure Julie that they were looking for her. But the police had said exactly the same to Julie when her son, Peter had gone missing. And he'd never turned up.

Emily had told her to ask Julie some questions. But she knew she had to choose her moment.

Julie veered from hysteria to a trance-like calm, and Jamilla waited for the sobs to subside before she began.

'Julie,' she said softly, 'has Carlo Natale been in touch with you at all?'

She shook her head vigorously.

'Did you know that Debby spoke to him a few days ago at the psychic fair at the Pavilion Hall?'

'No.' She regarded Jamilla with desperate, pleading eyes. 'She never mentioned it. Why didn't she tell me?'

'Carlo Natale's been watching this house for a while. You weren't aware of that?'

Julie gasped with horror. 'No.'

Jamilla decided to tackle the second question. 'Do you know a man called Alvin Cobarn? Or did Sinclair ever mention him?'

This time the light of recognition appeared in Julie's eyes. 'Councillor Cobarn. He's on the Arts Committee. Sinclair was trying to get funding for a street art initiative, and he met him a couple of times. I don't think anything came of it, but Sinclair said he'd been sympathetic.'

'How well did Sinclair know him?'

She shrugged. 'He never discussed anything to do with his work. All that stuff in his shed – all his jewellery making equipment – what shall I do with it?'

'Don't worry,' said Jamilla. 'We'll sort something out.'

Suddenly, without warning, Julie began to cry, her face contorted with grief. As she shrugged off Jamilla's protective arm, she started to wail, keening for her lost lover . . . and her absent daughter.

Joe passed the theatre on his way home. The fog had lifted, leaving a milky mist behind, and the audience had begun to pour out of the brightly lit building. They seemed remarkably subdued for a crowd who'd just enjoyed an evening out. Although 'enjoyed' probably wasn't the right word, from what he knew of the play. From the dates on the array of posters outside, *The Devils* only had two more weeks to run, but he wondered whether the drama surrounding the production, boosting ticket sales no end, would result in it being kept on longer.

When he arrived home he toyed with the idea of ringing Maddy. But he told himself she'd be helping her mother to come to terms with the disappointment of not seeing Carlo Natale. Joe, on the other hand, had seen too much of him that day and felt that he might actually be doing the women a favour by holding him in custody while they continued their enquiries.

The psychic had lied to them about his whereabouts on the night that Debby Telerhaye vanished. But if he had taken her for some reason, what was his motive? Joe could only think of one, and that possibility disturbed him. If he was right, it meant that Natale was dangerous. And wicked.

He shovelled down a meal from the freezer and walked to the Mitre, where he drank three pints quickly, like a thirsty man offered water in a desert. He sat alone in the corner of the bar, watching the other patrons. When he went to the bar again he exchanged a few pleasantries with the landlady, who asked him how the young lass from the other night was. It was clear that the women hadn't time to keep up with the local news, and he hadn't the heart to tell her that Debby was missing. He just said he hadn't seen her and went and sat down again with his half – he reckoned another pint would have been unwise, as Emily had ordered an early start.

The beer mellowed his mood as he walked home through the darkness. At least the visibility was almost back to normal tonight. Had the killer used the persistent fog to conceal his activities, or had it been a coincidence? He began to think of Sinclair, the only victim who hadn't been strangled. There was a slim possibility that it was suicide and he'd placed the badge in his own mouth to fool the police – a final joke: two fingers to the establishment? Hopefully, they'd find out for certain when Sally conducted the post-mortem.

The next morning Joe woke up with a slight headache, nothing a pint of water wouldn't cure. A fine veil of drizzle was falling as he walked to the police station, and by the time he reached his destination the headache had gone.

Natale had spent a second night in custody, but Joe knew their time was running out. They had to either prove something against him or release him, and Joe could sense Emily's frustration as she paced up and down the office giving the morning briefing. Natale was slippery, she said, and he had no alibis for Jonas Ventnor's and Sinclair Doulton's deaths. It was going to be hard to get evidence and break his existing alibis. But she was determined to keep trying.

There was also Jamilla's news that Sinclair Doulton had known Alvin Cobarn. Joe wasn't sure this was relevant, but Emily thought it might just be another piece in the jigsaw. Unexpected connections between suspects always aroused her suspicions.

A breakthrough came at nine thirty when some tedious routine checking threw up a gem of information.

Carlo Natale, under his real name of Charles Nuttall, was the owner of a cottage on the edge of a village called Torthwaite, twelve miles north of Eborby. However, according to the electoral register, nobody was actually living there.

Half an hour after the discovery was made, Joe was sitting in the passenger seat of a pool car beside Emily, who was driving too fast down the A1.

'He's kept bloody quiet about this, Joe,' she said, her eyes fixed on the road ahead. 'Why do you think he hasn't mentioned it?'

'How long has he owned it?'

'It looks as though he inherited it from his grandparents. Hasn't been occupied for years, as far as I can see. I called the local station, and they seemed to think it's used as a second home, but there's no record of him renting it out.'

'Maybe he keeps it as a secret bolt-hole.'

'Too bloody secret if you ask me.'

They'd reached the village of Torthwaite, which turned out to be a cluster of mellow stone houses huddled around an ancient church and an appealing stone pub with picnic tables outside for use in the summer months.

Emily's satnav led her to a lane three-hundred yards from the village centre. They drove down it a mile, but there was no sign of a cottage, just a farm gate set into a drystone wall separating the rutted lane from a field of sheep.

As they drove on, Joe began to think that they'd taken the wrong road, but Emily spotted another entrance and brought the car to a sudden halt. This one was flanked by a lofty hedge and the single wrought-iron gate looked rusty and unused. Beyond the gate was a winding overgrown path, but if there was a building at the end, it was well hidden by trees. Joe looked for a house number or a sign bearing the name of the property, but there was nothing.

'We might as well give it a try,' said Emily as she climbed out of the car.

'Looks pretty abandoned,' said Joe. Then he noticed another gap in the hedge fifteen yards up the lane. This was blocked by a double gate, rusty wrought-iron like the first, and when they reached it they could see tyre tracks leading into an overgrown drive. Someone had been here recently. They had driven through this gate and closed it behind them.

Joe and Emily left their car on the lane and took the closer, narrower path, walking to the accompaniment of birdsong and the distant bleating of sheep. Wood pigeons cooed comfortingly from the surrounding trees, and the scent of damp vegetation filled the air. It was a peaceful place. Or it would have been if they hadn't been dreading what they'd find at the end of the tortuous path.

They walked on until they saw a dilapidated cottage. Its brick walls were in urgent need of repointing, and the window frames were rotting away. However, the slate roof looked good and, with a bit of care and attention, the house would have been habitable. But as it stood, it didn't seem the sort of place a man like Carlo Natale, with his Italian suits and sporty Toyota, would choose as a weekend retreat. Joe wondered if it even had an indoor bathroom.

'I'm surprised he hasn't done it up,' said Emily. 'It's in a lovely spot. He could have flogged it as a holiday home and made a tidy sum.'

Joe didn't reply. Instead he left Emily and walked around the house, peering in through the windows. The curtains were open, and he could see the rooms were filled with heavy, dark wood furniture that gave them a cluttered, claustrophobic feel. In the poky living room there was a three-piece suite upholstered in green Draylon and fussy ornaments on the 1950s tiled fireplace. It was an old person's house, and Carlo Natale would have seemed out of place here.

By the time he reached the back door, Emily had joined him.

'It looks as though it hasn't been touched since his grandparents' day,' he said.

'Maybe he's sentimental, wants to keep it as it was when they lived here.'

'What do we do now?'

Emily grinned. 'We find evidence of a break-in so we have to enter the property to make sure everything's OK,' she said with a sly wink.

Joe followed her as she made another circuit of the house, stopping at the kitchen window. The frame had almost rotted away, and the opening section of the window hung precariously. Joe eased it open and used an old metal garden chair nearby to climb inside. He unbolted the kitchen door, and Emily stepped in. It was a kitchen from days gone by with dirty linoleum on the floor, a couple of tall cupboards, stainless-steel sink set in an old green base and a cooker with an eye-level grill, so clean it looked unused. The fridge probably dated from the fifties, and its curved shape was now back in fashion. Everything comes around if you wait long enough.

Emily opened a cupboard and wrinkled her nose. 'Some packets in here way past their sell-by date, but the tins'll probably be all right.' She picked up a packet of dried peas. 'Use by end of December 2004. Wonder when the grandparents died.'

'We can easily find out.'

Emily charged ahead into the narrow, gloomy hallway, opening the doors to the living room and dining room and peeping inside. It was Joe who made for the stairs, and she followed him up.

In the first bedroom the double bed was still made up and covered by a pink candlewick bedspread. When Emily looked in the wardrobe she found women's clothes bathed in a strong odour of mothballs. The smaller of the two wardrobes contained the clothes of a man, and Joe guessed this had been the grandparents' marital bedroom, presumably untouched since their deaths.

There were three more doors off the landing, and when Joe opened the first he realized he'd been wrong about the lack of a bathroom. But this one was basic with a pink suite and green gloss-painted walls. The second bedroom was similar to the first, only with a double bed and just one heavy oak wardrobe. Joe wondered whether Carlo Natale had spent much time here as a child. If he had, it would have been a bleak, lonely place for a growing, imaginative boy. Perhaps that's how he came to make a living from communing with the dead. Perhaps there were ghosts here that had kept him company.

The fourth door had a large key in the lock on the landing side, as if whoever had occupied the room had been locked in at some point. But it was unlocked now, and when Joe opened it he was shocked by what he saw.

It was a child's bedroom with shelves full of toys around the walls. Games, boxes of Lego that looked new, jigsaws and a train set laid out on a table in the corner.

'Probably belonged to Natale when he was a kid,' said Joe. 'Wonder why he's kept it like this? Do you reckon he lived here with his grandparents and it's some kind of shrine to his childhood?'

Emily stepped past him into the room. She touched nothing, but her eyes took everything in. 'You're wrong, Joe. A lot of this stuff was manufactured long after Natale was a boy. I think those Lego models must be around twelve years old. My nephew had some of them and passed them on to my eldest.'

Emily was the mother of three children, so Joe bowed to her superior knowledge.

'And some of these packs of Lego haven't been opened,' she said. 'What kind of kid would leave them like that?'

'Are you thinking what I'm thinking?' said Joe.

'No wonder Natale was so sure where Peter Telerhaye was. He had him. I'm getting a forensic team over here.'

'So what happened to Peter?'

Emily hesitated. 'That's what I'm afraid of.'

'I think Natale came here when he told us he was in Leeds. A car's been up that drive recently. The tyre tracks are quite clear, so we need to get a match with his car. We need something solid to charge him with, not just suspicions.'

'Do you think I don't know that?' Emily snapped. 'Let's get out of here. It's giving me the creeps.'

'Any sheds? Outhouses?' said Joe when they got outside. He looked round and spotted a dilapidated wooden shed, half hidden behind a clump of rhododendrons. When he went to investigate he saw that the door was hanging open, and inside he could see an array of garden tools hanging neatly on the wall, every one in its own place.

Underneath one hook he could make out the faint shape of a spade, lighter against the dark wooden background, the ghost of the implement left behind when it had been taken down. He pointed it out to Emily, and she gave a grim nod.

Joe left the shed and continued his search. The garden that had probably been Natale's grandparents' pride and joy had returned to a wilderness. But as he rounded a row of overgrown privets, he came to the drystone wall that marked the rear boundary of the garden. The grass was high here and dotted with weeds and wild flowers, but he could see the top of a spade sticking out of the ground next to the wall.

He glanced behind him and saw that Emily was following, uncharacteristically silent, as if she was dreading what they might find. They walked over to the spade and stopped when they saw a patch of bare earth where the vegetation had been cleared away.

The spade protruded from the soil, as if it had been abandoned by somebody who'd just begun to dig a hole there. Or maybe a grave.

Joe saw Emily take out her phone. They needed help.

TWENTY-SEVEN

There was nothing they could do until the examination at the cottage was complete. But they had Sinclair Doulton's post-mortem to distract them in the meantime.

Joe went to the hospital with Sunny because Emily was busy coordinating the search of the cottage. She'd ordered a forensic archaeologist to help with the excavation of the disturbed spot they'd found. If it was what she feared, she needed someone who knew how to preserve buried evidence.

Sunny stood beside him watching, apparently fascinated by what Sally was doing. He was miserable company, and Joe missed Emily's flashes of black humour that made the whole procedure more bearable.

Finally, Sally delivered her verdict. 'In my opinion his head injury was made with something like a hammer. It's murder, I'm afraid. Sorry to add to your workload.'

'Unless you killed him, you've got nothing to apologize for,' said Joe with a smile. 'Thanks.'

Sunny, standing beside him, issued a grunt of thanks.

'Boss won't be pleased,' were the only words he uttered on the way back to the station.

The child's skeleton was found a few yards away from where the patch had been dug. Emily Thwaite looked down into the sad little grave as the forensic archaeologist went about his work in the protective suit he wore to avoid contaminating the scene. She felt tears prick her eyes, but she tried to detach herself from the situation, to stay professional. But she thought of her own children and failed, and in the end she walked away, making the excuse that she wanted to see how the CSIs were getting on in the cottage.

But after twenty minutes of watching other people work, she knew she couldn't put it off any longer. She took a deep breath and returned to the grave.

'Boy or girl?' she said to the archaeologist, a balding man from Eborby University who had the look of a nervous accountant.

'Impossible to say when they're this young,' he answered. 'But DNA should tell us, of course.'

'Can you tell how old he or she was?'

'Probably around seven, judging by the teeth.'

The same age as Peter Telerhaye had been when he vanished. She thanked the man and put in a call to the station. She wanted to speak to Carlo Natale again. And he'd definitely need his solicitor.

An hour later she was sitting in the interview room facing Natale. Joe was at her side, having just returned from Sinclair Doulton's post-mortem. When he'd relayed Sally Sharpe's verdict, she'd received the news without comment: after all, she'd been expecting it.

Natale's solicitor was a woman in her thirties who looked sure of herself. But she didn't know what Emily knew.

'You own a cottage outside the village of Torthwaite,' she began, eager to get the interview started.

There was no mistaking the panic in Natale's eyes. 'It belonged to my grandparents. I haven't been there in years.'

'When was the last time you were there?'

'About five years ago. There's a woman in the village who keeps an eye on the place, but I really haven't had time to do anything with it. I've been meaning to put it on the market,' he went on, trying to sound casual. 'It's too isolated for my taste. And besides, I have my apartment in Leeds.'

Emily and Joe exchanged looks.

'What would you say if I told you that the body of a child has been found buried in the garden? We'll get a match with dental records, but we suspect the body is that of Peter Telerhaye. When he disappeared ten years ago you claimed to know where he was. Now I think you were telling the truth. You had him all along.'

'And you killed him,' said Joe quietly.

Natale stared into space for a moment, then he buried his head in his hands and began to cry softly. The solicitor put a hand on his sleeve then withdrew it, as though she wasn't sure what to do.

'Did you kill him?' Emily asked.

'No.' The word came out in a heartfelt cry. 'I'd never have harmed him.'

'But you abducted him?'

'You make it sound so sordid.'

'I don't know how I could make taking a seven-year-old boy from his family sound anything else.' Emily clenched her fists. This wasn't the first child abductor she'd come across who felt sorry for himself rather than his victim.

'It wasn't like that. I found him wandering on his own, and I took him back to the cottage. I gave him toys to play with. It was a treat.'

'Why?' Joe asked.

Natale stayed silent for a while. Then he whispered something to his solicitor.

'My client wishes to make a full statement,' the solicitor said. She sounded defeated, as if she was taking her failure personally.

'Very well,' said Joe. 'The tape's running. Tell us what happened.'

'It was a stupid idea, I can see that now.'

Joe asked him to speak up for the tape, and Natale cleared his throat.

'At that time my career was flagging, and I needed something to give it a boost. Publicity. I hit on the idea of taking someone – a child. They wouldn't come to any harm. They'd just stay somewhere for a few days and be spoiled. Then I'd take him somewhere and use my powers to see where he was. I had Scarborough in mind, and I thought that once I'd made my prediction, the police would pick him up and he'd be back with his mum and dad in no time, none the worse.'

'You'd have needed help,' said Emily.

'I had a lady friend. It was her idea, actually.'

'We'll need her name.'

'It's Cheryl. Cheryl Greatorex. And you won't find her because she died the year after it happened. She killed herself. Looking back, she was mentally unstable. But we can all be wise with hindsight, can't we? Anyway, we came across this little lad out playing on his own. We disguised ourselves so that when he was asked who took him he'd give a misleading description.' He gave a feeble smile. 'I wore a wig and a false moustache, and Cheryl wore a big blond wig and glasses.'

'So what happened?'

'We took him to the cottage.'

'Did you drug him?' Emily asked.

'We gave him a drink with some of Cheryl's sleeping pills crushed in it, just so he'd sleep during the journey and wouldn't know where he was being taken. He was fine when we got there. We'd already bought toys and done out a room for him. We made it a game. He kept asking for his mother, but when we said she'd gone away for a few days and she'd asked us to look after him, he was quite happy.' He smiled, as though he was recalling a pleasant memory.

'What went wrong?'

The smile vanished suddenly, and a spasm of pain passed across his face.

'One night he was crying, and when Cheryl went in to him she found him gasping for breath. Since then I've read in the papers that he suffered from asthma, but I had no idea. He'd seemed fine up till then.' He buried his head in his hands again. 'It all fell apart. But it wasn't my fault.'

'You should have called an ambulance,' said Joe.

'It happened so fast. He was dead before we could do anything . . . honestly.'

Emily looked away. She clearly didn't believe him.

'So you had a body on your hands,' said Joe. 'What did you do?'

'I had to change my plans,' he said after a few moments of silence. 'I told the Telerhayes he was at a derelict barn near Whitby.'

'It was searched. We found evidence he'd been there.'

'I know. There was a room above the barn, and I left one of his shoes there and cleaned the place thoroughly with bleach . . . as if someone had been trying to destroy evidence. Only, he'd never been there. He was at my cottage all the time.'

'A diversion.'

'I suppose you could call it that, but I thought it would confirm that my powers hadn't let me down – that he had been where I said he'd been.'

'You had a dead kid on your hands. What did you do?'

'I had to cover my tracks.'

'So you buried him,' said Emily. 'You didn't even give his mother a chance to hold his funeral and grieve properly.'

'That's why I traced Julie Telerhaye and came here. I wanted to put things right. I thought that if I could lead the police to his grave, his mother would have some sort of closure.'

'Closure.' Emily almost spat the word. 'Her son was dead, and you hid it from her.'

'It wasn't my fault,' Natale whined. 'It was natural causes. Could have happened any time.'

Joe ignored his excuses and carried on. 'The grave was on your property,' he said, watching Natale's face carefully. 'You had to move the body so you could pretend you had a message from the spirits to tell you where it was.'

'That's right. It was all overgrown, and it looked so different from when we buried him. I started to look for the exact spot, but it wasn't easy on my own. I intended to go back in a couple of days when I didn't have an evening show and have another go. I had to work in the darkness, you see, because I didn't want the people from the neighbouring farm seeing my car. I was planning to bury him in some woodland a few miles away.' A smile played on his lips. 'I found a lovely spot. Very tranquil.'

Joe thought he sounded almost sanctimonious. He began to go through the charges they could bring against him. But he wasn't sure whether murder was one of them.

'Did you abduct Debby Telerhaye?' Emily asked.

'No.' He closed his eyes. 'I told you she was with the dead, and since then things are becoming clearer. She's underground with people whose spirits departed centuries ago. She's trapped in the dark, and I feel fear.' He rose from his seat, ignoring his solicitor's warning hand on his sleeve. 'And she's in danger. Great danger.' He collapsed back into his chair, and his eyes glazed over as if he was in some sort of trance.

Joe and Emily watched and waited.

'Ghosts,' Natale said after a few seconds had passed. 'You've got to find the ghosts.'

Emily stood up and announced that they were going to take a break. Joe followed her out into the corridor. He could tell she was irritated. She leaned against the wall and rolled her eyes.

'Got to find the ghosts. It's all bloody theatricals. Well, it won't wash with me.'

'But he's probably right when he says Debby's in danger.'

Emily grunted. 'You don't need to be a bloody clairvoyant to work that one out.'

There was a plastic bucket in the corner of the room. She hadn't been told its purpose, but Debby had used it to relieve herself, and now the place stank of excrement as well as death. The light was too dim to work out what colour the bucket was, but her eyes were slowly becoming used to her surroundings.

She was underground all right. The only shaft of light came from a tiny barred window set high in the far wall. At night that light turned a sickly yellow, which she guessed meant that there was a street light outside. This gave her new hope. Where there were street lights, there were people.

At first she'd assumed it was a cellar, but now she wasn't so sure. There were stone rectangles set like tables around the walls. At first she thought they looked like altars, but she soon realized that they were tombs. There were a couple in the centre of the floor as well, one with a recumbent figure: a sleeping knight. This was a vault – a place of the dead. And her main fear was that she'd soon join them.

She thought of Perry's weird accommodation. He was strange, but was he responsible for this? Could this place be underneath his strange house? He hadn't mentioned a basement, and she hadn't seen an entrance, but it was the only explanation she could think of – that this was part of some sick art project. Either that, or Carlo Natale was trying to silence her. She'd tried to call out both their names, but it was as if she'd shouted and screamed into a void. Then came the sleep, the heavy unnatural sleep that kept her unaware of anything for most of the time. She suspected the food she was given was drugged, but she'd been too hungry to refuse it. Besides, sleep filled the time. While she was sleeping she wasn't afraid.

Her phone was gone and she never wore a watch, so she had

no concept of time. Only the street lamp and the demands of her stomach gave her any idea of the passing of the hours, and she was feeling hungry now. Surely, she'd be fed soon.

She heard the faint creaking sound that heralded food, so she pushed herself up off the mattress and crawled over to a square of faint light that had appeared suddenly, like a sunbeam through thick clouds, at the top of the steps in the corner. From experience she knew the tray would be left on the top step and she picked her way over slowly, feeling a sharp pain as she bashed her knee on the cold stone.

Every time she'd reached the top she'd pushed the trapdoor with all the strength she could muster. But it had never budged.

The arrival of food had become the highlight of her day now, and after tearing the wrapping from the supermarket sandwich, she stuffed it into her mouth. It was rubbery cheese and the bread was past its best, but it still tasted good. There was a plastic bottle too. Coke.

When she'd finished her feast she pushed at the trapdoor again, just to make sure. Then her head began to swim so she crawled back to her mattress and shut her eyes.

Next time, she thought, she'd be ready for him.

The security guard who patrolled the station car park by night was used to boredom. And perhaps it was preferable to the alternative. Trouble didn't appeal to him much; he'd much rather settle down with a good book until the time came for him to patrol the perimeter. Filling in applications for jobs more suited to his qualifications took up much of his time, but he always welcomed the hourly stroll which was a chance to stretch his long legs.

It was quiet. It always was at three in the morning, apart from the occasional drinker sneaking in to urinate against the far wall on his way home from a late night out. Sometimes there were women too, always in a group, always shrieking loud enough to wake the dead. If he ignored them, they always left in their own good time. Avoiding confrontation was his mission in life.

But tonight was different. Nobody would want to hang about longer than necessary, with the cold mist hanging in the air like the fug from some giant bonfire. Except one person. He could see someone over by the wall who had been there too long to be answering a call of nature. The bastard was drawing. A graffiti artist. This had to be dealt with. But he needed some help.

The City of Eborby was always conscious of its image as a Mecca for tourists, so things like this were always taken seriously. And if he asked a nearby police patrol car to pop by and apprehend the culprit, it would pass the problem on to someone else.

Ten minutes later the figure was still there, working on his defacement of the wall with the concentration of a craftsman while the security guard watched from his hiding place in a shadowy doorway. Even when the patrol car made its stately way into the car park, the figure didn't move. Not until the car door slammed loudly and the policeman got out.

The security guard watched the ensuing chase, glad that he hadn't become involved. The vandal was a young man who looked as if he might fight back, so it wouldn't have been worth it.

Only when the culprit was safely in the back of the police car did he step forward and have a word with one of the officers, keen to be seen to have done his duty.

'Thanks for reporting it,' the officer said. He jerked his head towards the wall. 'Seen what he's done?'

The security guard flashed his torch at the wall, but in the place of the usual mindless tag he'd been expecting to see was a chalked figure drawn with great skill. A man with arms extended, as if pleading for aid. Water was dripping from his sodden clothes and hair, and the eyes sunken into the death-pale face were tightly shut.

A drowned man. Why would anyone want to draw a picture of a drowned man?

TWENTY-EIGHT

Long-buried skeletons weren't really within Sally Sharpe's field of expertise, so as soon as the child's skeleton arrived at the mortuary, she'd put in a call to a forensic anthropologist she knew.

First thing the next morning she rang the incident room with the verdict, and as soon as Joe had finished speaking to her he rushed to Emily's office.

'That was Sally. Natale might be telling the truth about Peter Telerhaye's death,' he began. 'There are no signs of violence on the body and nothing to contradict his account.'

'Apart from the poor little thing being buried in the garden of the man who abducted him,' Emily answered bitterly.

'Doesn't mean he wasn't telling the truth,' said Joe. 'It was a publicity stunt that went badly wrong.'

'And resulted in the death of a child. He's not going to get away with that.'

She compressed her lips. Joe sensed her anger. As far as she was concerned, Natale was responsible, whether or not he actually meant to harm the child. Joe knew she was right, but he couldn't help having some pity for the man who must have had the shock of his life when his stunt backfired. But he reminded himself that Natale had continued gulling the vulnerable public afterwards, so perhaps he wasn't worth his compassion after all. Natale had been charged with abduction and concealing a death. That would do to be going on with.

Carlo Natale swore that he had no idea where Debby Telerhaye was, and Joe tended to believe him. The family liaison officer at her mother's house had just reported back that there'd still been no word. She could be anywhere. The only thing he was sure of was that she was in danger. He was about to try the number of one of Debby's friends – a girl from college they hadn't yet been able to contact – when a uniformed officer entered the incident room and hurried across to his desk.

'We made an arrest in the early hours,' the constable began. 'Lad caught scrawling graffiti in the station car park.'

Joe wondered what this had to do with him.

'Turns out he's someone who's already been questioned – name of Perry Antrobus. Calls himself an artist.' The last sentence was pronounced with heavy sarcasm. 'Mind you, it's not just scrawl. He's good – a bit like that Banksy.'

The constable obviously fancied himself as a bit of an art connoisseur. Joe waited for him to elaborate.

'He was drawing a drowned man. Creepy, in my opinion.'

'Is it still there?' Sinclair Doulton had been pulled out of the river. It could hardly be a coincidence.

'We didn't wash it off. Unless the people at the station . . .'

'Get on to them right away and tell them not to touch it. I want it examined and photographed.'

The constable seemed to twig. 'You think it's connected with this case? With that girl's stepdad who drowned?'

Joe didn't answer the question. 'Is Perry Antrobus still here?'

'Yes. We kept him in overnight. Criminal damage.' He grinned. 'Only, he claims it's art.'

'I want to see him. Have him brought to the interview room, will you?'

Ten minutes later Joe and Emily were sitting face to face with Perry Antrobus. There was a smug half-smile on the boy's face, as if he was privy to a secret they didn't share.

'What were you drawing on the wall when you were arrested?' Joe began.

'A ghost.'

'The ghost of Sinclair Doulton?'

As Joe said the name, Perry suddenly looked wary. 'Is that who it was?'

'Didn't you know?'

'How could I? I just heard some poor sod had been pulled out of the water.'

'You knew Sinclair. You supplied him with materials for his jewellery.' Joe paused. 'Incidentally, one of those Saint Galert badges was found in his mouth.'

Perry's eyes widened in alarm. 'That's got nothing to do with me,' he said quickly. 'Anyway, my picture doesn't even look like him. I heard someone had drowned, so I drew a drowned man. It's just another ghost.'

'Ghost? What do you mean?' asked Emily.

Perry looked at her. 'You wouldn't understand.'

'Try us,' said Joe.

'It's a concept. Eborby's obsessed with ghosts. There's ghost walks, books about ghosts, all this boasting about it being the most haunted city in England. Eborby thrives on its history. The past is its life blood, and I'm celebrating all those lives that have been lived in its streets over the centuries and how people become immortal by leaving their ghosts behind.'

'You believe in ghosts then?' said Emily. Joe could hear the scepticism in her voice.

'I believe in art,' Perry replied. 'Think of it as my tribute to generations gone by. The people who made this city.'

'That's all very well,' said Joe. 'But what made you choose these particular ghosts? As you say, Eborby's full of them. Why choose the nun from the theatre, the hanged actor?'

Perry shrugged. 'Who said I did those?'

'Did you?'

'No comment.'

'And now you've drawn a man who may be connected with the recent murders.'

Perry raised his eyebrows, a picture of innocence. 'I didn't even know it was him. Honest.'

'His name's been released to the press.'

He sniffed. 'I never read trash. I merely selected the newest of the city ghosts . . . the initiate into the brotherhood. They say ghosts are people who've died suddenly with unfinished business on the earth. The drowned man fitted my project perfectly.'

Perry began to pick at his fingernails, as though the questioning was boring him. Joe suspected his studied nonchalance was an act. But was it because he was caught drawing on a wall, or was it something worse?

'So you claim you know nothing about the death of Sinclair Doulton.'

'He was just a business acquaintance. Why should I kill him?'

There was a knock on the interview room door, and Jamilla

crept in, trying to be unobtrusive. She had a photograph in her hand, and she placed it on the table in front of Emily.

Emily studied it for a while and pushed it towards Joe. It was an image of Perry's handiwork of the previous night. The drowned man. It could have been Sinclair Doulton but, on the other hand, it was a generic image – a pale figure in sodden rags dripping water from its green-tinged flesh, the face vague, almost blank. It was good enough to be an illustration – the drowned mariner returned from the sea.

He handed it to Perry. 'This is the picture you drew on the wall.'

'So it is.'

'If you don't read the news, how did you know that the body had been found?'

'Good question,' he said, patronizing. 'I must have heard it somewhere. Someone must have told me.'

'Who?'

'I'm not saying any more. You'll either have to charge me or release me.'

'We can charge you with criminal damage.'

'Whoopee. I can hardly contain my excitement. I'll tell the magistrate how sorry I am and how I only wanted to contribute to the artistic life of the community, and I'll either get let off or receive a slap on the wrist.'

Emily stood up. 'After stealing from the cathedral, I think you're pushing your luck.'

Joe watched her face redden. Perry Antrobus was beginning to get to her.

'I told you I was sorry. It won't happen again. I'm going straight. From now on, I live for art.' He looked at his watch, and Joe sensed a sudden anxiety, as though he realized he should be somewhere and time was running out. 'Look, I've been here all night. Can I go now?'

'Is there somewhere you've got to be?'

'I've just got to see someone, that's all.'

'Who?'

'My sister. She doesn't know where I am. She'll be worried.'

Emily began to move towards the door. Joe followed, but then he turned round to face Perry, who remained forlornly at the table.

'Are you covering up for someone?' he asked. He saw a flash of something that looked like worry pass across Perry's face. He had hit the target.

'No.'

When he was alone with Emily in the corridor, he leaned towards her and whispered, 'I think we should release him, have him followed and find out where he goes. Or, rather, who he goes to.'

Emily thought for a few seconds, before nodding in agreement.

The varying light trickling through the small barred window at the top of the wall told Debby whether it was night or day, and from now on she intended to count the times that tiny space darkened then brightened again. The last couple of times she hadn't drunk from the open can of coke, and her head felt clearer, which proved there must have been something in the drink to keep her subdued and acquiescent. But the downside of her new alert state was boredom, and fear had made it hard to sleep in the dark hours. Instead, she sat on the mattress and waited, listening, her ears attuned for any tell-tale sound that would herald her captor's arrival.

She'd explored her prison, searching for anything that might give her some hope of escape, and she'd found a potential weapon, a piece of loose, carved stone she'd prised from one of the tombs. It seemed to be the hand of some recumbent stone figure, and although it wasn't large or heavy she'd experienced a small thrill of triumph when she'd manage to wrest it from the place where it had lain for centuries. She felt so weak that she wondered if she was up to attempting an escape. But she thought of her mother. After what happened with Peter, she'd be grieving, thinking that some terrible curse had struck her twice. She hoped Sinclair was supporting her, but if she knew anything about the toe-rag, he'd probably have abandoned her to spend more time down the pub with his mates. Her mother needed her. She'd have to try.

While she'd been down there, she'd had plenty of time to think, and she'd come to the conclusion that Carlo Natale was her captor. She'd made a nuisance of herself, and this was probably his way of punishing her. He hadn't allowed her to see him, and this gave her hope. If he intended to kill her, it would hardly matter if she knew his identity.

She slumped back on the mattress and felt tears pricking her eyes, wondering if this was what Peter had gone through. It was something she hadn't considered before – what her brother had actually suffered. All she'd known was that he was probably dead. Unless somebody had taken him to adopt him, to replace some precious lost child. That was the hope her mother had clung on to – that he was still out there somewhere, happy and alive.

A noise suddenly shattered the silence. The grating of wood against stone that heralded the arrival of food.

This was her chance. After picking up the stone hand and weighing it in her fingers, she levered herself off the mattress and moved quickly towards the staircase. If she could get to the top before the trapdoor opened, she could bring her weapon down on the hand that delivered the tray and make her bid for freedom.

However hard she tried to walk in silence, she could hear her own footsteps as the soles of her shoes hit the hard floor. She contemplated taking them off, but there wasn't time.

When she reached the stairs she heard a click as the key turned in the trapdoor's lock, and she crouched on the fourth step down with the stone hand raised, ready. As soon as the trapdoor opened, sending a shaft of daylight into the vault, she threw herself forward with a primitive howl.

She let go of the stone, hurling it at the light, but there was a loud crash as the trapdoor slammed shut and the light vanished, leaving her sprawled on the steps in darkness.

Her captor had been too quick for her. This time.

TWENTY-NINE

Perry Antrobus had feigned a triumphant swagger when he'd been with the police, but it was only a way of concealing his fear. Bad things were happening. Things he hadn't planned. His concentration, so essential to an artist of any kind, was shattered, and he feared he wouldn't be able to carry on and complete his project.

When they released him again, pending further enquiries, he stood outside the police station for a while, wondering where to go. Today would have been cathedral shop day, but there was no chance of that now. He saw now that trying to make a few extra bob by selling those trinkets from the shop had been a big mistake. But it had been suggested by a stronger will, and he'd yielded. Just as he always did.

They'd given him his mobile phone back, and now he used it to try his sister. At this time of day she was usually at home. But there was no answer.

He walked back to his house with a vague feeling of unease, and when he reached his destination he unlocked the door.

At first everything looked normal in the gloom. Then he stepped behind the drapes at the back of the room and opened the small oak door that led out into the small cobbled courtyard. He crossed the yard and pushed open a door set into the stone wall on the opposite side: an unobtrusive little door that led into a small chapel that had once belonged to the monastic house. When he'd moved in it was being used as a storeroom, but his sister had cleared it out and claimed it for her own. She liked its privacy and the fact that nobody but Perry knew it was there. When the police had searched, he was sure they hadn't found it, or had dismissed the door as belonging to another property.

The room beyond the door was hung with bright throws, with fairy lights around the walls and threaded through the old iron bedstead. He called his sister's name, but there was no answer. Then he heard a scrabbling sound, followed by a whimper.

He could see her now, crouched in the corner holding her face. As he got closer he saw blood glistening on her hands. She was hurt.

He could hear a repetitive banging now. A pounding which seemed to be coming from the back of the room. But as far as he knew there was nothing there, only the place she used as a makeshift wardrobe, hidden behind a battered junk shop screen.

'What's that noise?' he asked. But she didn't answer. Instead she rocked to and fro, her face hidden from him.

He knelt on the cold stone floor beside her and asked if she was OK. When she didn't answer he stood up and shifted the screen a little. All he could see behind it was a rack of clothes, but the noise continued, although it had subsided to a gentle tap tap.

He pushed the rack, and as it moved to one side on its castors he edged his way past, trying to locate the sound. When he spotted a wooden trapdoor set into the floor he stopped. This had always been his sister's space, and he'd respected her privacy so he'd never investigated too closely. This was unknown territory.

The noise started up again. *Knock, knock.* And after a few moments he summoned the courage to answer. He wasn't afraid of ghosts; he worked with them; they were his inspiration. But he was afraid of human beings. Each time he'd met Sinclair Doulton in that dodgy pub to trade his stolen trinkets for hard cash, the vague ambience of violence had made him nervous. 'Hello. Is someone there?'

'Help me.' The voice was feeble, like an injured child's.

He attempted to lift the trapdoor, but it wouldn't budge, and he saw that it was secured with a padlock.

He turned to face his sister. 'There's somebody down there. Have you got the key?'

She didn't answer. But he knew by the look on her face that she'd done something terrible.

He fumbled for his phone. He needed help. As soon as he ended the brief call, he grabbed his sister's arm, and she squealed with pain.

'What have you done?'

This was the moment he'd been dreading all his life. The moment when the monster in her would rise again.

Joe decided to go home to have something to eat before returning to the police station for the evening shift. In spite of his head acknowledging that Carlo Natale was a criminal who had abducted an innocent child, as well as being a fraud and a liar, a small part of him had derived some comfort from his claim that Debby Telerhaye was still alive. Although he'd never have admitted this to Emily.

But his professional head told him firmly that nothing Natale said could be trusted, and the only spirits he'd ever encountered were to be found in bottles. He had always believed in a life beyond the seen, but he doubted whether wandering souls would ever have any truck with Natale's brand of show business. He also believed in evil – he saw it every day in the course of his work – and human weakness. Natale had preyed on the vulnerable, which in Joe's opinion was just another form of wickedness.

When he arrived at his silent flat he saw that the light on his answering machine was flashing. He knew who it would be. Maddy had been trying to reach him on his mobile all day, but he had ignored her calls.

He listened to the messages. In the first one she sounded calm, almost casual. 'I've been trying to reach you. Can you give me a call?' There were four in all, each one sounding more urgent, more needy. He helped himself to a bottle of Black Sheep and drank it while he made himself an omelette. He wasn't in the mood for speaking to Maddy. He had too much on his mind.

Emily had agreed with Joe's suggestion that they put a tail on Perry Antrobus, in the hope that he'd give himself away. The plain-clothes constable had reported back that he'd returned to his address near Mungate, and Emily had told him to keep watching while she arranged for another search of the premises. But by the time Joe had left the office there'd been no further update.

Joe took another bottle out of the cupboard. He was drinking when he was technically on duty, but he felt he needed another. He prised the top off and took a swig. It tasted good, and he felt the tension in his body melting like ice in sun.

His mobile phone rang, and he looked at the caller's number. It was Hen Butler. He looked at his watch and calculated that she'd be at the theatre preparing for that evening's performance of *The Devils.* He wondered why she was ringing. But there was only one way of finding out, so he answered the call. 'Hi, Ms Butler. What can I do for you?'

'It's probably nothing, but . . .' Hen sounded unsure of herself.

'Why don't you tell me what's bothering you.'

'You know when Charlotte was attacked the other night . . .?'

'Did you see something?'

'No. That's the point. I'd nipped into the next dressing room to borrow a hair grip from another member of the cast around the time she said it happened, and . . . Well, I didn't hear anything. The door to my dressing room creaks because nobody's ever bothered to oil the hinges, and I didn't hear it opening, which means that whoever attacked Charlotte never left.' She hesitated. 'Either that, or . . .'

'Could the sound of the hinges have been masked by her screams? She did scream, didn't she?'

'Yes. But Louisa was in the corridor when the screaming started. She didn't see anyone leaving either. I've asked her. There was nobody there.'

'So what do you think happened?'

'Either Charlotte was lying or she did see a ghost.'

'As far as I know ghosts have never been known to attack people.'

'Unless . . . Well, Louisa was there.'

This was something Joe hadn't expected. 'You think she might have . . .?'

'I don't think she likes Charlotte. I wonder if she was trying to scare her so she could bring in a replacement. It's just a thought. I'm not accusing . . .'

'Of course not,' Joe said quickly. He guessed it had taken a lot for Hen to make this call. He knew she respected Louisa, which meant that the incident must have preyed on her mind for some time before she summoned the courage to report it.

But there was another possibility.

As soon as the call was ended, his phone rang again. When he saw it was Emily, he took a swig from his bottle. He was due back at the station in forty-five minutes, so whatever she wanted must be urgent.

'Joe,' she began, 'there's been an anonymous call. A man saying there are screams coming from Perry Antrobus's place. I've listened to the recording of the call, and I think it sounds like Perry himself. But that doesn't make sense. The patrol hasn't called it in, so maybe it's a hoax. He's playing another of his tricks.'

'We shouldn't take any chances. I think we should get over there.'

'OK. I'll pick you up.'

The line went dead, and he stared at the phone for a moment before making another call. There was something he had to know, something that might stop them making a big mistake.

'No.' The single word came out as a howl of anguish.

She closed her fist on the key and tightened her grip. Her brother wouldn't undo her work, not when she'd taken so much trouble.

Her cheeks were damp with blood and tears. The little bitch had hit her with something. She was injured, and her main fear was that it would prevent her from turning up at the theatre that evening, which would ruin everything. She needed to look in the mirror to see how bad it was. She'd done it all so she could take her rightful place in the world. Her proper role. If the bitch in the basement had spoiled that, she deserved all she got. Maybe she should have disposed of her quickly, but she'd wanted to take her time. The others had been rushed. Necessary. But Debby Telerhaye's death would be a work of art.

'What have you *done*?' Perry was kneeling by her, tears running down his cheeks.

'I did it for you. For the project.'

'I never asked you to kill anyone. If I'd known what you were doing, I would have stopped you!'

She didn't reply.

'Who's down there?'

'That girl you brought back. The one who saw me in the undercroft. I couldn't take the risk.'

'You have to let her go.'

She wasn't listening. 'I thought we could both do it this time . . . watch her spirit leave her body . . . create our very own new ghost.'

Perry struggled to his feet. 'This has gone too far. It's over.' He began to back away. 'The police have already questioned me. They think I did it.'

'I never thought you were a coward.' He saw contempt in her eyes. The wound on her forehead had stopped bleeding, and the blood was crusting on her skin.

'It's not a game any more. It has to stop,' he said. 'You need help.'

He put a hand on his sister's arm. She was older than him, but he'd always felt responsible for her. She veered between seeming completely sane, even ordinary, and bouts of cunning, controlled madness. He loved her, but he hated what he knew she was capable of. He'd known she was different ever since he'd found her with the tiny limp body of the kitten their parents had bought for them when they were little. She'd suffocated it with a plastic bag; killed it out of curiosity, she'd said. Curiosity and intense jealousy of the attention the cute little thing was receiving. He'd covered for her then, saying it had been an accident. He'd never told, and he'd been shielding her from the consequences of her actions ever since; humouring her, sometimes even taking the blame.

But now it had to end.

'I'm letting Debby out,' he said softly. 'And you're not going to stop me. I've called the police.'

'You hate the police,' she whined like an injured child. 'You've always said . . .'

'Give me the key,' he whispered.

He didn't see the knife she was clutching in her other hand until it was too late and it had pierced his flesh.

He heard his sister scream, as if she was shocked by what she'd just done. Then he slumped on the floor and the world went silent.

THIRTY

The constable watching Perry Antrobus's address had been told to wait for backup, and when Emily's car drew up, Joe saw him standing by the door of a little medieval building that looked out of place huddled amongst the red-brick houses. The man rubbed his gloved hands against the cold as he reported that everything was quiet right now. He'd heard a man's raised voice a few minutes ago, but he hadn't been able to tell where it came from.

Joe had never been down this street before, and he had no idea that such an interesting building existed. But Eborby was like that. The past leapt out at you when you least expected it. Somehow it looked just the sort of place Perry Antrobus would choose to live, and he wondered how he'd managed to secure it.

But now he knew the identity of Perry's sister, everything was starting to piece together. His only regret was that they hadn't checked out the addresses of everyone at the theatre earlier and found the connection. But hindsight is a wonderful thing.

A patrol car had followed them. The driver was Sergeant Una O'Kane, a woman Joe had always thought of as formidable, even on the verge of scary. She was accompanied by a well-built uniformed constable, and he felt glad of their presence. The person they were about to confront had killed three people and possibly abducted a third. Emily thought Debby Telerhaye was probably dead, but Joe still clung to hope.

He banged his fist on the door, so hard that it hurt. The modern lock was probably the weakest point in the sturdy oak door, and Emily instructed the largest constable to break it open while she and Joe stood back and watched.

Eventually, the lock yielded, and as the door burst open, the constable stumbled into the building.

They walked in after him, looking around. The place looked like a medieval hall, stone built and filled with art equipment. The cart Perry used to transport his living statue gear and art equipment stood near the door, and there was a mattress covered by a duvet against the left-hand wall halfway down the room. A few old chipboard kitchen cupboards stood in one far corner, and in the opposite corner was a niche, the sort Joe had seen in churches to accommodate the tombs of important men and women.

He walked slowly to the back of the room, and when he reached the niche he saw that stones had been removed to reveal a wooden coffin. He took a deep breath and lifted the lid to be greeted with the sight of the mummified corpse the officers who'd searched this place had mentioned. At first he thought it might be some horror-film prop that Perry Antrobus found amusing to have around his place, but on closer inspection he realized it was the real thing. He pointed it out to Emily and saw her eyes widen.

Apart from Perry's gruesome house guest, it was a utilitarian space with no sign of female habitation, which made Joe doubt his assumptions. But when he walked away from the open tomb he saw the threadbare velvet drapes on the back wall billow slightly, as though there was a draught. He pushed them to one side and saw a little door, ajar and letting in a weak glimmer of light. He pushed at it, and when it creaked open he signalled Emily to follow.

He stepped out into a cobbled yard, enclosed on all sides by stone walls. There was a door set into the wall on the other side of the yard . . . and it was standing wide open.

When Joe reached the threshold he stopped and took in his surroundings. There were fairy lights and bright fabrics. This must be the sister's domain. He froze, listening, sensing there was someone in the gloom.

The heavy silence was broken by a banging sound followed by a sob and a faint moan. Joe walked towards an old screen decorated with Victorian scraps, turned to sepia with the years, which blocked off the corner to the right of a large iron bedstead. The knocking was continuous and rhythmic now, and the sobbing started up again, a desperate, hopeless sound.

As he shifted the screen to one side, the knocking stopped.

The one thing he hadn't expected to see behind the screen was Perry Antrobus lying unconscious and bleeding on the cold stone floor next to a rack of women's clothes. Joe knelt by him and felt for a pulse. He was still alive. Just.

Joe could see a bloody gash through his black T-shirt near his heart, and behind him he heard Emily calling for an ambulance.

When she'd finished, she squatted down beside him. 'Suicide attempt?'

'No sign of a weapon.'

'He could have hidden it before he collapsed.'

Joe wasn't convinced. When he asked Emily why he'd go to that trouble, she replied that he was an artist. Perhaps it was some sort of statement; a final joke against the police.

Before Joe could reply, the knocking started up again.

'Where the hell is that noise coming from?' Emily asked. She began to search round, pushing shoes and carrier bags aside so she could get to the wall. 'It could be coming from next door,' she concluded.

'No. It's somewhere nearby. Look over there.'

Emily saw what he was pointing at – a trapdoor in the floor a few feet away, secured by a padlock. She twisted round and called out to Una O'Kane who had followed them in and had taken it upon herself to guard the door. 'Help me get this up, will you? You might need a crow bar or something.'

'This looks like some sort of chapel,' said Joe as he examined the padlock. 'It could have a vault. A burial place.' As he said it, Carlo Natale's words flashed through his head. *She's with the dead.*

It took five minutes to break open the padlock, during which the knocking ceased. Joe watched as Una and a couple of colleagues hauled the trapdoor open. Then he peered down into the void and saw a pale little face looking up at him. Debby Telerhaye's eyes looked large and desperate.

And when she saw Joe she started to cry.

The paramedics led Debby out, a blanket around her shoulders. Perry Antrobus had already left in the first ambulance, headed for Intensive Care at the hospital with ear-piercing sirens blaring. He was still alive, but it was touch and go.

There was still no sign of a weapon, but Joe was unconvinced by Emily's theory. Hen Butler's phone call had told him the killer's identity. Emily might think Perry was guilty and that he was safely in the hospital, but Joe knew there was another, shadowy, intelligence behind his actions; somebody who'd felt compelled to kill Perdita Elmet and then hadn't been able to stop.

He followed Debby out and touched her shoulder gently when he caught up with her. But she jumped and swung round, terrified, and he cursed his clumsiness.

He had one question to ask her that might convince Emily that it wasn't over yet.

'Is Perry responsible for this?'

Debby shook her head.

'Was it a woman?'

Debby froze. When she spoke, the words emerged in a hoarse whisper, as if she'd lost the habit of speech. 'The last thing I remember was a woman spilling my drink and buying me another. A few minutes later I felt faint, and she helped me outside. Could that have been . . .?'

'Can you describe her?'

At first, Debby shook her head. 'I don't believe it. She looked so . . . ordinary.' Then slowly, with a great effort, her fuddled brain provided a description which, although vague, told Joe he was right.

And it looked as if the killer had managed to escape through a side entrance to the little chapel that led on to the street. But Joe knew there was only one place she'd go.

THIRTY-ONE

Julie Telerhaye had wept when she'd been reunited with her daughter. She'd clung to Debby like a drowning man to a lifebelt, as though she would never let her go. Her son, Peter, was lost forever, with no hope of getting him back. But Debby was safe. And with the death of Sinclair Doulton, all they had was each other.

Joe had left Jamilla Dal with the depleted little family. There was some joy in the Telerhayes' situation, but there was also a barrel-load of grief, so he didn't envy her.

It was five to seven when he and Emily arrived at the theatre with uniformed backup, and the half had just been announced over the tannoy. They made straight to Louisa Van Sturten's office, only to find it empty.

'Surely, she wouldn't just turn up to work as if nothing had happened,' Emily said.

'She's been keeping up the act ever since she killed Perdita Elmet,' Joe said. 'Here in the theatre she can become someone else.'

'Even after she's tried to kill her own brother.' Emily pressed her lips together. 'We should have checked out her address.'

'We had no reason to. We just thought she was a witness.

Besides, Perry lied about his address at first, so we'd have been none the wiser.' She hesitated. 'She should be here. Let's check the dressing room.'

Joe suddenly felt apprehensive. If they were right, she was unpredictable, and by now she'd be desperate. They were both wearing stab vests, and Emily wriggled as she walked, complaining that she found it uncomfortable. But she had no choice. As far as they knew, the woman they'd come to arrest was armed.

They walked slowly down the backstage corridor, alert for anything that didn't seem right. A radio played softly somewhere: a hit from the 1960s. And a male voice held a one-sided conversation in the dressing room that had once been allocated to Jonas; his replacement, talking to someone on his mobile. There was a low murmur of female voices from the room Hen shared with Charlotte, but Joe sensed that something was wrong in there.

He was about to knock on the dressing room door when Emily shook her head and put her finger to her lips before placing her hand on the doorknob.

She pushed the door open. Hen Butler was sitting on a stool by the large mirror, her make-up spread out on the counter in front of her. She was already in full costume, and her hair was hidden beneath a skull cap in preparation for the wig she wore during the performance. Louisa Van Sturten stood in the centre of the room with a worried frown on her face.

'We're looking for Charlotte,' Emily said.

'Aren't we all,' said Louisa. She looked like a woman with problems. 'The half was called five minutes ago, and she hasn't turned up. If you'll excuse me, I'm going to have to brief her understudy . . .' She looked at Joe and Emily accusingly. 'Unless you know something.'

'We just need to know where she is,' said Emily, who hadn't time for long explanations. 'Have you any idea where—?'

'I was telling Louisa,' Hen interrupted. 'Her costume's gone. The stage manager says she saw her come in half an hour ago, but nobody's seen her since.'

'Where have you looked?' said Joe.

'In the dressing rooms and the backstage area. The usual places. We're on in twenty-five minutes! She should be here.'

'I'm afraid you'll have to cancel tonight's performance,' said Emily.

Louisa looked as if she was about to protest, but instead she asked why.

'Charlotte's been involved in a serious incident. We think she might be hiding on the premises. I've called for backup. This theatre will be crawling with police officers soon. I'm sorry,' she added, noting the director's horrified face.

Louisa took a deep breath. 'I don't suppose I have any choice.'

'I'm afraid not.'

There was noise outside the room. The backup had arrived.

'Has anyone looked in the basement?' Joe asked.

He saw Louisa and Hen look at each other. 'Not yet,' Louisa said.

They left the two women together and hurried out into the corridor to join the other officers. Sunny was with them, and he seemed to have assumed command, sending them off in different directions. When he saw Emily, he looked at her quizzically, but she nodded as if to say *carry on*.

Joe told him that he'd take the basement. Hen had seen a nun down there, and he'd have laid money on that nun being Charlotte. She'd probably used it as her own personal refuge. He asked a couple of uniforms to go with him as backup, and Emily brought up the rear.

As soon as he opened the door, Joe flicked the switch to his left, and the place was bathed in watery fluorescent light that left the sides and the corners in darkness. He walked down the steps, glad of the echoing footsteps of the officers behind him, glad that he wasn't alone in that place.

The props stored there created shadows of their own. Each large piece of scenery could serve as a hiding place, as could the network of old stone walls, shoulder height in places. She was there somewhere, presumably armed and ready to spring out at whoever was first to find her. Joe turned and issued a whispered warning. *Be careful. She's dangerous.*

They fanned out, moving cautiously, breath held; everybody listening for some tell-tale sound that would betray her whereabouts.

Slowly, they worked their way towards the shadows at the

back of the huge room. Joe moved forward, making for the foundations of the convent that stood in almost complete darkness. She'd appeared there once. It was her place.

He saw a movement: something rising slowly from the ruins. At first it was nothing more than a dark shape, the shade of a long dead nun. Then Joe saw Charlotte's long pale face against the darkness of the robes. He held up his hand; a signal for the others to stop.

'Charlotte. We've been looking for you.' He kept his voice level and calm. 'You have to come with us now.'

There was no answer.

Joe waited several moments before he spoke again. 'Tell us why you did it, Charlotte. What had Perdita ever done to you?'

This time she spoke, the voice of a little girl: petulant and self-excusing. 'She stole my man when we were in Leeds. Then she took the part I should have had. I had to watch her going on night after night, knowing I'd be better.'

'You were jealous of her?'

'I knew I could do better.'

'Was that worth killing her for?'

'Perry wanted ghosts. I gave him one.'

'Was that the only reason?'

'She took him from me.'

'Who?'

'Carlo. He was special, but he went with her.

'And you wanted him to yourself.'

She didn't answer.

'How did you move her body?'

'I used Perry's cart – the one he uses for his living statue things.'

'I think Perdita was hoping to meet up with her latest man after the play on Friday night, but you told her you wanted to talk to her. Am I right?'

'Yes.'

'You gave her a drink. Water, was it?'

'I gave her my water bottle. Acting's thirsty work.'

'The water you gave her was drugged. You drugged all your victims.'

'They're not victims, they're ghosts,' she said sharply. 'I got it online. You can get all sorts of things online.'

'What about Jonas? Why did he have to die?'

'He should have minded his own business. He guessed what had happened, so I had no choice.' There was no hint of regret in her voice.

'And Sinclair Doulton?'

'He was watching, and he knew what I'd done. He tried to blackmail me. Not for money, because I don't have any. He wanted other things instead,' she said, wrinkling her nose with disgust. 'And I knew that girl had seen me in the undercroft, so I couldn't take the risk. She was going to be my gift to Perry. He collects ghosts, you see. They're his special project.'

'And you provide them?'

No answer.

'Why did you kill Perry?'

'He betrayed me. I was going to let him see a ghost actually being created. I was going to let him watch her die. But he said . . . He said I shouldn't have done it.' Her voice was breaking with emotion now. 'He said I was ill. He was so ungrateful.'

Joe walked towards her. 'It's OK, you're safe now,' he said gently. 'But you'll have to come with us.'

She let out a howl and began to cry, a terrible primitive keening followed by desperate sobs. Joe had reached the wall that she'd used as a shield. It came up to his waist, and he could see her a few feet away. She was holding a knife – a sharp kitchen knife, grasped so tightly that her knuckles were white. She stared ahead, as though she was in some hell of her own, hardly aware of his presence.

'Perry's still alive,' he said. 'They say he'll be OK.'

'You're lying.'

Joe was stunned by the swift change in her mood. She was defiant now, and the knife was pointing straight at him.

He looked round and saw the team closing in. She had nowhere to go. He held out his hand. 'I'm not lying. He's in hospital. Give me the weapon, Charlotte. It's over now. You'll be looked after, I promise.'

At first he thought she was going to come quietly. She bowed her head with nunlike meekness and stood perfectly still, as though in prayer.

Joe was unprepared for her ferocity when she lunged at him with the knife. He'd known he should have ordered her to drop it on the floor, but he hadn't wanted to break the spell. He felt the blade make contact with his arm and saw the gash in his leather jacket. There was no pain at first, then he felt a stinging where metal had pierced flesh. He heard wild shouts, and he was aware of uniformed arms grabbing at the girl's flailing limbs. Then there was a piercing scream, and he felt a warm shower of liquid on his face.

When he looked up he saw Charlotte lying on the ground with a dark, gushing gash staining the pure white wimple at her throat. And, in spite of the panicked efforts at resuscitation going on around him, he knew that she was dead. That had been her intention when she'd hidden herself down there. She'd wanted to become a ghost.

THIRTY-TWO

Joe had needed stitches, but his favourite jacket had been the real casualty. The right sleeve was ruined, and it could never be worn again, much to his consternation.

The other casualty had been Louisa Van Sturten's production of *The Devils*, which had been cancelled for the rest of the week. Losing two of the cast to murder had been bad enough, but when a third had been unmasked as the killer it proved too much even for the redoubtable Louisa. However, she was determined to reopen on Saturday once Charlotte's understudy had had the chance to rehearse. She ignored any talk of curses or ghostly appearances heralding dreadful deaths. She was a rational woman. Luck hadn't come into it. Besides, recent events had been fantastic for ticket sales.

There is always an aftermath to any serious investigation, and Joe and Emily spent the next week or so putting the finishing touches to reports and paperwork. Emily had been unusually quiet. Joe knew what happened that evening had shocked her.

One thing that surprised him, however, was the reappearance of Alvin Cobarn on the scene. He'd been lying low while the investigation was going on, but now he was starting to creep back into the local paper: an opening here, a statement about the future of the city's public libraries there. Joe guessed that recent events wouldn't keep him down for long. But whether his marriage would last, he had no idea. He thought of Regina Cobarn and felt sad on her behalf. He hoped things would work out for her, with or without her unfaithful husband. Perhaps, after her suicide attempt, he'd recognize her unhappiness and do something to make amends. But that would take a miracle, and Joe knew that miracles were rare.

On Friday night he left the police station late and found that mist was shrouding the city again, dancing like grey ghosts between the buildings and turning the car headlamps into the glowing eyes of strange, slow moving beasts. He was glad he was walking. Even after so many years of living in Eborby, driving in it made him nervous.

He reached his flat at eight thirty and stood on the threshold for a second, listening to the silence. It was a habit he'd got into, a precaution, just in case an intruder was waiting in the darkness.

He switched on the lights. His unwashed breakfast things were still in the small kitchen off the living room, but these days there was nobody to criticize his slovenly habits. He was alone. And the silence felt threatening, so he switched on the TV, just for the sound of another human voice.

He hadn't heard from Maddy for several days. He presumed she was still with her parents, providing support. He had snatched Carlo Natale from them, their source of comfort. But that comfort had been false. He tried to convince himself that he'd done them a favour, but at least Natale had given them hope.

He took a bottle of Black Sheep from the cupboard, but before he could open it, he heard the door bell ring. When he saw Maddy standing there, it was as if his thoughts had conjured her, and he was surprised at how glad he felt.

He asked her in and offered her a drink. He only had beer. She rolled her eyes fondly and suggested they go out somewhere if he hadn't already eaten. She'd spent the day with her parents but had refused her mother's desperate offer of a meal, and now she was starving. There was an eagerness about her words, and he wasn't sure whether he was pleased or alarmed. At that moment he was just glad of her company. Maybe he'd have been glad of any company.

They decided on a pub meal at the Star, but as they walked past Singmass Close, Joe's eyes were drawn to the place where Perry Antrobus had drawn the ghost of Enoch Bartholomy. There was no trace of the drawing now. It had vanished with the rain. Vanished like a ghost.

Maddy seemed happier. Her mother was coming to terms with the fact that Carlo Natale was a fraud and was channelling her grief by starting work for a charity that helped people whose relatives were killed or went missing abroad. Joe said nothing. He didn't want to tell her that Natale had predicted they'd find Debby Telerhaye amongst the dead. For all he knew, that had just been a lucky guess.

By the time they'd ordered dessert, he was starting to feel uneasy. Her eyes were a little too bright, and her reaction to any joke he made, however feeble, was a little too attentive. When they'd finished eating, she placed her hand on his. 'This is my treat,' she said. 'To celebrate the new job.'

Joe tried to argue, but she didn't listen. Instead, she took out her credit card and went to the bar to pay.

He'd said nothing about her coming back to his flat, but she seemed to take it for granted, and as they walked she put her arm through his. He felt it wasn't right, but when they reached his flat he let her follow him in. What he had to say couldn't be said in the street.

She sat down, completely at home, her eyes shining with excitement, as though they were on their first date.

'I've missed you,' she said. 'I know it was me who broke it off when I went down to London, but . . .' She paused. 'It's something I regretted almost as soon as it happened. My parents weren't the only reason I came back to Eborby, if you want the truth.'

She looked up at him hopefully. He hadn't even taken his coat off, and he was still standing, holding his keys.

'I'm sorry, Maddy.' He sat down in the chair opposite her, fidgeting with his keys, wondering how best to express what he needed to say. 'There are a lot of things about me you don't know; things I never told you. If you did know, you'd probably want nothing to do with me.'

She frowned. 'We were together for over a year. I can't believe there's anything I don't know about you . . . certainly nothing bad.'

He could hear desperation in her voice. Was he making a mistake? He'd had plenty of time to think about it while they'd been apart, but now he felt himself wavering. Was living a life of solitude really better than hiding an uncomfortable truth that he'd almost forgotten himself; a truth that he'd managed to live with for many years?

'I killed someone once, Maddy.' He blurted out the words before he had second thoughts.

Maddy gaped at him, as if he was some stranger who'd just intruded on her personal space. 'I don't believe you,' she whispered after a few moments. 'Who did you kill? When?' Her eyes widened in recognition. 'Didn't your sister-in-law accuse you of killing your wife? Was she right? Did you do it?'

'No,' he snapped, a spasm of pain passing over his face.

'Then who?'

'I can't tell you. But I did it to save someone . . . a child.'

Maddy looked relieved. 'In that case . . .'

'It's not what you think. It wasn't in the line of duty. It was years ago, while I was training to be a priest. I came across . . . something terrible – someone abusing a child – and I told someone else and . . .'

Maddy latched on quickly. 'And the person you told dealt with him? Is that it?' She looked at him, willing it to be true.

'Yes. But I knew this person was hot headed. I knew what was likely to happen, so I was responsible. Maybe losing Kaitlin was my punishment.'

Maddy put her arms around him and kissed the top of his head. 'You can't blame yourself.'

'But part of me meant it to happen, don't you see? In my heart I wanted that man to die for what he'd done.'

'Who was he?'

'It doesn't matter.'

She tightened her embrace, and they sat for a while in silence before he spoke again, pushing her away gently. 'I think you'd better go.'

She stood up. 'I'm not giving up on you.' She looked round.

'Do you mind if I stay tonight? Only, I don't fancy going home to an empty flat.'

'I'll take the sofa,' said Joe quickly.

Maddy looked at him. 'In that case I'll have another drink. Red wine if you've got any.'

He rose from his seat, unable to meet her gaze. The partial lie had backfired, and she now thought he was some sort of hero who'd dealt out summary justice to a child abuser. It was a story that was partly true, but it wasn't the worst thing he'd ever done. He'd intended to share the truth about his last day with Kaitlin with her, but he'd lost his courage at the last moment.

That night he slept on his sofa and awoke next morning with a sore shoulder.

Perry Antrobus knew he was a murderer. He'd killed his own sister . . . as good as. He'd known she had to be stopped whatever it took, so he'd put in the anonymous call to the police. Ever since she'd become involved with Carlo Natale she'd become more and more unstable. It was almost as if she'd been possessed by the spirits he claimed to have been able to contact.

It had started when she'd gone to see Natale after their mother's death two years ago. He messed with her head, controlled her, until, in her vulnerable state, she had become obsessed by him. She'd followed him around the country, watching him and becoming violently jealous of any woman he paid attention to. She'd kept track of his relationship with Perdita Elmet. That was why she auditioned for *The Devils*, because she'd wanted to keep close to Perdita, whose involvement with Natale had inspired her festering hatred.

Natale had kept Charlotte on a string, making sure he gave her just enough attention to feed her obsession. She had become his creature, and her sick mind had thought she was doing what he wanted, ridding him of the woman who'd trapped him by becoming pregnant. No doubt he'd told the police he had no idea about Perdita's pregnancy, but he'd be lying, like he always did.

It had been her dealings with Natale that had placed the ghosts in her mind. And Perry had gone along with it because it had seemed like a brilliant art project, but he hadn't realized then how far his sister's damaged mind was willing to go. He'd denied the truth to himself for so long . . . until he'd heard Debby trapped in the vault he hadn't even known existed and he'd had to face up to the horror of what Charlotte had done.

He often thought of Debby. He'd heard she'd moved away with her mum to make a new start. He'd also heard how Natale had concealed her little brother's death. The man was bad news. He was glad he was going to be locked up. It's a pity the police hadn't stopped him before he'd got at Charlotte. If it hadn't been for Natale, he might have been able to get her some help. Things might have been different if she'd never met Carlo Natale.

He had his chalks with him. The police had taken his cart away for forensic examination because she'd used it to transport Perdita's body, so his living statue act was more difficult these days. He had also received a suspended sentence for stealing from the cathedral shop, so he knew he had to keep his nose clean. For the time being. But they hadn't taken away his chalks.

It was dark now, and the mist was coming down again. This was perfect. He didn't want to be seen.

He reached the wall at the side of Wheatley Hall. It was an ancient wall with timbers set into the brickwork. This was the right place. She would be immortal here until her chalk ghost faded. Since her death he'd sensed her presence. She was still out there somewhere.

He began work, and when he'd finished he stood back and flashed a torch at his creation. It was a nun with Charlotte's thin, pale face. He thought it best to put her in the clothes she was wearing when her spirit had left her body, and he was pleased with his handiwork.

Carlo Natale was in prison and would be for some time. But Perry was patient. His project required just one more ghost. And one day, that ghost would be Carlo Natale.

Perry Antrobus, the emerging artist, had plans.